The book of Horses and Unicorns

The book of Horses and Unicorns

Jackie French

Angus&Robertson
An imprint of HarperCollins*Children'sBooks*

Angus&Robertson
An imprint of HarperCollins*Children'sBooks*, Australia

This is a combined edition of two titles: *Ride the Wild Wind* (first
published in 2002) and *The Book of Unicorns* (first published in 1997)

This combined edition first published in Australia in 2014
by HarperCollins*Publishers* Australia Pty Limited
ABN 36 009 913 517
harpercollins.com.au

HarperCollins*Publishers*
Level 13, 201 Elizabeth Street, Sydney NSW 2000, Australia
Unit D1, 63 Apollo Drive, Rosedale, Auckland 0632, New Zealand
A 53, Sector 57, Noida, UP, India
1 London Bridge Street, London, SE1 9GF, United Kingdom
2 Bloor Street East, 20th floor, Toronto, Ontario M4W 1A8, Canada
195 Broadway, New York NY 10007, USA

ISBN 978 1 4607 5013 1 (paperback)
ISBN 978 1 4607 0442 4 (e-book)

Cover design by Christa Moffitt, Christabella Designs
Cover image by shutterstock.com
Author photograph by Kelly Sturgiss
Printed and bound in Australia by McPherson's Printing Group
The papers used by HarperCollins in the manufacture of this
book are a natural, recyclable product made from wood grown in
sustainable plantation forests. The fibre source and manufacturing
processes meet recognised international environmental standards,
and carry certification.

Contents

Ride the Wild Wind

To Angela, Noël and Fabia
with love and gratitude:
the spirit of the book is yours!

Contents

The Golden Pony

Six thousand years ago...

Spring sunlight streamed across the snow and through the trees. This was a world of white and green shadows. The sled sped through the forest, avoiding the melted patches of grass tufts and broken branches.

'Da!' The girl signalled her father to stop.

The man pulled at the reins. The two reindeer halted as the rope tugged at their antlers, and shifted impatiently in their harness. 'Zushan, what is it?'

The girl pointed. 'Over there,' she breathed. 'Horses!'

The big man followed her gaze. Four horses stood motionless among the trees, a stallion and three mares, their heads raised nervously, waiting to run. Their coats were dappled with black like the shadows, and gold like sunlight gleamed through their coarse winter hair.

'I've never seen horses that colour before,' whispered Zushan. 'Not as bright as that.'

The man nodded. He slipped quietly from under the furs on the sled and pulled out his spear. One step, two ... the snow squeaked under his felt boots.

Suddenly the stallion broke and ran. The mares followed him, darting through the trees as the man cast the spear.

For a moment Zushan thought it would fall short. Her father was strong, but horses have tough hides. It was hard enough to drive a spear through horse skin even at close range.

One of the mares screamed. She fell to the ground, the spear through her neck, the snow turning red around it. The horse struggled frantically, trying to get to her feet.

The stallion reared. He reared once at the hunter, then galloped back and reared defiantly over the sled, as though he knew the attack had come from there. His hooves were wide and sharp. There was no time to scream or run. For a moment Zushan thought the hooves would slash down at her face, but instead the stallion turned and galloped through the trees, his mares with him.

One horse remained. A smaller horse, all legs and floppy ears and straight dark mane. The falling body of the mare must have hit it, for it struggled in the snow, trying to find its feet.

'A foal,' breathed Zushan. 'An early spring foal ...' She leapt from the sled and ran after her father, her brown felt boots slushing across the snow.

The big man pulled his spear from the horse's neck, then thrust it in again. The horse gave a dying gurgle;

her struggles stopped. The foal whickered in alarm. It managed to get to its feet just as Zushan's father lifted the spear again.

'No!' yelled Zushan, grabbing his arm.

Her father stopped. 'What's wrong?' he demanded quickly. 'The stallion didn't hurt you?'

'No, no, nothing like that. Just please don't hurt the foal!'

Her father blinked and lowered his spear. The foal staggered a few steps then stood there shivering. 'Why not?' the big man asked quietly.

Zushan hesitated. Why not indeed? The foal would soon die, separated from the other horses and without its mother's milk. Either the wolves would sniff it out, or it would starve alone in the snow.

'Let me look after it!' she said suddenly.

Her father stared. 'Look after a horse! What use is a horse, except for eating?'

'I don't know,' said Zushan, confused. 'No use, I suppose. It's just so lonely in the tent. There is no-one to cuddle up to, since Mama and Zerik died ...'

The man's gaze softened. 'It's been a hard winter,' he said quietly. 'But there will be others to cuddle up to at Auntie Meran's tent, I promise you. How about we keep a young reindeer from the spring migration, eh? You can cuddle it all you want to and train it to pull a sleigh.'

'I want the foal,' whispered Zushan. 'Its mother has died too.'

'If we take the foal we will have to leave most of the meat,' her father began. 'Oh, very well, shh then ...'

The foal felt warm. Its heart beat heavily against hers under the deerskin rugs. It still struggled now and then, but mostly it lay still, as though it knew the only safety now was in Zushan's arms.

The reindeer stamped and nuzzled at the snow, looking for lichen. They took no notice as Zushan's father pulled the skin from the horse's body, then cut the meat from the bones into rough chunks with his stone knives. The reindeer were used to the smells of blood and hunting.

Beside the sleigh the mare's bones and guts steamed in the snow. There was no point taking any but the best meat — rump, thigh, the long strips along the backbone, and the kidneys, heart, tongue and brain. There was a limit to what the reindeer could pull. As it was, Zushan's father would have to run behind.

He cast a longing look at the pile of bones. Horse marrow was rich in fat and it had been a hungry winter. Perhaps he could carry some of the bones in a sling on his back. The child could do with some fat. As for the guts, well horse guts were no use, unless they were dried and used to carry melted fat or seeds, and any animal's intestines could be used for that.

Zushan's father felt a brief regret that it wasn't a reindeer's body lying in the snow, instead of a horse. If those had been reindeer guts, they could have eaten the fermented lichen in the belly. Normally humans couldn't digest lichen, but once it had been partly digested by the reindeer, it was good to eat.

The child could do with some greens, thought her father. It would be weeks yet before the first herbs would poke up through the snow and months before the berries would ripen. Reindeer antlers could be used for tools too … Horses gave good meat bones and hide, but they weren't much use otherwise. The big man sighed. At least there was the horse skin. A good colour it was too, all gold and black. Most horses were mouse-coloured or grey. Winter skins were warmest; Meran would be glad of it.

The foal whinnied. Zushan shushed it and stroked its golden head. Now she was close she could see faint dark stripes through the gold. Unlike the bigger horses, the foal had no shaggy winter coat. The young horse was the most beautiful animal Zushan had ever seen. 'I'll call you Sunlight,' she said.

It was as warm inside Auntie Meran's deerskin tent as Zushan's father had promised, and filled with comforting people smells and warm breaths; especially at night, when everyone slept together on the deerskin mats under the white fox skins. It had been so cold these last months with just her and Da.

There was always someone next to you in Auntie Meran's big round tent when you woke up in the dark.

The moisture from their breath condensed on the roof of the tent and fell back in long warm drips, plop, plop, plop, all through the night, while the reindeer snorted and stamped their hooves outside. Reindeer rarely strayed once they had been tamed.

It was good to be in a crowded tent again, thought Zushan. Auntie Meran had four children, but there was room for her; especially as Uncle Tari had gone north with Da and the other men to hunt the reindeer that poured across the land on their spring migration.

The men would spend weeks hunting and butchering, hanging the best skins out to dry high in the trees where wolves and other meat eaters couldn't reach them.

Later, when it grew warmer, their families would travel north to join them, and other camps would meet there too. The reindeer would pull the sleds across the grasslands, avoiding the forest country where branches might block their way. Auntie Meran's big sled, which carried the tent, furs and all her family, needed ten reindeer to pull it, with everyone taking turns to run behind and help push when the long curved wooden runners caught on bushes.

Everyone in the summer camp would spend weeks slicing the meat and drying it on wooden racks for winter, and cracking the bones and boiling them up for fat. The fat was poured into bags of reindeer guts that had been soaked in water till they were clean and soft.

These bags were then tied at the top and bottom to keep the air from the fat.

The rest of summer would be spent hunting other game and gathering berries to dry for winter. The big summer camp was a time for gossip and laughter, music, marriages and stories, before the camp split up and the families returned to their winter camp sites.

Last winter had been lonely, as Mama and Zerik had died of the coughing sickness. A lone hunter had stumbled coughing into camp. Mama and Da had taken him into their tent to care for, then the sickness took them and the other families who had shared their winter camp, too. Zushan and Da had recovered, but so many from their camp had died. That was why Da had brought Zushan to Auntie Meran's: to try to leave the memories behind.

The colt grew too fast to keep inside the tent at night, though Auntie Meran had allowed it for a few days till Zushan grew used to the strangeness. Now the young horse straggled around the camp on its long legs, eating porridge mixed with reindeer milk from Zushan's hands, and poking his nose into other pots in case it found something good.

'Look at the creature,' laughed Auntie Meran, as the colt butted Zushan's waist, hoping for more porridge, 'it'll be as tall as you soon!'

Auntie Meran was a round comfortable woman who laughed a lot, which was a good thing, thought Zushan. You could either laugh at the colt when it upset a bag of grain into the mud and slush, or yell at it, and laughing was definitely better.

Old Farna snorted. 'What use is a horse, I'd like to know,' she said. But she hobbled over and fondled the colt's floppy ears and scratched along its back as she said it.

'No use at all,' stated Blani. Blani was Auntie Meran's oldest son. He was angry because the men had said he was still too young to accompany them on the reindeer hunt this year. 'You could never train a horse to pull a sled, or even carry a load.'

'Why not?' demanded Zushan

'A horse is too stupid to train, that's why. And they're too small. A horse doesn't have a reindeer's strength.'

It was true that horses were smaller than reindeer, thought Zushan, but she refused to believe Sunlight was stupid. 'I bet they can pull a sled,' she insisted. 'And they could carry small loads! See how broad his back is.'

'It's as skinny as yours,' jeered Blani.

'It will be broader when he grows up!' said Zushan hotly.

'And so will yours,' said Auntie Meran soothingly. 'You will look as fat as a pook pook bird with all its feathers ruffled by the end of this summer, you see if you don't. Now Blani, off and check the fish traps and Zushan, check the snares we laid yesterday before the wolves get there first!'

It was as good to get away from camp sometimes as it was to be among people again, Zushan decided, as she trod through the slush under the trees, while the colt danced ahead of her then behind, nuzzling the ground for the first spring shoots.

Zushan ate as she walked too. It was habit, especially now in spring, to reach up and strip catkins from the willows, bend down to pick young thistle leaves or the unfolding stems of ferns, and use her stone knife to peel off some strips of bark, its inner layer sweet with rising sap.

Now that the snow had melted, she could see the small pools and bogs again, thick with sedge and bulrush stems. The new spring stems were crisp and sweet, and Sunlight butted her to get his share.

It was a noisy world now. Spring was in full song. The snow lingered only in deep drifts on the shady side of trees. The world was full of the cracking of ice and the yelling of the birds, and the rustles and cries of animals. Icicles dripped from the twigs, and snow melted in the branches. Streams ran down every possible channel, bringing a thousand new smells of thawed droppings and decay.

Winter smelt of ice, thought Zushan, as the colt leapt over a snowdrift, but spring smelt of the remains of last summer and of the summer to come.

The first snare was empty; the dried sinew looped around the tree lay limply on the slush. The second was empty too, but it was torn as well. Evidently a wolf or fox had found the contents before she did. Zushan untied it then tied it around another tree further on. There was no use leaving it in the same place; it had already caught something, and the smell of fear and death would scare other small animals away from it.

The colt butted her again, as though to say, 'Come on slow foot!' Zushan laughed, and rubbed his ears. 'You've got four legs and I've only got two!' she informed it. The colt whinnied back as though to say: 'And that's a very poor arrangement!'

'I'll race you then!' said Zushan. She ran through the trees, her felt boots thudding against the grass and slush, but the colt soon overtook her, and danced circles around her as she ran.

Zushan leant puffing against a tree trunk. 'Ooof,' she said. 'You have too much energy!'

The horse whinnied again, just as though he understood her. Maybe he did, thought Zushan. Blani was wrong. No reindeer ever *listened* to her the way that Sunlight did.

The third snare held a hare, still struggling to free its leg from the noose. Zushan wrung its neck quickly and expertly, then used her stone knife to slice between the sinew of one leg and slipped the other leg through the hole, so that the legs formed a loop and made the limp body easier to carry.

She was glad she'd found the hare. Spring was a fresh green time, with air that sometimes felt too rich to breathe, but it was a time of shortages too — winter's stores were used up and there was little fresh food around. Even fish were hard to trap in early spring. Blani might well bring home nothing, she thought with satisfaction. Even though her hare was skinny after winter, it would feed them all.

The colt nosed at the hare, in case it was good to eat.

'Nope,' said Zushan, holding it high out of his reach. 'Horses do *not* like hares!' The small horse snorted with disapproval and kicked his legs high.

One more empty snare, then a fox and a weasel in the next two. Fox's meat was sour, but the fur was good; especially in winter when it was soft and white. Weasel meat was even worse than fox — you had to be really hungry to eat weasel — but the fur was softest of all. She'd use the fur to trim a hood, decided Zushan, if Auntie Meran had no other use for it. Weasel fur felt lovely around your face and was so fine that snow and ice just slid off it.

'Come on!' she yelled to Sunlight, who was nosing in a snowdrift. 'That was the last snare! Time to go home!'

The little horse ignored her.

'Sunlight! Home!' She walked towards him, as the colt looked up then danced towards her.

Zushan looked more closely at the snowdrift; it was white against the new spring growth and larger than any drift she'd passed. But *was* it a snowdrift? Surely it was too large for this late in spring, and the shape seemed wrong as well.

Zushan stepped closer. It wasn't snow at all, she thought excitedly, it was a sheep! Perhaps it had been lying there frozen all through winter, the white of its fleece mingling with the last of the snow.

Zushan prodded it. A whole sheep was a prize, especially in spring when animals were lean after winter. This sheep would still have its autumn fat and all its wool. Wool was used to make felt. It was rolled and pounded till the cloth was thick and waterproof and more pliable than leather. Wool boots kept out the cold even better than leather, and were more comfortable too. But most wool was simply gathered from bushes as the sheep dropped it in their summer moult. This would be better than anything Blani might bring home!

If she could get it home.

Zushan hesitated. If she left the sheep and ran to get help, a wolf might find it before they got back. The snow was melting fast, and even in an hour or two there would be enough of the sheep above the snow to invite the attentions of others. But all the way back to camp was a long way to drag a frozen sheep over uneven ground. It would take both her hands. She would have to leave the fox and hare and the soft-furred weasel. If only she had brought a reindeer to help carry the load …

The colt danced in front of her, bored. Zushan gazed at it. No, the young horse couldn't take the weight of a sheep on its back, Blani was right about that, though Sunlight would when he was an adult, she thought stubbornly. But he might … he just might …

Zushan unwound the plaited felt belt from her waist and tied part of it around the bodies of her animals.

'Sunlight!' she ordered, 'Come here!'

The colt skipped towards her, expecting food. 'No, you silly horse, stand still.' She tied the rest of the rope around his middle in a rough harness. The horse kicked up his legs, thinking it a game. The rope slipped and the hare slithered over the young horse's tummy. He neighed in surprise and fear, and pranced away from her.

'No, it's alright you silly horse,' soothed Zushan. 'Come back here! That's right.' She scratched the little animal along his back, and the place he liked best around his ears. 'Now, you just stand still and I'll fix this up ... see? It doesn't hurt and it's not heavy.'

The colt kicked again, and once more the bundles tumbled. Zushan hesitated, then undid the long strips that held her leggings. The wind blew cold about her bare legs, but they would warm soon enough as she pulled the sheep. She untied the rope that held her hair back too and knotted all the ropes together.

'Sunlight! Here boy!' The little horse approached again. This time Zushan tied the rope in the same way her father would fix a reindeer harness — around the neck and chest, with the load attached to the harness so that it balanced on either side of Sunlight's back.

The foal kicked up his legs and pranced around the trees, half frightened, half fascinated by the weight on his back, his head shaking backward and forward as he tried to see it. But this time the load stayed in place.

Zushan laughed. 'It's alright!' she cried. 'You'll get used to it!'

The young horse looked at her. He seemed to be considering her, as though he were thinking: 'Do I trust this human enough to do this or not?' Then suddenly he halted, and trotted closer again.

Zushan looked back at the sheep. The snow was melting quickly. She took hold of the sheep's forelegs and tugged.

Nothing happened. The sheep lay where it had lain all winter, frozen in the snow. Sunlight butted her, as if to say: 'Can I help too?'

Zushan tugged again. She felt something give, as the sheep moved slightly. Suddenly the sheep gave way so abruptly that Zushan and the horse fell together in a mass of legs and arms.

Zushan got to her feet, laughing. The little horse whinnied, and it seemed to Zushan that perhaps he was laughing too.

'Now, home!' she ordered, as she began to tug the sheep across the slush and snow. The small horse bucked again and craned his head around to try to see the bundles on either side of his back. Then he noticed Zushan was ahead of him, and trotted after her.

It wasn't easy. The way was rough; the sheep's fleece kept catching as it began to thaw, and Zushan had to keep untangling it from twigs and bushes and lifting the body over rough bits. The strange weight on his back kept frightening the little horse too. He would trot a few steps, and then remember and grow skittish again. He had to be coaxed along.

But finally the camp was in sight, the round tents silhouetted against the pale spring sky. The reindeer were nuzzling at the ground for grass and lichen, the white of their winter coats giving way to summer brown.

'Ahoh!' yelled Zushan triumphantly.

The reindeer raised their heads, their antlers dark against the sky. Aunt Meran looked up from the fire where she had been cooking a fish — one very small fish, thought Zushan happily. Blani looked up too, and old Farna and all the others.

'It's a sheep!' yelled Zushan. 'A whole sheep! And Sunlight has more things too!' She laughed as the little horse trotted beside her, carrying his load as steadily and obediently as any reindeer.

It was a good summer after that.

The colt grew taller and broader. He carried small loads regularly now, not heavy ones — perhaps just a skin scraped clean of fat and membrane, ready for tanning — and trotted after Zushan from one end of the camp to the other. But there would be time enough for Sunlight to carry proper loads, thought Zushan proudly, when the horse reached his full sturdy growth.

'I would never have believed it,' said Auntie Meran in wonder, watching the little horse trot obediently after Zushan as she carried firewood back from the trees. Blani said nothing but he gave Zushan the best helping of fish whenever he caught one, as though in apology. Blani wasn't so bad, thought Zushan cheerfully, once he got over his disappointment at being left out of the hunt.

'You should tether that horse,' advised old Farna, 'or put him in the yard at night like the new reindeer, or he will wander off.'

Zushan shook her head. 'But he likes it here!' she said. 'We're friends. We're his family.'

Old Farna shook her head. 'Friends you may be,' she said, 'but one day he'll wander off.'

Zushan smiled. Sometimes she dreamed that one day Sunlight would pull a sled, just like a reindeer, or even carry her on his back once he was fully grown. But she never mentioned that in case everyone laughed. But one day, she said to Sunlight in her mind, one day we'll show them all …

Yes, it was a good summer. The camp moved northwards to join the hunters, as did the other camps of the region, and the young horse came too, trotting behind the sleds with the spare reindeer. Unlike them he carried no packs of furs or dried meat; Auntie Meran judged he was still too young to carry anything far.

It was wonderful to see Da again; to be with so many people and enjoy laughter and roast thick reindeer steaks every day and sit around fires that sparked into the night. The rivers ran thick with fish and foam, and berries ripened on their low bushes away from the trees.

Berry-picking was best of all, thought Zushan. You could eat as you picked, as long as you were careful to watch out for the bears who loved the berries too. More than once the young horse neighed nervously, as he scented danger on the wind, and each time Zushan hesitated till she too caught sight of the lumbering brown bears and was able to edge around them safely.

Towards the end of summer, the camp split up again into family groups, and they all headed back to their winter territories. Half a moon after that, Da took the sled with three large reindeer and headed east. By the time the moon was small again he had returned, and a woman shared his sled.

'This is Fanshan,' he said to Zushan.

Fanshan held out her hands. They were square muscular hands; hands that spent their time gutting fish and making felt and slicing meat for drying. 'I hope we will be friends,' said Fanshan, and Zushan saw her smile and knew they would.

It was a good summer until the end.

The moon hung low in the sky, a hunter's moon, but there was no need to hunt tonight. Autumn had been rich this year, and the last month busy. The bags in the tents were filled with seeds and lily roots, and yellow fat which had been melted and strained and mixed with dried berries and strips of lean dried meat. Bundles of dried fish lay on the outer layer of the tents as well, tied together with plaited felt rope so they didn't fall off in the wind. Soon, after the first freeze and snow fall, it would be time to hunt and fish again. They would leave the freshly killed meat to freeze under piles of snow and rocks where they could find it later in the winter, and put the frozen fish next to the dried ones on the roof of the tent.

Zushan snuggled into her furs and listened to the breathing of her father and Fanshan. It was good to be in their own tent again, and Fanshan had promised her a new brother or sister by next spring too. Outside the tent she could hear the shuffle of the colt's hooves as he nosed around the tents. Horses, it seemed, didn't sleep as long as human beings.

A sudden whinnying broke the silence. For a moment Zushan thought it was the colt, calling for help perhaps. Then she realised it was further away.

Another whinny, but this one was closer. Sunlight calling back ...

Zushan leapt from the furs and out of the tent. The frozen ground bit at her feet and the cold air stripped the warmth from her arms and legs. The fur tents were so warm that you needed to wear little inside; out in the night air the wind was breathing ice again.

'Sunlight!' she yelled.

The colt glanced at her. He was on the far side of the encampment now. Dimly in the moonlight Zushan could see other horses, their pale hides gleaming in the night.

'Sunlight! Please!'

The colt snickered softly, as though in apology. Then he was gone.

Zushan's father staggered from the tent, 'Zushan, what's wrong?' he cried. Fanshan crawled through the tent flap too.

'It's Sunlight!' cried Zushan. 'He's gone!'

Fanshan held her as she sobbed. 'But darling, you knew this must happen! A horse isn't a reindeer, after all! Horses don't live with people!'

'I should have hobbled him,' sobbed Zushan. But in her heart she knew she could never have hobbled Sunlight, or kept him in a pen. Sunlight was a wild animal who had chosen to stay with her and if he now chose to live with his own kind, she might cry, but she could never really wish to keep him prisoner.

One year passed and another and another, each year following the same pattern, but each one different. The golden horse didn't return.

Each time a hunter brought horse meat back to camp, Zushan was afraid it might be Sunlight. But each time the horse's hide was dun or brown, or shaggy white in winter, not the colour of Sunlight, the horse she had loved.

Zushan grew taller. Boys began looking at her sideways at the big summer camp, and she looked at them as well. Soon, she knew, she would choose to go to another family's tent, or perhaps some boy would join hers.

Her family was larger now. Her brother Hari toddled round the winter camp, following everyone as they worked, falling into puddles and pulling over baskets, just like the colt had so long ago. Zushan had a sister too, still a baby, but growing fast.

It was cold this winter, the coldest winter since her mother had died. But this year there was no illness. The food bags were full, there was fresh meat frozen under the piles of stones around the camp and frozen fish on the roof. The big tent was full of laughter and stories, and the children played around the camp in the winter sunlight.

It was a clear day when it happened. The wind had dropped. The snow had frozen firm and crisp on the ground, tinged with blue as it reflected the sky; the pale high sky of winter. The air was as crisp as ice stretched thin.

Zushan's father left the tent first and stared at the early morning sky. 'There'll be a storm by evening,' he decided, looking at the faint wisps on the horizon, 'but it should stay clear till midday. Enough time to check the fish traps at any rate.'

You had to break the ice to check the fish traps in winter, even though the holes were covered with reindeer hide so the ice didn't freeze too thick, but most times there was something to bring home. Fresh fish was a welcome change from dried meat, or the frozen fish that was shaved so thin that the raw flesh melted on your tongue.

He banged on the hide of the next tent. 'Worri!' he called, 'are you going to sleep all winter? There are traps to be checked!'

A tall man crawled out of the tent, then two men from the next.

'Hari go too!' yelled Hari, crawling through the tent flap. Zushan made a hurried dive and grabbed him. 'Oh, no, you don't,' she informed him, bearing him down onto the fur rugs and tickling him. 'Next year you can go help the men with the fish traps maybe, or the year after that!'

I might be gone to my own tent by then, thought Zushan, with a touch of wistfulness. But the thought was exciting too.

It was a busy morning. In the brief spell of sunshine the bags of moss used as a toilet had to be emptied, scraped out with fresh snow and lined with more moss. Clean snow was gathered and melted on the fire of wood, reindeer droppings and long-dried bones. By mid-winter the snow around the camp was trodden and dirty, and it took a while to fetch enough fresh snow to melt.

Leather bags of snow and grain and herbs and dried meat were slung across the fire, to cook slowly in the heat. As long as the fire didn't burn too high, the water seeping through the leather would stop it from burning. The grain would swell and soften, and the dried meat too.

When the storms blew long and furiously and it was too cold to go outside, the family could survive in their warm tent on dried meat, shaved raw fish and dried berries mixed with fat. But it was good to have warm food instead and today, with luck, there might be fresh fish to grill, or meat from the snares.

Zushan helped the others pack more snow on the big windbreak around the camp, then set out to check the snares. Many animals hibernated in weather like this, or migrated south, but the sun might have tempted a few out to scrape away the snow and find greenery below, or to prey on others.

It was a silent world, away from the camp. The trees stretched green and brown above the snow, but they too carried their burden of snow. The only sounds were the occasional thud, as snow slipped off a branch, or a crack as an overladen branch broke.

Zushan settled her hood further down her face, not so much for warmth — in the gentle sunlight there was no need — but to shade her eyes from the glare of the snow. On a day like this, the reflected sunlight might burn your skin as well.

Here and there prints made patterns in the snow: bird tracks and, once, the prints of a fox, weaving through the trees. Zushan hoped he hadn't found the contents of her snares.

As she had expected, most of the snares were empty but one held the small, hard, frozen body of a hare; ice glistened on its fur. Zushan unlooped the plaited sinew from its leg. The animal was winter thin. It must have caught its leg in the snare yesterday or even the day before, thought Zushan, and froze to death when it grew cold again.

A sudden wind blew a gust of coldness against her face and sent beads of ice rolling across the snow. Zushan looked at her tracks in the snow. Already the wind was filling them with ice. Soon there would be no record of anyone walking this way, or any animal either.

The storm would come soon, thought Zushan, as she carried the hard body of the frozen hare back to camp. She hoped there would be time to cook the hare before the weather broke, though it would keep fresh — and frozen — outside the tent, until another break in the weather.

She was nearing the camp when she heard the scream. Zushan broke into a run. 'What is it?' she cried.

Fanshan ran from the tent. 'It's Hari! I can't find him! I was feeding Taran, and Hari was playing with the knuckle bones, but when I looked again he wasn't there!'

Auntie Meran glanced at the sky. 'The storm is coming! We'd better find him quickly,' she decided. 'We'd best all take a different direction. Fanshan, you stay here in case he wanders back. You,' she said to Zushan, 'go that way, through the trees. I'll head downstream to the river and tell the men to hunt for him too, and you and you go upstream. Keep a lookout for his tracks — there may be some in the shelter of the trees, where the wind hasn't got to them — but if you don't find anything by the time the sun is below the branches, turn back. We can't have anyone else getting lost as well, and the wind will rise soon!'

Zushan nodded. She slipped into the tent and filled her pouch quickly with the dried berry and fat cakes. Hari would be cold, and hungry too, and food was one way to keep the cold from taking you.

'Find him. Please find him,' whispered Fanshan.

Zushan nodded and trudged back the way she had come, though the wind had blown away all traces of her prints now.

'Hari! Hari!' The cries drifted across the snow, slowly growing fainter as the other searchers moved away.

Luckily the snow was still firm, thought Zushan gratefully, as the thin crust of ice crackled under her feet, so there was no need for snowshoes. If it snowed too much today, then no-one would be able to go anywhere for days without the wide flat willow and leather shoes that stopped you sinking down into the slush. But now at least, it was still possible to walk without them.

Zushan peered through the trees. No footprints, no small figure in the distance ...

'Hari! Hari!' Only her voice could be heard now. Zushan hesitated. Surely Hari couldn't have gone this far without a sign!

Suddenly she saw it. A footprint, small and deep, in the soft snow next to a giant tree. The trunk had sheltered it from the wind.

Zushan ran over to it. The track was pointing outwards, away from the camp.

What should she do now? Run back and fetch the others, so they could search this area too? But that would take so long! Or should she keep on going? Surely one small boy could not have gone far!

'Hari!' she yelled. 'Come here at once!

Nothing answered her, not even an echo. The snow had swallowed her words.

Zushan ran through the trees. Yes, there was another print ... and another. Above her the clouds hovered green and grey, lower and lower in the sky.

Snowflakes began to fall. Zushan ran on. There was no choice now. She had to go faster ... faster ... She had to find him before the snow covered every sign.

'Hari! Hari!'

'Zushan! Zushan, I'm here!'

Zushan blinked into the thickening snow. Something darker than the snow huddled against a tree trunk.

'Hari!' Zushan raced over to him. 'Are you hurt? Are you alright? Oh, you're in for it when I get you home. Why did you run away? Naughty, naughty boy.' But she was hugging him as she scolded.

'I want go to home,' wailed Hari. 'I want my mummy and my dadda and ...'

'I'll get you home now, don't worry. Can you walk?'

Hari shook his head. 'My legs are cold. They won't go, Zushan.'

'Well, try,' said Zushan.

Hari nodded.

Zushan took his hand. It felt tiny in hers. 'You don't even have your over-gloves on!' she scolded as she helped him up. 'It would serve you right if the ice giants got you.'

'What are the ice giants?'

'They're monsters who live down under the ice and they gobble up naughty boys!' It was better to think of ice giants, thought Zushan, than real dangers like snow and cold and wolves ...

Just as she thought the word, a howl broke the silence. Zushan froze. How far away had it been? Not far, she decided. The snow muffled all but nearby noise.

But the snow might protect them too. If the wolves couldn't hear them or smell them, they wouldn't attack.

'Shh,' she whispered to Hari. 'Better not talk now. Just walk, alright?'

Hari nodded. He stumbled next to her, one step, two, then fell again.

'Oh, alright,' whispered Zushan, lifting him up and holding him against her. Better just the sound of one pair of feet anyway; any noise might bring the wolves closer. She wondered how far wolves could smell in the snow. Wolves could smell far better than humans, but perhaps the coming blizzard would hide their scent.

The snow was falling ever harder now. The flakes were larger, till they weren't flakes at all, just a steady whiteness falling from the sky. It lay thicker on the ground too, so every step was an effort.

How many steps to home? wondered Zushan. For the first time she began to fear that with the burden of Hari in her arms, she wouldn't make it safely back to camp.

She had to keep her sense of direction. That was the greatest danger in the snow. The sun had been on her left. Now it should be on her right but the sun was nearly hidden by the snow; only a bright patch of whiteness low on the horizon showed where it was.

That way ... it had to be that way ... Zushan plodded on through the whiteness.

At least there were no streams between her and the camp; often the ice would collapse as you walked over them. That's if she was headed in the right direction ...

Zushan glanced up at the horizon again, but now the last of the sun's brightness had vanished. The world was a featureless white all around.

In a white-out like this she might walk right past the camp and miss it. She would have to call and keep calling, and hope that someone heard her, that their voices might guide her ...

But there was no point calling out yet. Zushan had no way of telling time or any way of counting her steps but she had a clear sense of how long it had taken her to come this way, and a clear sense, too, of how long it might take to get back. No use yelling till she was nearer camp. She would just exhaust herself, and she and Hari needed all her strength now.

Another step, another — her legs were screaming as she pulled them through the snow; her arms and back ached with Hari's weight. But at least the front of her was warm where his small body pressed against hers. That meant he was warm too. If only they could make it home, they would survive. 'Here.' Zushan reached into her pouch and pressed a blob of fat and berry between Hari's cold lips. She took a mouthful herself too. The food would help ... for a while.

It was an effort to lift her feet now. The fresh snow sucked at them, and weighed them down. It was ankle-height already.

A dark shape loomed in front of her. A tree. She changed course to avoid it, then carefully tried to find the right direction again. If she bumbled into a tree, its weight of snow might fall on her, might suffocate them both.

The cold had seeped through her clothes, her flesh, her bones. Hari must be even colder ...

Another shape grew out of the whiteness — another tree. But this shape moved.

Zushan blinked. The fur of her hood had kept most of the snow from her face, but her eyes felt frozen, and there was snow on her lashes too. She blinked again and tried to see through the whiteness.

The shape moved again. A white shape in the thicker whiteness, long and lean, with dark eyes that gleamed through the snow. Something growled, almost too low to hear.

Wolf!

The wolves must have heard her ... they must have tracked her, even in the blizzard.

Zushan looked round frantically for a weapon. A fallen branch, a bone — anything! Wolves were naturally timid and rarely attacked humans, except when they were starving in mid-winter and hunger drew them out, even in a blizzard, except when the humans were alone and tired in the snow.

The wolf growled again. Another moved behind it.

Zushan screamed, but the snow swallowed the sound.

If she flung herself on the ground, over Hari, perhaps they would just take her, not him. But no, only starvation would bring the wolves out now. They'd take what they could find and even if they didn't, Hari would soon die alone here in the snow.

The wolf stepped closer, his nose low, his eyes watchful. Zushan yelled again, her arms tight around Hari.

But this time her cry was answered. A long whinny sounded through the trees. Hooves thundered through the snow, and a gold body reared through the whiteness.

The hooves lashed down, just missing the wolf, which ducked hurriedly away. The hind hooves lashed out as well, and the stallion reared again. The wolves dissolved into the snowstorm, and were gone.

The stallion paused and looked around. Dimly Zushan could see the shapes of other horses — mares — but they kept their distance from the human.

The golden stallion stepped closer.

'Sunlight?' whispered Zushan.

The horse whickered softly. He turned to go.

'Sunlight, please, no. You have to help us.'

The horse stopped at the sound of her voice. He faced her, the dark eyes blinking off the snowflakes, the nostrils wide as he remembered her smell.

'I can't carry Hari back,' whispered Zushan. 'Not through the snow. I'm not sure I can even find my way back. Please help us.'

The golden horse gazed at her, proud and wary. This was no young foal, romping with his playmate. This was a stallion, leader of his band of mares, a wild horse who did as he pleased.

Zushan staggered towards him, Hari in her arms. There was no time to think or plan. No way to fashion a sled or reins or tether. All she could do was hope the memory of their friendship held.

What had Blani said all those years ago? A horse is stupid ... No, this horse was not stupid. The stallion knew exactly what she asked of him. Suddenly he whickered, and tossed his head at her. He stepped closer. Zushan felt his warm breath on her skin.

She touched the broad gold back with her mittened hand. The horse started but he didn't move away.

Slowly, slowly, Zushan put Hari on the warm straight back, just as she would load furs onto the taller, stronger back of a reindeer. Then she lifted one leg over the stallion's back as well.

Her toes could just touch the ground. She was taller than the horse now, she realised. But he was much, much stronger than her.

The stallion shifted uncomfortably. For a moment Zushan thought he was going to buck them off and gallop off into the snow, leaving them cold and alone. But suddenly it seemed as though the memory of weight on his back returned to him.

The stallion began to move, slowly at first, as though he wasn't quite sure how to move with the unexpected load, and then more confidently. The mares followed. Zushan could hear their footsteps, muffled by the snow, and the huff of their breathing.

The world grew even whiter. The stallion lifted his head, his nostrils flaring. He changed direction slightly, and plodded on, head down into the snow.

She could feel the warmth of the horse through her clothes now. It was as though a small fire burnt under the shaggy golden coat.

What if he wasn't taking them to the camp, wondered Zushan, but to a sheltered glade where the horses saw out the blizzard? What if he didn't realise that she and Hari needed tents and the warmth of other humans to survive?

'Hari?' she whispered. The child whimpered in her arms. At least he was still alive, thought Zushan. 'Don't go to sleep!' she whispered. 'You'll die if you fall asleep in the snow.'

She had to keep him awake, she thought. She had to keep awake herself.

But soon there was no room in her mind to think. All she could do was hold on to Hari, hold on to the dark tough mane, and try not to fall asleep in the cold that sapped her strength and her thoughts.

Whiteness ... whiteness ... impossible to hear the mares behind now. Impossible even to hear the footsteps of the stallion. Even her own breathing seemed to vanish. Perhaps she had dissolved into the snow, and Hari too and all that was left was whiteness, silence and more white ...

Zushan shut her eyes. It seemed she dreamed, or perhaps it was not a dream. A young girl rode a horse, much as she was riding now. But this horse was larger and so tall her legs dangled at his sides, and brown not gold with no stripes along his spine and across his withers. The snow had gone, and in its place was grass, more grass than the world could ever hold, hill after hill of grass and the horse was galloping, pounding across the hills with the girl on his back and ...

'Zushan! Zushan! Hari!' The voice was faint but clear.

Zushan opened her eyes. 'Over here!' she called. 'Over here!' Hari cried out softly in her arms.

The stallion stopped. He lifted his head and neighed softly. One of the mares neighed back.

'What ...?' began Zushan, and then she understood. Slowly, stiffly, she slid off the broad back and gathered Hari into her arms again.

'Thank you,' she whispered to the stallion. The blizzard was so thick now she could only just see his eyes, dark and watchful above the golden nose.

The horse looked at her. It was a long look, as though he knew that something had begun today that would change life for every other horse, and every human too. Then he lifted his head and called his mares and trotted off into the white.

'Zushan! Zushan!' There were more voices now and faintly the pungent smell of burning bones from the fire. The camp must be very close.

'Here!' yelled Zushan again. She began to plod through the snow with Hari in her arms.

What should she tell them, she wondered. 'I was saved by a horse and he carried me on his back.' No, they'd never believe her. They'd think she'd been dreaming, dazed by cold and white. Perhaps she had.

No, she thought. The memory of the warm gold hide was too strong. The smell of horse lingered on her clothes as well.

It was no dream. The world had changed today, but no-one else could ever understand.

Strangers on Horseback

The strangers arrived in fog. The air was like grains of wheaten flour, drifting in long thin clouds along the cliffs above and forming a thick sea down in the valley, so that it was impossible to see the grapes or olive groves below.

Only the yellow road that snaked through the fog to the big house was visible to Milon, as he limped around the endless circle, leading the white horse that pulled the harness which turned the stones and ground the barley into flour.

The other slaves laughed at Milon for leading the white horse. Even the steward snorted and told him he was wasting his breath — why not sit with a whip and let the lash force the horse to do its work instead?

But even though his leg ached, Milon found it impossible to strike the horse. Simon worked best when you spoke gently to him, when you walked with him, and Milon found comfort in the warmth of the horse too, as they walked endlessly together. Simon had been his only friend since his first weeks in the slavery. It was as though they were both slaves together. The other slaves were older and none remembered being free. At times it seemed to Milon that the horse also had his memories. Maybe he had once galloped in a real partnership with his rider, instead of being harnessed by a nose ring to a grinding stone.

Simon worked best when Milon was with him and, as the steward said, a crippled boy wasn't useful for much else.

Sometimes, when no-one was watching, he even hugged the horse. Its size and strength were a refuge. For a while he'd even been able to cry into the horse's white hide, but he hadn't cried for a long time.

Sometimes you got used to pain.

The days all felt the same now. Only the work changed from season to season, as he led the horse while it pulled or ploughed or carried. Today they would grind the barley from the autumn harvest, and tomorrow they would grind the barley too, and the day after that, though the fog might clear by then, and he could watch for eagles on the cliffs above, or glimpse the other outdoor slaves down in the olives or vineyards.

Even gazing at an empty road was better than watching his own thoughts or thinking about the pain in his leg; better by far than his memories. He could always dream that any moment now someone miraculous would ride out of the fog — his father, perhaps, somehow unharmed. That was the best dream of all, though it hurt as well. Or perhaps the rider would be an uncle, one that he'd never known, a traveller who had escaped the massacre and spent his life hunting for his nephew.

'I vowed on my brother's grave that I would never rest till I found you and set you free!' he'd cry. He'd throw down gold at the Master's feet and together they would ride off to … to somewhere else. Somewhere like the past, when there had been soft beds and more than barley gruel to eat, and laughter and dreams of years to come.

The fog thickened slightly. The white horse in his harness plodded round and round the muddy track, leaning into the harness attached to the grind stones and Milon limped before him. No-one would come, of course. No-one would ever come …

The fog shivered slightly. Milon halted and the white horse stopped too. Something *was* coming up the road that led to the big house.

It was a cart drawn by two great horses, as white as Simon, with a high canopy hung with embroidered curtains, which gleamed gold and red in the thin white light. It seemed almost as though the horses chose which way to go. No hand guided them from inside the curtain.

Behind the cart came a rider. No, several riders, six perhaps, or seven. Milon squinted through the fog.

The horses and the cart halted at the gate that led to the house's outer courtyard. One of the riders dismounted and hammered on the courtyard door. Milon watched as the door opened. A slave's face peered out then disappeared, to be replaced by the Steward's harsher features.

Suddenly the courtyard doors were flung open. The strangers must be important, thought Milon, whoever they were. The Steward bustled out, gesturing to the slaves behind to take the horses to be watered, fetch the Master, fetch the wine.

One rider stayed on his horse. He seemed to be asking a question. The Steward gestured up towards Milon. Milon hurriedly began to lead Simon again, limping round as fast as he could in the damp air, as the rider cantered up towards them. Lazy slaves were beaten — worse; Simon might be beaten too.

The horse's hooves echoed through the fog — a brown horse, with a slender man on his back. Milon blinked, and realised that the man was a girl.

'Ho, boy! Which way is the horse pasture?'

Milon stared. It was impossible not to, even if it meant a beating afterwards. He had never seen a girl on horseback before, or a woman either. Women remained in their quarters with their spinning wheels and kept their gazes lowered.

This girl rode like a man. She was dressed like a man too, or a strange foreign man anyway, in linen trousers embroidered down the leg, and a fur-trimmed tunic. Her hair was fine as cobwebs and red as flame, with a soft round cap that was embroidered too. A gold brooch like a snake held her cloak, gold snake bracelets pushed high up on her arms, and she wore a single earring like a crescent moon.

'The horse pasture!' repeated the girl impatiently. Her accent was strange, like music, as though her words followed a tune.

Milon gathered his words together again. 'There is no horse pasture,' he said, feeling his tongue too big in his mouth.

The girl frowned. She was Milon's age, or perhaps a year younger. 'Where does your horse graze at night then?'

'With the sheep,' said Milon, feeling even stupider.

The girl sighed theatrically. 'Then perhaps you'll tell me where the sheep pasture is? I can't see anything in this fog.'

'It's just above us. You'll hear the sheep before you see them, but you can't miss it, even in the fog.'

'Thank you,' said the girl carelessly. 'I want to have a look at the pasture before we put the horses out.'

'It's good grazing,' said Milon. 'At least at this time of year.'

'Good,' said the girl. But she didn't leave. She gazed at him for a moment and then at Simon, plodding in its endless circle. 'That's cruel,' she said abruptly. 'A good horse shouldn't be treated like that.' She gestured to the ring that was through the horse's nose. 'A horse like that shouldn't be forced to walk in a circle to grind the grain, either. What are donkeys for?'

Milon shrugged. 'He was lame when the Master bought him, the same time as he bought me. That's how the Master got him cheaper than a donkey.'

That's how he got me cheap too, he could have added, because I limped like Simon. He said instead: 'But he refused to work in harness till the Master ordered him to have a ring.'

'That's even crueller then. A horse should work for love of you, not because he fears pain if he stops.' The girl leant across and stroked Simon's white neck. He whinnied at her softly, and for a moment Milon felt a tug of jealousy. The horse was his friend, not hers.

'He's a good horse,' said the girl. 'There's no sign of a limp now.'

Milon shrugged. Every day he was afraid the Master would notice the horse was no longer lame and take him for a riding horse, or worse, sell him for far more than he had paid.

The girl hesitated. 'You're a thrall?'

'A slave,' said Milon shortly. A thrall was sold to pay a debt and worked till the debt was paid, but a slave was ... just a slave. Always a slave.

The girl examined him. It would have been unbearable if she'd looked at him with pity. But she simply looked curious.

'You don't look like a slave,' she said at last.

Milon almost smiled. He gestured at his rough chiton, his bare feet with their callouses, the hair untrimmed for two long years

'I don't look like a slave?'

The girl shook her head impatiently. 'You're dressed like a slave. But your expression, the way you talk ...'

'Sometimes I forget,' said Milon.

'Forget what?'

'How to be a slave.'

'Ah,' said the girl.

'Sometimes I think the horse forgets too,' said Milon impulsively, before he realised what he was saying. 'Sometimes he gazes down the mountain, as though he remembers running free, just him and his rider ...'

The girl stared at him. Milon flushed.

The girl slid off her horse suddenly, stepped over to the white horse in its harness and stroked its nose. 'How long have you been a slave?'

'Two years.' Since the massacre, since my family died, since the spear stabbed my leg, since they took me to the slave market to stand while passers-by stared at my scars or offered money ... but he didn't say that.

The girl absently stroked the swollen flesh around the horse's nose ring. 'My name's Zanna,' she said abruptly.

'I'm Milon. Son of Milon,' he added, for the first time in two years. What did it matter who a slave's father was? But suddenly he wanted to claim a family now. 'And this is Simon.' He stroked the horse's white neck. Simon whickered gently in his ear.

'Simon?'

'I had a friend called Simonides,' said Milon shortly.

'And the horse is your friend now. Well, Milon's son,' the girl said, looking at him straight in the eyes, 'why do you stay?'

Milon blinked. 'What?'

'Horses are tethered. You're not; a man can choose what he does. Why don't you run away?'

'I can't run.' Milon gestured to his leg. 'I limp. That's why I lead the horse after the harvest, or milk the sheep in summer. I'm no use for any other work. Even if I ran, where could I run to? They'd find me, bring me back. Escaped slaves are branded, didn't you know?'

'Is that what they do around here? I wouldn't know. We haven't been in these parts before. We're traders,' she added.

'I thought most traders came by boat.'

'Boats!' Zanna looked scornful. 'We're horse people, we always have been. We trade things that come from the far east road, like bronze mirrors and silk — it's even finer than linen that's been beaten thin on the rocks. Do you know what mirrors are?'

Milon nodded. 'They show your reflection like pools of water do. My grandmother had a mirror.' For a moment he wondered who had it now.

'You won't find those on boats,' said Zanna with satisfaction. 'But we trade other things too. It depends where we've been, where we plan to go. Aunt Anitha takes the omens and decides, or just lets the horses choose which road to take.'

'You let the horses decide?'

'Sometimes. Why not? It's what our ancestors have always done.' She laughed, high and clear as a bird. 'The horses led us up here, through the fog. We were going to go right, along the plain, but the horses took the cart to the left, so we followed.'

'But there's nothing up here,' said Milon. 'Just farms. No-one who could afford the sort of things you bring.'

'So what? Tomorrow we'll go back down again.' Zanna laughed again. 'The world is our home. It doesn't really matter what room we're in today.'

'You don't fear bandits?'

Zanna grinned at him. 'There are eight of us — all armed! Spears, javelins, arrows ...' She gestured at her horse and for the first time Milon noticed the bow and arrows lashed to the saddle.

The shock must have shown in his face; Zanna's grin grew wider. 'I'm not one of your soft village women! My arrows shoot straighter than any man's. My mother is the same.'

'Your father doesn't mind?'

'He'd mind if she didn't!' Zanna glanced down at the house. 'I must go and check out the pasture before it gets dark, or Aunt will have my hide.'

For a moment grief felt like a spear thrust, it was so sharp. The girl was the first person in two years to talk to him as a person, Milon realised, not a slave. Suddenly he desperately wanted to thank her, to do her some service in exchange.

'Your horse,' he said suddenly. 'It has a cut on its leg.'

'What?' The girl looked down. 'It's only a small one. We must have brushed against a thorn bush in the fog. I'll wash it later.'

'Thorn bush scratches fester,' said Milon. 'Perhaps you don't have them where you come from?'

The girl shook her head.

'But there is a herb, it grows in a mat by the rock, the leaves are furry, greyish and they smell sweet when you crush them. If you boil them, they make a good wash. It won't fester at all if you do that.'

The girl gazed at him again. 'You know medicine?'

'My father was a horse doctor. A good one,' he added.

'And you're a slave,' said the girl, as though deciding something. 'Well, Milon, Milon's son, I must go.' She mounted in one swift movement. A minute later she and the horse had vanished in the fog.

The shed smelt of mould and damp. Outside the fog grew thicker in the darkness. The air clung and chilled and crept inside your skin. Milon huddled into the musty straw and listened to the talk around him.

Only four slaves slept in the hay shed. The others were farm workers, older and tougher. The difference in age and experience made Milon more lonely in their presence, not less. The household slaves slept indoors, the Steward in his small room off the kitchen, and the women in the women's wing, where they could hear if one of the Master's grandchildren cried in the night.

'Came out of the fog, they did.' It was Old Heron's voice. 'Took me by surprise so I nearly dropped the prunings. Must've taken the wrong turning in the fog, rich folk like that ...'

'Did you see their horses? Never seen so many horses, so fine and big.'

'Women too, right up there on their backs. Reckon the Master'll ...' Old Heron broke off.

A lantern was approaching across the dark courtyard, a puddle of gold light in the fog-smudged dark. The Steward's harsh face appeared at the door. 'Milon,' he said shortly, 'you're wanted.' He turned and was halfway back across the yard before Milon caught up with him.

The thick wooden door to the inner courtyard was open. It was the first time Milon had been inside. He caught the scent of damp cold herbs, their scent almost smothered by the fog. A pattern of fish and dolphin tiles flashed by in the lamplight and then came the wall of the house.

The house was an old one, built of mountain stone. One of the house slaves opened the door.

A hall with a tiled floor. A smell of marble, and beeswax, so that Milon felt a pang of memory. Those were the smells of home.

Another door. The Steward scratched at the door and opened it. 'Here is the boy, Sir.' He ushered Milon in then stood back against the wall in case he was needed to pour the wine.

Milon looked around. It was a long room with painted walls and it was well furnished: couches, a table with a wine jug, a bowl of white sheep's cheese and wheaten bread and raisin cakes. Milon's eyes caressed the raisin cakes. He could almost taste them.

'Well,' said the Master. 'Is this the boy?' It was only the second time Milon had seen him up close, a tall man with black and grey hair and shaggy brows and a smooth combed beard.

'I imagine so,' said a voice calmly, an older, richer voice than Zanna's, but with the same accent.

Milon stared. A woman lay on one of the couches, just as a man might do.

She was the fattest woman Milon had ever seen. Her face was oval, like a swollen egg, the eyes like tiny bright-blue raisins in the fat. Her cheeks were tattooed blue as well. Her face merged with her neck and her neck with her body. Layer upon layer of gold necklaces like leopard claws dropped below her chins; her tunic was thin linen, with embroidery at the base. Like Zanna she wore linen trousers underneath, sandals with gold buckles and studs, and a single crescent earring. Her hair was red like Zanna's too and gathered in a long thin braid that poked through a hole in the top of her pointed cap.

She gazed at Milon calmly, looking him up and down. The small blue eyes were shrewd. Milon wondered if there was straw in his hair or clinging to his clothes. But he kept his hands still.

'Well,' she said. 'So this is the boy.'

'A good worker,' said the Master, smiling as he sipped his wine. 'Well worth the price.'

'I doubt it,' said the woman. She must be Zanna's aunt, thought Milon, the one who took the omens and decided with the horses where to go. 'But I'm prepared to pay it. My niece has sense. If she says we should buy the boy, we should. And perhaps that is why we took the turn up here, in the fog. There is usually a reason, if you wait. '

'A fine girl, your niece,' purred the Master.

The big woman shrugged, sending ripples through her fat. 'Perhaps she will take the omens after me. Or perhaps she will decide to marry instead, like her mother. But, yes, she is a girl to be proud of.' She flicked a finger. 'Come here, boy.'

Milon walked forward. 'I plan to buy you,' she said, 'and for a ridiculously high price. Have you anything to say?'

Milon's heart shuddered. He tried to steady his breathing. 'You'll take me away from here?'

'We will. We will also free you. I'll not have any slave travel with us, to steal away while we sleep. You'll come freely, or not at all.'

The world tilted even further. It was as though the fog had gathered even in this room, as though it was impossible to see.

Dimly he heard the Master start to protest, and the fat woman cut him off. 'If I buy him, he is mine to free or not.'

Freedom, freedom, freedom ... Suddenly the fog cleared, as though a sharp wind blew inside his brain. He could see tomorrow almost as though he was there, walking down the road beside the wagon, the farm behind him, and Simon left on the hill. Another slave watched Simon working now, a slave who held a whip, while Milon wandered free ...

And suddenly Milon knew what he must do.

'No,' he said.

'What! How dare ...?' The Master began to struggle to his feet. The fat woman waved him back. Either her presence — or her gold — commanded him. He sat down again.

'No?' asked the woman quietly.

Milon shook his head. 'If you buy me and free me, I won't really be free. I'll be yours, because you bought me.'

The Master began another protest. Again the woman waved him silent.

'Is that all you have to say?' she asked. It was impossible to tell her reaction from her tone.

'No. Please ... if you have the gold to spare, will you buy the horse? The white horse. He's in the sheep pasture now with yours.'

'A white horse? White horses have always been special for us,' said the fat woman slowly. 'Why should I buy a horse instead of a boy?'

Milon hesitated. He knew what he felt, but it was hard to put it into words. 'Because ... because a man can choose the things he does,' he said. 'Mostly, anyway. But a good horse works for man and should be protected by him. Simon is a loyal horse. He shouldn't have a ring through his nose. He should be galloping across the plain, not pulling a pole in a small circle on the mountain.'

'Is that the only reason?' asked the fat woman.

Milon hesitated again. Finally he added, 'Because Simon is my friend. What can a slave give a friend? This the one thing I can do for him.'

Milon heard the Steward gasp behind him. Perhaps he'd get a beating later. But at the moment it didn't matter.

The woman was silent for a moment, her eyes half closed so they were almost lost in the fat. Then she opened them again, and Milon forgot the fat in their brightness.

'So,' she said slowly. 'You're young to have learnt that lesson. No, you can't give someone freedom. You can help them take it, that's all. Well,' she added, more briskly, 'let it be done then.'

She turned a careless gaze at the Master — far more careless than she'd given his slave. 'I presume if you'll sell the boy, you'll also sell the horse.'

The Master's eyes grew calculating. 'A horse is worth much more than a boy,' he said. Milon noticed he didn't mention that he thought the horse was lame. 'Especially a white horse.'

'A white horse is no more valuable to you than a brown one,' said the fat woman. 'Nevertheless — shall we say six times the weight of gold I offered for the boy?'

The Master's eyes widened with shock and pleasure. The woman nodded, as though he'd spoken. 'That's settled then.' She reached into a pouch at her waist and fumbled briefly, then beckoned the Steward. 'Give these to your master,' she instructed.

The Steward gaped at the coins, then crossed to his master.

'Come here, boy,' said the fat woman, as the Master gazed at his gold. She bent her head. 'We leave here tomorrow morning. We'll travel west along the road, and down the mountain,' she whispered, too softly for the Master to hear. 'Surely a boy who wants his freedom can run as far in a night as horses can walk in a day?'

Then she straightened, and hunted for the plumpest raisin cake with her fat fingers, as though Milon didn't exist.

The Steward grabbed Milon's shoulder. It was difficult to read his expression. He seemed half angry at Milon's effrontery, and half awed at the amount of gold offered for one lame boy. But the Steward was experienced at keeping his emotions to himself.

Would his own face be as blank as the Steward's, wondered Milon, after forty years of slavery?

'Back to the shed,' grunted the Steward.

Neither the fat woman nor the Master glanced at either of them as they left.

It was impossible to sleep. Milon lay among his straw, listening to the snores on either side of him, the distant bleat of sheep, and an owl booming far off up the mountain, the sound louder and clearer in the fog.

Freedom, offered to him like a honey cake on a plate. And he had turned it down. But ... was it really freedom? Had he really turned it down?

Wherever his words had come from, he knew that they'd been right. Your soul must be free as well as your body, and if his body had been bought again, he knew he would never feel free.

But what had the fat woman meant — 'a boy who wants his freedom can run as far in a night as horses can walk in a day'. Did she mean ...? Surely she meant...

It was almost dawn before exhaustion overtook him and he slept.

He had thought Zanna might come to say goodbye. He had no reason to think so, but he had. But she didn't come.

Milon ate his barley gruel, sour and thin as always. This morning he was told to watch the sheep, up on the hill. They would be lambing soon, so there would be foxes about. The grinding would have to wait until the master bought a donkey with the traders' gold.

The sheep pasture was a green flat, high up on the mountain. It looked as though the cliffs had hiccupped as they rose and left one grassy clearing. It was bordered by cliffs and fallen rocks from some long past rockfall — a high and silent place, especially in the fog.

His leg ached by the time he reached it, but then it always ached in damp weather. He gazed around the clearing. The sheep glanced up, damp and dust-grey as the rocks, then ignored him. There was no sign of the traders' horses. Simon was gone as well. The traders must have taken him already.

Milon sat on a rock and tried to rub the pain from his leg. He hadn't thought, last night, what the loss of the horse would mean to him. He had only thought of what he could do for his friend.

A raven yelled above, hoping for lambs; an old ewe bleated warily, then bent her head again. Milon had never felt so alone. He hadn't realised how much he would miss the horse. Every creature needed friends, he thought; even the sheep had each other.

He had to think, but it was hard to think. Slaves had no need to think, just to obey. It had been two years since he had wondered how tomorrow might be different from today.

'A boy can run,' she'd said. But though she'd glanced at his scarred leg under the shabby chiton, perhaps she hadn't realised he was lame. Milon would never run again.

If he tried to escape and was caught he would be beaten, so badly that perhaps he would die. A lame boy slave was no great loss, and his death would be an example to other slaves who might dream of freedom too. And if he lived a hot iron would burn into his forehead, to brand him in case he ever escaped again.

And if he didn't escape, what then? Day after day would pass, and every one the same, till he grew like Heron; an old slave still sleeping among the straw.

Thinking was easier now, he found. For there really was no choice at all.

The night air seeped into the shed, fresher than the smells of sweat and musty hay. The last lamps had been extinguished in the house. Milon stood up cautiously and trod warily through the hay. It rustled beneath his feet, but made no more noise than the mice that hunted seeds beneath it. The snores of his companions didn't falter.

Milon hesitated at the door. The watchdogs slept in the courtyard. They knew him but they would bark if they woke up. He must be quiet; he must get over the wall with no noise at all.

He crept along the wall. Yes, here it was, the foothold he'd noticed many times before. If he put his foot *there* and his hands *here* he could haul himself up. Now if only there were another foothold ... and another ... yes, here was one ...

It had been two years since he'd climbed a wall. He had forgotten his lame leg. All at once his knee refused to take his weight. His leg grazed painfully against the rock as his fingers grasped desperately at the stones.

A dog barked below him and then the other.

Milon froze. The barking was frantic now, as below him the dogs leapt at the shadow on the wall.

A spark of light flashed inside the house, then became a lantern's glow. Footsteps ran across the inner courtyard; the door to the outer courtyard opened. The Steward gazed out, holding his lantern high.

The light shone on the leaping dogs, the boy clinging to the wall. Shadows danced around the courtyard.

'What is it?' It was the Master's voice from inside the house.

The Steward looked straight at Milon, his face expressionless. For one long moment he didn't move. Then he turned.

'It's nothing, sir!' the Steward called. 'The dogs have cornered a rat, that's all. I'll quieten them down. Here, boys, here!'

The dogs bounded over to him. The Steward lifted the lantern higher, so it shone to the top of the courtyard wall. He was lighting his way, Milon realised.

His hands were trembling almost too much to move. But he forced himself to take another handhold, to shove as hard as he could with his good foot. The next shove took him to the top of the wall.

He glanced back. The Steward still stood there, the lantern in his hand, the dogs at his feet, his face still blank. The habit of hiding his thoughts was too strong to break now. Who was the Steward? Milon wondered suddenly. Had he been born a slave? Or sold for his father's debts perhaps, or his own? He'd never know. He could never ask the Steward now.

The Steward would be beaten in the morning, when the Master realised Milon had escaped. But suddenly he raised his hand. It was a gesture of farewell. It also said: this is all I can do for you boy. Don't waste the only thing I have to give. Milon nodded. He would have liked to smile, but it was as though he had forgotten how. He would have liked to wave in return, but both hands were needed now.

Milon slithered over the far edge of the wall, till he was hanging by both hands, then dropped. It was further than he thought. His good leg yelled with pain; his bad leg screamed with agony and collapsed. Milon rolled in the dust, then scrambled to his feet.

His bad leg refused to hold him. Milon gazed around frantically. Yes, there they were, the poles used to knock the olives from the trees. He hopped over to them and chose the thickest one, then hobbled down the foggy road.

The world was dark and foggy and painful. His knee swelled, so he could feel the swelling rubbing at his good leg as he limped along. His other leg felt bruised. Something wet trickled down his arm. Blood? But it was too dark too see and anyway, there wasn't time.

A boy wo wants his freedom can run as far as a horse can walk ... A boy can limp ... how far? At least it was downhill.

If only he could see the stars, thought Milon, he could watch them as they moved across the sky, and work out how long he'd stumbled on, how close it was to dawn. But the fog still hid the sky. He couldn't even watch the horizon, to see if dawn was coming.

Milon struggled on.

If only he hadn't urged the trader to buy Simon, he could have crept up to the sheep pasture instead. He could have escaped on horseback, instead of limping through the dark. That way they could both have escaped.

But a good horse is valuable — far more so than a boy slave. The traders might accept an escaped slave. Milon doubted they would welcome a horse thief.

The bleeding stopped, but he was sweating now. The sweat ran in hot rivers down his chest, then grew cold as it reached his legs. All he could see was blackness and the slight furring of the fog. The road was a dim shadow at his feet, but at least he could make out the dusty rise to either side, so he didn't veer off the road.

For a while he tried to dream, as he stumped along, but it hurt too much to dream of the past, and the future was unknown. Who were the traders he was running to? At least they must be better than what he had left behind. At least they had horses and could travel fast, and out-run the men who would hunt for him.

If only he could reach them ...

How long till dawn now? The fog thinned slightly, or was daylight seeping through the world? Milon could make out the olive fields on either side now. Were they still the Master's? No, he'd come too far for that. He tried to remember the country he'd passed when he'd first come to the Master's farm. But he had been too dazed in the rattling cart to notice what had been on either side.

The fog was definitely lifting. The road was steeper too, dappled with moon shadows and so rutted with ancient cart tracks that his staff slipped and twisted and jarred his leg.

His body yelled at him to stop, to rest. His throat screamed for water. Perhaps the road would cross a stream. If he stopped he might hear one gurgling nearby. But there was no time to stop.

Milon glanced upwards. For the first time in many nights he could see the stars. But they were fading now. Over in the east the grey light was eating up the dark.

The other slaves woke at dawn. After that even the Steward could not hide the fact that Milon had vanished. The Master, his sons and neighbours would be searching for him at first light.

For a moment Milon wondered if he should leave the road. The olive trees would hide him from anyone on the road. But in the fields the way was rougher; it would slow him down too much. No, better to make one desperate throw for safety and the traders than to cower among the trees, waiting for capture.

Dawn was pale pink tongues of flame. The birds yelled around him, celebrating the day. Milon could see the plain below him now, green trees and small square farms and the road a thread of yellow ribbon through the green.

There was no sign of the traders.

Perhaps they were around the next bend, or the next, camped by the side of the road with tents and fire, warming drinks and food before they started on their way. Any moment now he'd see them, smell their fire, hear their horses whinny. Just round the next corner ... or the next ...

And slowly Milon realised that no matter how much he hurried, a boy could never limp the distance that a horse could walk. His body refused to let him stop, but slowly his heart and courage seeped out of him, till there was only emptiness, bitter as wormwood, and the certainty of capture and loneliness forever more.

He hardly heard the hoof beats at first. His leg was throbbing and his heart was pounding too. The thudding of the road was like the thudding of his body. Milon froze. For a moment he wondered which way the sound was coming from. Perhaps the Master had borrowed a neighbour's horse, was already galloping to seize his slave. Even if it was a traveller coming the other way, he'd best get off the road.

It was too late. The horse rounded the corner and galloped towards him before he could even try to hide.

It was Simon.

The white horse whinnied. He was already stopping, even before his rider, her red hair gleaming in the morning light, could pull at the reins.

Zanna grinned at him. 'Like a ride?' she asked.

'I ...' It was impossible to speak. His heart seemed about to burst from his body. Zanna pulled out a damp flask and handed it to him. Milon took it gratefully. It was honeyed wine and water, cold and sweet, with barley meal to thicken it.

A hawk hovered and fell in one flashing swoop above them. A young goat called to his herd beyond the trees. The day had begun.

'I knew you'd come,' said Zanna.

Milon managed to find his voice. 'How?' he asked hoarsely.

Zanna met his gaze. 'You didn't have the eyes of a slave. I wanted to come and find you last night. But Aunt said, no, you had to free yourself. She said it was important. But then Simon started whinnying.' She stroked the horse's neck. 'I said to Aunt: "Look, he's telling us that I should go." And Auntie laughed, and said, alright, we'll let the horse decide.'

Milon smiled. It felt strange at first, then he felt it spread across his face. He handed back the flask. 'How far do we have to go?'

Zanna laughed her bird-call laugh, high and sweet. 'Down to the plain, to Olympia or Corinth perhaps, or across the world! Who knows? We go where the white horses take us, where there are goods to buy or sell.' She held her hand down to him. 'Come on, climb up. It'll be a good life, Milon son of Milon, I promise you that.'

Milon took her hand and pressed his other on the horse's strong white back. It had been two years since he had been astride a horse. But his body remembered. The white horse snorted. Someone, Zanna perhaps, had removed his nose ring. His reins were plaited leather, red and gold and brown. It had been two years for Simon too, thought Milon, since he had been ridden as a good horse should be. But Simon remembered as well

Zanna tugged on the reins as Milon held on behind. The white horse turned and cantered down towards the plain.

Half a Million Horses

The rider came at midday, moving with unbelievable speed across the spring-green plain, at first just a dark smudge against the clear blue sky, but growing larger and larger, till Sui could make out the giant animal he rode.

'Mama! Someone ... something ... is coming!'

Mama straightened, and gazed where Sui pointed across the wheat patch. The wheat was waist high and needed constant weeding now the soil was warmer.

The animal was almost as tall as the courtyard wall behind them, and brown like the wall too. But this was a glossy brown, not the dull brown of dirt and mud. Its legs were long and pounded against the ground, so the echoes rang around the courtyard long before the rider drew close.

'What is it?' wondered Sui.

Mama brushed the dirt off her hands. 'A horse.' Mama had lived on a farm near the city before she married Da; she had seen many strange things. But nothing else, thought Sui, could be quite so large or powerful as a horse.

And a man sat on it, just as she had sat on the big sow when she was small. But the sow had twisted so she fell off. This man balanced sure and strong on the great beast's back, despite its speed. As Sui looked, he tugged at the ropes in his hands, pulling the horse's head back, so it changed direction suddenly and skirted around the wheat patch and the short green millet, then it stopped in the dust by the courtyard wall.

The rider dismounted. His face was streaked with dust and sweat, but even so it was clear he was different from anyone Sui had ever known. His cheeks were wider, his nose more narrow and his clothes were strange too; not made of goatskin like all the clothes that Sui had ever known, but some thick, almost shiny, material, which showed deep red and blue, despite the dirt.

She glanced back at the horse. There was a sort of leather cushion on its back, where the rider had sat, and the cushion rested on a strange rich cloth. Two bags of leather hung on either side. Sui wondered if they held bedding, or food perhaps.

The rider was panting. He leant against his horse for a moment and wiped dark sweat from his forehead. 'Your headman,' he gasped, 'I must see your headman!'

Sui's mother bent her head politely. 'I will take you to ...' she began, just as Auntie Fai bustled through the courtyard door.

Auntie Fai was the oldest of the aunties. She was thin and hard and her hair was thin too, pulled back tightly into a grey knot at her neck. Her face was like an apricot that had rolled behind the fireplace and dried there all winter.

'What is going on here? A guest! Why didn't you call me at once! Excuse her, honoured guest ...' Auntie Fai's tiny mud-black eyes measured the rider's clothes and horse, and judged him to be honoured indeed. 'Please come inside. I will take you to Great Uncle.'

The rider nodded. 'Thank you,' he said briefly. His voice was strange as well, the familiar words were spoken slightly differently. He followed Auntie Fai through the gateway without a second look at Sui and her mother.

The giant horse clopped after him.

Sui sighed, then pinched herself. What had she expected? That he'd gaze into her eyes then immediately ask Great Uncle for her hand! It all came of listening to Mama's story of how Da had taken the pigs into the city market to sell, and seen Mama along the road and brought her back to the farm as his wife.

But that had scarcely had a happy ending, thought Sui. Da had died and Mama had to live among strangers, with the aunties and uncles who thought no-one would be good enough for their darling younger brother.

It would be horrible to live among strangers, decided Sui, no matter what Auntie Fai said.

Great Uncle lived in the biggest of the huts inside the courtyard, surrounded by apricot trees and dusty hens that pecked and made dust baths in the dirt. Sui watched as Auntie Fai ushered the rider inside then bustled out again. She gestured to Sui sharply.

'Call the others!' she ordered. 'The rider says he has something important to say, and Great Uncle insists we all be there as well.'

'Yes, Auntie.'

Sui sped through the apricot trees, calling through each doorway, then out the courtyard gate again and past the pig pen and the dung pile, to the grassland behind the farm where Cousins Donizen and Ushan were tending the goats.

'A guest!' she called. 'A rider on a giant horse!' She stumbled slightly over the unfamiliar word. 'Great Uncle says we all must come!'

The boys nodded and began to call the goats, to herd them back inside the courtyard. Sui left them to it and ran back. She hesitated at the courtyard gate, then hurriedly dipped her hands in the big earthenware tub of water that always stood there in case the animals were thirsty, and washed her face and tried to smooth back her hair. Sui had good hair, Mama said, thick and black, but there was so much of it that it kept escaping from her plait.

Except for the cousins, the family were already seated when she got there. The aunties and uncles and older cousins sat on the wide bed platform, and Cousin Tasha's children sat on the floor. Mama sat on the floor too. Mama no longer had a husband to provide for her or make sure she had respect.

Mama's face was pale and so were the faces of the aunties and uncles, as though shock had bleached all the colour from their skin. What had the rider been saying, Sui wondered, to make them look like this?

Sui sat down beside Mama. Light streamed over the rough mud windowsill. If she craned her head, Sui could just see the horse in the courtyard. Someone had taken the leather seat off its back and tied its rope to an apricot tree. The chickens clucked round its long legs, as though they too wondered what sort of beast had arrived.

The horse's rider sat in the seat of honour, next to Great Uncle.

'What has he been saying?' whispered Sui to her mother.

'He says an army is coming,' whispered her mother.

'An army!'

'A giant army, coming to attack the city! He says they will kill us all on their way there!'

'But that's ...' began Sui, then stopped, as Auntie Fai's stern eyes glared at her.

Great Uncle was shaking his head. 'I am sure it cannot be as bad as you say,' he protested. 'If we surrender and say we will pay their taxes, surely the army will let us live.'

The rider's face twisted with remembered pain. 'In my town Genghis Khan built a temple out of the bodies of those who had surrendered. His soldiers piled them high, then plastered them with mud to make walls to bake in the sun. Those he let live were taken to become a living shield, forced to advance on the next town in front of the army and protect the soldiers behind from arrows.'

Cousin Tasha began to cry, muffling the sound behind her hands. Auntie Lazza hugged her close to comfort her.

'How did you escape?' demanded Great Uncle.

'I was one of those he let live. I lived with the army for three weeks, till they came to the next town. I was made to run in front of the horsemen. When the arrows from the city killed those around me, I lay down and pretended to be dead. For three days the army passed over me as I lay there in the sun, protected by the heaped bodies of my friends. On the third day the world was quiet. I looked up and all I could see were crows and the slain and the ruins of the town.'

'And your horse?' asked Auntie Fai, glancing sternly at Cousin Tasha and her tears. 'Where did you get the horse?'

'Its leg was hurt. It could no longer gallop with the army. The soldiers had left it behind. But I had worked with horses, back in my old life when the world was sane. I cut the arrow out and ... and we both survived.'

'What did you eat?' asked Sui.

'Shh,' ordered Auntie Fai, shocked at such forwardness.

The rider almost smiled. 'It's a good question,' he said. 'One hundred thousand men and half a million horses eat the world empty.'

'Half a million!' exclaimed Auntie Fai. 'There aren't so many horses in the world!'

The rider shook his head. 'Every soldier in Ghenghis Khan's army has five horses, so if one is hurt or tired he can change at will. They say there are a hundred thousand men in the Mongol army ... After they had passed there was no grass, no animals, no grain stores left.

'But the crows came to feed on the dead, and I ate the crows. It rained that first night and soon there was grass again. And there, with the bodies of my friends around me, I swore I would ride from town to village, from village to city, and warn them of the danger and that is what I have done ever since. Genghis Khan's army moves quickly, but not as fast as one man and a good horse can travel.'

Great Uncle sucked his toothless gums thoughtfully. 'But are you sure the army will come this way?' he insisted. 'We are far away from the road to the city. No-one comes this way from one harvest to the next.'

The rider shrugged, making his strange bright tunic rustle. 'I'm sure,' he said. 'The army isn't like a caravan of traders straggling along the road. When it comes, the army will fill the plain from horizon to horizon. Until you have seen a hundred thousand men and half a million horses, you can have no idea how an army can fill the world. I have already warned the city elders and they have sent out warnings too.'

'So you have warned us,' said Great Uncle heavily. 'But what should we do with your warning? Run to the city?'

The rider shook his head, so his long dusty hair brushed against his tunic. 'There is no hope for the city. None at all.'

'Then what?' demanded Great Uncle.

'Run. Hide,' said the rider.

'How can we outrun an army? We have no horses to carry us away! We have nowhere to hide either.' Great Uncle gestured out the window, as though the rider could see the empty plain and bare brown hills beyond the courtyard wall. 'We have no caves, no forests, no mountains to flee to. What can we do?'

The rider hesitated. He glanced at Sui then looked away. 'I could take one person away with me on horseback,' he offered. 'Or even two, if they are small.'

Sui glanced again at the horse out the window. Even an army seemed less frightening at the moment than the thought of trying to balance on that great creature's back. She had never seen an army nor had any clear idea of what one might be like. But the horse looked very big and all too real.

Great Uncle studied Sui and the children on the floor thoughtfully. 'Maybe,' he said doubtfully. 'How far away do you think the army is?"

The rider shrugged. 'They will be here in fifteen days perhaps. No more.'

'Then can you wait a day with us? If we can find no other way of escape by then we ...' Great Uncle's voice quivered, then he forced it firm again, ' ... then we would be most grateful if you would take two of us to safety.'

'No!' screamed Sui in her mind. But she said nothing. To leave her home, her family, the village ... everything she had known. But if she wasn't one of the chosen ... if the rider took little Dalan or Shai instead, then she would die among the crushing hooves of half a million horses.

Great Uncle nodded at Auntie Fai. 'Our guest will be hungry,' he said. He smiled grimly. 'We may as well feast now. What we don't eat, the army will.'

The aunties left first, with the children. The oldest of the uncles, Jaim and Ballar, stayed in the hut. The sound of their voices floated across the dust of the courtyard, where the hens scratched unconcerned by any thought of armies. Surely Great Uncle would find a way to save them all, thought Sui. Great Uncle knew everything, or almost ...

Auntie Fai nodded at the horse. 'The beast will be thirsty,' she said. 'You had better give it some water.'

Sui inspected the horse nervously. 'How do you know?' she asked.

'All animals drink,' said Auntie Fai impatiently. 'Hop to it!'

'Yes, Auntie,' said Sui obediently.

Sui fetched the spare wooden water bucket and trudged out to the well. Usually the cousins fetched the water for the pig-pen households in the morning, balancing it on a pole they carried between them on their shoulders, though they all took turns in carrying water for the young turnips or wheat or millet. Sui glanced at the horizon, almost expecting to see the army in the distance, a brown wall of monsters like the horse inside their courtyard.

But the horizon looked as it always did — hills like dirty skulls on one side and a thin black wrinkle where the green plain met blue sky on the other.

Surely it was impossible that an army could be so close. Life just didn't change so suddenly. The rider must be tricking them, thought Sui. But Great Uncle believed him. Great Uncle would not be taken in by trickery.

The well had been dug long before even Great Uncle was a child, and lined with rocks dug from the soil. It was surrounded by a thick straw and mud wall, like the courtyard and hut walls, and these walls too were topped with a roof of thatch made of dried wheat stems, to stop the rain washing the thick dried mud away.

Sui lowered the well bucket into the darkness. The water level was high now in spring. Later in summer the rope would fall deep into the ground before it splashed below, and your arms ached long before you'd got the bucket to the surface.

The well was too dark to see far down it, no matter how far you leant over it thought Sui. Maybe …

Sui hauled the water up from the blackness, and ran back into the courtyard. Her mother was bending over the fire, poking twigs into it so it burnt more quickly. A freshly killed goat, already cut into chunks, hung on the spit above the flames.

Sui looked at it hopefully. It had been months since she had tasted meat, not since the last festival. But the rider and aunties and uncles could easily eat one goat between them, and they were unlikely to offer any to her. Sometimes she envied Auntie Fai, who had the job of chewing Great Uncle's meat so it was soft enough for a toothless man to swallow. At least she got to taste the meat, even if her stomach didn't get its goodness.

'Mama?'

Her mother turned. 'Yes? What is it, Chicken?'

'Could we all hide down the well? It's dark down there and no-one would see us …'

Her mother shook her head. There were tears in her eyes, Sui saw. Mama's tears made the army much more real …

'The army will need to use the well to get their water,' she said softly. 'But it was a good idea.'

'But where else can we hide?' cried Sui.

The tears seemed to freeze in her mother's eyes. 'I'll ask Great Uncle to choose you to escape,' she whispered. 'He told me once that you are the cleverest of all the family's young ones. I'll tell him it is important that he choose those best able to survive.' She bit her lips so hard the skin around them turned white. 'Now take the water to the horse, as Auntie told you to.'

Sui nodded. She hefted up the bucket and walked across the courtyard. The horse raised its head and whinnied softly as she approached.

Sui hesitated. Its teeth were enormous, yellow-brown, broad and blunt. Its mouth looked like it could chew your arm up in a single bite.

The horse whinnied again, and Sui saw its eyes.

They were brown eyes, the biggest, gentlest eyes that Sui had ever seen.

She stepped forward cautiously and placed the bucket on the ground. The horse blew through its nose at her, and lowered its head to the bucket. Its short brown hair looked smooth ... almost without thinking Sui stretched out her hand and stroked the giant neck. The skin felt warm and very strong.

There was a step behind her. 'So,' said the rider. 'You have made friends.'

'I ...' Sui began to apologise, then realised the rider was smiling. The smile looked strange, as though his face wasn't used to smiling, but it was a kind smile nonetheless.

'Yes,' she said simply.

'Good,' said the rider. 'My name is Timur,' he added.

'I'm Sui.'

'I know,' said Timur. 'Your Great Uncle told me.'

Sui wondered why they had been discussing her. Perhaps her mother was right, perhaps Great Uncle was considering her to be one of the two to escape.

But she didn't want to go! She wanted to go back to yesterday, when there was no thought of armies on the horizon. And, as that was impossible, she wanted her whole family to survive, to stay living right where they were, on their farm by the brown hills on the plain.

The rider, Timur, was still standing next to her, stroking his horse.

'Does the horse have a name too?' asked Sui.

'I call him South Wind,' said Timur. 'The wind blew from the south as we rode away from the ruins and the smell of death. The wind smelt clean and strong. Even an army can't stop the wind.' He shrugged, and looked at the horse with so much love that Sui almost felt she should look away. 'Sometimes, when I'm on his back, I feel like we are the wind too.'

'Please,' she said. 'May I ask another question?'

'If you like,' said Timur.

'How do they live, this great army? How can they find enough food or shelter?'

Timur shrugged. 'They carry tents with them, giant felt tents, made of wool that is pressed under their saddles as they ride. And as for food, well, they hunt game and steal stores from the villages and towns they conquer. But mostly their horses feed them.'

'Their horses?'

Timur began to untie the bags from either side of the horse's back. 'The horses feed on the grass as they travel and they give their riders milk and blood ...'

'Blood!'

'From the big vein in their neck. It doesn't weaken the horse if they only take a little each time. They carry dried horse meat too, in the pockets of their trousers, and dried mares' milk in leather bags. When they have to cross a river, they blow air into the bags so they float across the river and help the men across.'

'What about the women?'

'There are no women with the army — or not for long.' Timur looked away, as though he didn't want to meet her eyes. 'The Mongol women are back home in the far north desert lands, looking after their cows and sheep and goats. It is the northern desert that makes the men so tough.'

'Would they really kill us?' whispered Sui.

Timur did meet her eyes this time. 'Yes,' he said.

'Sui. Stop bothering the guest!' cried Auntie Fai.

Timur smiled his unpractised smile again. 'She's not bothering me,' he said. But he nodded to Sui briefly, and went back to Great Uncle's hut.

Sui crossed the courtyard to her mother and knelt next to the fire. 'I've been thinking,' she said.

'Yes? You're a thinking little chicken, aren't you? Always so full of ideas.'

Her mother spoke like they were already parted, thought Sui. 'I thought, what if we build a giant bed platform and we could all hide in it?'

Her mother stroked her cheek. 'I think the soldiers might suspect something if they saw a giant bed platform and no-one about,' she said.

'We could hide in a pile of straw then!'

'It is true that the wheat is waist high; we could cut it and make a pile of straw big enough to hide in. But the horses would trample it, and the soldiers would take it for them. And, no, we can't hide in the grain bins, because they'll take the grain too.'

Her mother had been trying to plan too, thought Sui. Everyone was, of course, not just Great Uncle. She gazed around the courtyard, at the hard-packed dirt and the dirt-coloured walls, and the dusty chickens that were dirt-coloured too. If only the family were the colour of dirt as well! They could press up hard against the courtyard walls and no-one would see them. If only when they had built the walls for Cousin Tasha's hut last year, they had built them hollow, so they could hide inside …

And suddenly the idea came to her, so clear and simple it was as though it had been floating in front of her, waiting for her to pluck it from the air. Without thinking she leapt to her feet and ran across the courtyard.

'Sui!' called her mother. 'What are you …?'

It was too late. Sui was through the door before she realised her bad manners. No-one ever entered Great Uncle's hut without knocking and asking his permission. And she had just run in …

'Sui!' Great Uncle looked startled; it was the first time Sui had ever seen him look surprised.

'You impertinent girl!' Auntie Fai bustled behind her. 'You come out at once now, and …'

'No,' said Great Uncle. 'Sui is a polite girl. She must have some reason, don't you child?'

'Please,' said Sui. 'I had an idea.'

'Ah yes,' said Great Uncle affectionately, and Sui realised for the first time that Great Uncle really liked her. Great Uncle never showed favourites, but now …'She is full of ideas, this child,' Great Uncle said to Timur. 'Just like her father, who was like my father … well child, tell us this idea!'

Suddenly Sui felt her tongue grow too big for her mouth. 'I just thought …' she mumbled.

'Speak up!' said Great Uncle.

'I thought of a place we could all hide.'

'And where is this place?' Great Uncle spoke kindly, but without much hope.

'In the walls.'

Great Uncle looked at her, puzzled. 'The walls are solid mud child. We can't hide in walls.'

'But … but we could make new walls. Like we did when we made the new hut for Auntie Tasha. But we could make them hollow and hide inside them …'

Auntie Fai snorted behind her. 'Impossible!'

'No,' said Great Uncle slowly, sucking at his gums as he always did when deep in thought. 'Not impossible. It doesn't take long to make a wall, and we have fifteen days. There would be time for them to dry too, so they don't look too new.'

'But how would we breathe inside a wall?' demanded Auntie Fai, forgetting the politeness due to Great Uncle.

'We could leave small holes in the walls,' suggested Sui. 'Too small to see but big enough to breathe through.'

'And we stand in the walls for …how long did you say it took for the army to pass?' Auntie Fai challenged the rider. 'Three days? Without moving or drinking or eating? It is impossible!'

'Is it?' asked Great Uncle softly. 'Think, Fai. If you must choose between standing for three days inside a wall or dying with the armies of Genghis Khan, which would you choose?'

Auntie Fai fell silent. She looked at Sui, then back at Great Uncle. 'I can stand for three days,' she said finally. 'And if I die of thirst or hunger, at least I die with dignity and not at the hands of soldiers. But the children — how can they be quiet for three days? And if just one of us cries out, they will find the rest.'

Great Uncle stood up. 'You will take cloth and tie it across their mouths, so they cannot cry,' he said. 'And you will tie their legs and arms as well, so they cannot move. Each of us will have a gag across our mouths too, in case we cry out in our sleep or in a daze.'

'But what will we live on when the army has passed?' cried Auntie Fai.

'We will tie up the hens and the roosters,' decided Great Uncle, 'and as many of the goats and pigs as we have room for, and hide them in the walls too. We will keep the wheat we have left from last autumn's planting, and the turnip and onion seed, and the millet seed that would feed us till the next harvest, and keep it to plant too.'

'And the apricot trees?' asked Auntie Fai. The apricots were one of the village's main foods

Great Uncle smiled grimly. 'You can't put a tree into walls,' he said. 'Perhaps the soldiers will cut them down. We can only hope they will sprout again from the roots. Now, call in the family, it is time to plan and work.'

The children took turns carrying the water and helped the women mix the mud and straw, and the men took lumps of soft mud and piled them one on top of each other. But instead of the usual single wall, this time they built two walls, side by side, with a hollow in between just wide enough for a person to stand. They pulled the roof beams and the thatch from Cousin Tasha's hut to put on the new one, and knocked the walls of the old hut down, so no-one in the army would wonder why a hut stood roofless in the village.

Timur worked with them. 'I'll stay while you build the walls,' he promised.

'Thank you,' said Great Uncle simply. 'We need your help.'

It was true. While one wall took only a day to make, a double wall took twice as long, and the walls had to dry for at least ten days, or they would be too soft and fall down if they were even nudged a little from inside. There were still all the usual jobs to do as well, the grass to be collected for the pigs, and the goats to herd, though the backbreaking job of weeding the wheat and millet had been abandoned. What was the point, when the armies' horses would eat them before they had a chance to bear grain?

Even Great Uncle worked at the walls, though he needed a stick to walk, and his joints were almost too stiff to move in the mornings.

Sui heaved another bucket up from the well. The water smelt cold and fresh and she was hot, despite the wind from the hills.

'Let me carry that for you.'

Sui started. Timur had the ability to walk so softly you didn't know he was there. Sui wondered if it had come from having to lie so still for so many days, as the army passed over him. Would she have the same quality, she wondered, if she too survived after the army had passed?

'It's alright,' she said awkwardly. 'I can manage.'

'It's no trouble. I want a drink anyway.'

She handed him the bucket and watched him drink. He didn't look so strange now, mud-streaked as they all were. Or perhaps, she thought, she had got used to his strangeness.

'Where did you live before?' she asked suddenly.

'A long way north and east. I have been travelling for what,' he shrugged, 'perhaps three years now.'

'How old were you when the army captured you?'

'About your age.'

Sui blinked. Timur smiled grimly. 'You thought I was older? Well, I am now.'

He began to walk back to the farm. Sui followed him. 'Timur ...' It was the first time she had used his name.

'Yes?'

'Was your village like our farm?'

'No. It was a town, oh, much, much larger than your farm here. We had a farm just outside the town walls, but our farm was bigger than yours too. We raised horses.' He glanced up at South Wind, peacefully tearing at the grass outside the courtyard walls and ignoring the goats who grazed on either side. 'I've never been without a horse. I don't think I would have survived without South Wind. I don't think I would have wanted to survive.'

'I ...' Sui stopped. She had been going to say that she hated horses. Horses were going to bring pain and death. If it wasn't for horses, the armies would never find their small farm on the plains. But how could she tell that to Timur?

And it wasn't true, she realised. She hated the idea of horses — giant creatures with armies on their backs. But South Wind was different. He was powerful but he looked friendly too, nibbling at his grass in the sunlight.

For a moment she wondered what it would be like to ride on the great horse's back like Timur, and race with the wind as he had done. She thrust the thought away. It would never happen now. She and her village would live ... or they would die ... but in either case, Timur and South Wind would be gone.

'Sui!' Auntie Fai bustled up towards her. 'What are you doing, lazing about? We need more water!'

'I'm sorry, Auntie.' Sui took the bucket from Timur and carried it over to the mud puddle and tipped it in, then began the walk back to the well again. She glanced up at the horizon automatically, as they all did now. The blue sky gazed back at her. The green plain was still.

By the third day the hollow walls were finished and the new hut was capped with wooden beams and thatch. The walls gaped at each side of the doorway. Such small gaps, thought Sui, but they were wide enough to wriggle into and, as Great Uncle said, if the walls were any thicker some soldier might wonder why and investigate. Now they could only hope the walls would dry before the army reached them.

She looked across the plain again. It was still empty, apart from an eagle hovering high above the hills.

'Sui! Dinner!'

Sui walked slowly towards the fire. The family ate together now, instead of in their separate huts. Even Great Uncle ate with everyone else. They ate well too. All the remaining seed had already been walled up with the precious plough, and the dried apricots and beans and dried goat's curds and withered turnips from last harvest.

But Great Uncle said the older goats and hens and pigs would never survive being walled up for three long days, and there was no point leaving their meat for the army. There was meat to eat every day now, with only green herbs and wheat shoots to accompany it. Sui had never thought she might get sick of eating meat and long for millet porridge.

Great Uncle sat in his big wooden chair and Timur, as their guest, sat next to him in the only other wooden chair the farm had. They sat on the upwind side of the fire so the smoke didn't blow in their faces. Sui sat next to her mother and took the bowl she handed her. She sniffed at it. Goat again, an old one by the look and smell of it, and tough. She took a chunk between her fingers and began to nibble it.

Great Uncle cleared his throat, as he always did before formal pronouncements. 'We have to thank you,' he said to Timur. 'Without your help the walls would not have gone up so quickly.'

Timur shrugged, so his strange thick robe fell in creases around him. 'I did little enough.'

'It means a lot,' said Great Uncle quietly, 'that a stranger would stay to help us. There is nothing that can be done now until the army approaches. All we can do is wait. You are free to leave, if you wish. You have helped us all you can.'

Sui started. It hadn't occurred to her that Timur might leave so soon. But Timur shook his head. 'I'd like to stay, if I may,' he said to Great Uncle. 'I'll go when we see the army coming across the plains. That will still give me time to escape.'

Great Uncle looked at him strangely. But all he said was, 'If that is your wish, then we welcome you.'

So the days continued. The wheat grew unweeded — there was no point tending it now when half a million horses would gallop over it. For the first time in Sui's life there was little to do, except collect grass for the pigs, and firewood and mushrooms from the hills, and watch the horizon and wait.

The trees were stunted in the gullies between the hills, but at least they *were* trees. Down on the plain the winter wind was too harsh for any tree to survive, unless they were protected by a thick mud wall, like the village apricot trees. But at least there was plenty of firewood; the weight of snow broke many branches and when the snows melted they lay shattered on the ground.

Sui tied up another bundle of wood with a roughly cured strip of goatskin (it was easier to carry many small bundles than one large one) then slowly climbed the next hill. She could see the village from here and the far hills too and even further along the plain. It was strange to see Auntie Fai and Mama and all the others so small below her.

There were birds up here too, hunting for lizards among the rocks, and last summer she'd seen a fox slink across a gully. The swallows darted above her, hunting flies. They made their mud nests below the rooves of the huts every summer.

Would there be any swallows left when the army had passed, she wondered? She supposed not, and no trees or foxes or other animals either. The army would take everything ...

'Sui?'

Sui started. 'I didn't hear you!'

'I've learnt to walk softly. What were you thinking about?'

Sui gestured about her. 'The trees, the animals. What will we burn if they take all the trees?'

'Trees grow again. You can burn dried horse droppings, like the army does.' He grimaced. 'It stinks a bit, but burns quite well. There will be plenty of horse droppings once the army has passed.'

Sui gazed out over the plain again. 'It's all so quiet,' she said. 'Are you really sure they are coming, Timur? What if they decided to go another way?'

Timur shook his head. 'They always head for the largest city. And the largest city is to the south.'

'What's it like?' asked Sui. 'No-one from our farm has ever been there, except for Da. Even Mama never went inside the city walls.'

Timur shrugged. 'Big. Some mud walls and mud houses like yours, but larger.'

'Aren't all walls made of mud?'

'What? No, of course not. The walls on our farm were made of stone.'

Sui frowned. 'You can't stick stones together. The walls would fall down.'

'Not little stones, like you find in the soil here. Big rocks, and we use burnt shells to stick them together.'

Sui thought it sounded quite impractical. 'Did you eat the horses on your farm?'

'Eat them! No, they were for riding, though we milked them sometimes.'

'You raised horses for armies to ride!' cried Sui, horrified.

'No! For other people, to … to get from one place to another. And farm horses too.'

'Farm horses?'

'You know, for ploughing the ground and carrying the crop to market.'

'The uncles take it in turns to pull our plough,' said Sui.

'Well, horses do it faster. Horses are much stronger than people, so you can plough much more ground and then you have wheat to sell too, so you can buy things.'

'What sort of things?'

'More tools, metal pots, dresses made out of silk or hemp instead of goatskin.'

It all seemed unreal to Sui. As unreal as the army galloping across the plain … if there were an army. If it weren't all a dream. Perhaps horses pulling a plough was a dream too. How could a giant horse be harnessed up to a tiny plough?

'Timur …' she began.

'Hush,' said Timur suddenly. Then he pointed across the plain.

Sui squinted into the distance. 'But there's nothing there!' she exclaimed. Maybe, she thought, all he had been through had made Timur imagine armies in the clouds. 'It's just a dust cloud,' she said reassuringly. 'They blow across the plain sometimes.'

'In spring?'

'Well, no. In late summer, when the grass is dry.'

'But the grass is green now,' said Timur softly. 'That dust comes from horses' feet. Half a million horses ...'

Sui gazed at the horizon again. The cloud was thicker, wider, than it had been only a few moments before. Black specks rose above it.

'Crows,' said Timur, and his voice was grim. 'They fly above the army, waiting for the dead the army gives them.'

'How long ...?' began Sui.

'They'll be here by nightfall. Hurry! We must go down!'

'First of all the cooking pots and the bowls,' ordered Great Uncle. 'Yes, that's right. Ballar, make sure there is another batch of mud mixed to seal the gaps — it would be bad if we ran short at the last minute. Sui, catch the hens ... we'll put them in the walls last, but they need to be tied up ready. Fai, have you got the leather bindings? We'll start with the goats ...'

'Sui?'

Sui turned. It would be the last time, she thought, that Timur would speak so softly behind her.

'I have to go,' he said.

'I know.'

'If I stay ...'

'If you stay you might die too and there is no need for you to die.'

'If I stay South Wind will die. You can't put a horse in a wall.'

'I know,' said Sui.

'Come with me! We'll ride west then north, into country that the army has already conquered. I have gold in my saddlebags — the cities gave it to me in thanks for warning them. We'll find a place to farm, somewhere safe ...'

For a moment Sui could see it, like dawn light in her mind. The two of them, riding with the wind, building a house of stones together and raising hens and horses ...

'More binding on that sow!' ordered Great Uncle. 'She'll twist loose otherwise, that's it.'

'No,' said Sui sadly. 'I can't come with you.'

'Why not?'

Because it was my idea to hide in the walls, she thought, and if it fails I have to be here too. 'Because ... because if ... if we live through this, it will be hard afterwards. Very hard. I have to be here to help.' This is my family, she thought, and I love them, even Auntie Fai.

Timur took her hand. His face had lost all the life that had flowed into it since he had been at the farm. He looked like the blank-faced stranger of fifteen days before. 'Goodbye,' he said. Then he walked away.

Sui watched him leap up onto South Wind. The horse reared once, as though excited at the ride to come. Then the horse was galloping through the wheat field. The man who rode him didn't look back.

'Sui ... we need to hurry.'

Sui turned. It was Auntie Fai, but her voice was gentler than Sui had ever heard it.

Sui nodded. 'I'll catch the hens,' she said.

The animals were tied securely and hidden in the walls. Great Uncle watched Dalan and the other children take a final drink. 'Now no worrying if you make a mess in your clothes,' he told them. 'No trying to cry out. You understand? It will be dark in there and frightening. But remember the whole family will be near. And when the men have gone, we will be free again.'

Little Dalan and the others nodded. They couldn't really understand how important it was to keep quiet and still, thought Sui. But the gags would keep them quiet anyway, and the ropes would stop them moving. She watched as one by one they were bound and pushed through the gap into the wall.

Now it was her turn. She hugged each of her aunts and uncles, then Auntie Fai. The old woman's face crumpled like dried goatskin. 'Good life to you,' she whispered. 'You are a good girl, Sui. A good girl.'

Great Uncle laid his hand on Sui's head. 'If the family survives it will be due to you,' he said quietly. 'Never forget that, Sui.'

Sui nodded. She should say something, she thought. But words seemed too small for everything she wanted to say.

Great Uncle hesitated, then spoke again. 'I am glad you stayed, Sui. I am glad you didn't go with the rider. The family needs you — will need you. You have ideas — just like your father, like my father. Too few people have ideas. Never be afraid to tell your ideas, even though you are a girl. Now hug your mother. Quickly. We must hurry.'

Sui turned to her mother and hugged her too. 'I will be standing next to you,' her mother whispered. 'We'll make it, I know we will.'

Sui filled her own mouth with old soft leather, then tied her gag over her lips. Auntie Fai bent and tied the ropes around her ankles.

'They're too loose!' objected Sui.

Auntie Fai shook her head. 'You need to be able to move in them after the soldiers have gone,' she said. 'You're not a little child, Sui, who needs ropes to stop you breaking the walls in panic. Your ropes are just to support you, to wake you, if you fall asleep. But you must be able to shuffle out of them too.'

Auntie tied the ropes around her arms. Sui shuffled towards the wall, then gazed up one last time at the horizon. The cloud of dust was wider, higher. Below it the plain rippled, as though the earth was dark and shivering.

The army was nearly here.

Sui looked south, but there was no sign of Timur. The hills must had hidden him from view. She took one last glance at the wide clear sky, at the swallows diving and looping through the air with no knowledge of the terror to come, then shuffled into the darkness.

The dark gap smelt of damp and pig and goat and fear. She shuffled further inside. Another step, another ... her shoulder bumped into someone in the dark. Dalan — she could feel him flinch. She wanted to say something to reassure the little boy, but there was no way to make a noise. In a short time any noise could kill them, any movement too ...

She moved a little to her left. Yes, there was a hole in the wall, too small to see through, but at least it let in a tiny gleam of light and, more importantly, air. She settled next to the hole and waited.

Someone else shuffled in beside her. Mama — she had said she would be next. But there was no way to be sure if it was her or not. More noises, further along the wall, then suddenly the slopping, slapping of fresh mud, sealing the outside.

Sui took a deep breath. The air was already stale, already smelt of sweat and urine. Dalan must be terrified ...

But there was nothing she could do, but wait.

Inside the wall grew hotter and hotter still.

What if they didn't come, she thought. What if they swerved across the plain and went some other way? How long should they wait?

The space inside the wall grew even hotter.

A child further down the wall made a noise deep inside its throat. An almost sobbing noise, choked by the gag.

What if the soldiers heard it, thought Sui, panicked. What if the gag slipped and the child cried louder.

But there was nothing she could do.

The sweat dripped down her face and down her legs. Her legs ached already and her arms. It was impossible to stand so still. She had to move, she had to get out, get out, get out ...

Then she felt it.

It was a vibration first, the sort you'd feel on the bed platform with lots of other people in the room. The whole ground was shuddering.

For a moment Sui thought the wall had moved. And then she realised.

It was the army, coming closer.

She could hear them now. It was like thunder across the plain. But thunder boomed and went away. This thunder went on and on.

Terror put strength into her bones. She waited for the sound of men, of yells and cries, but she could hear nothing but the beating of hooves.

How far away were they now? she wondered. How far away could you hear the sound of half a million horses?

The sweat grew cold about her face and feet.

Slowly the thunder grew louder and louder still. The noise filled her ears; it filled the world. But now she could make out hoof beats too, like South Wind's hooves but magnified half a million times.

Someone shouted, outside the wall. A horse whinnied. Another answered, and another.

The first riders must be searching the farm, Sui realised, hunting for prisoners or hens or other food, for anything the army might find of use.

Another shout, triumphant this time. What had they found, thought Sui desperately. She tried to make out the words, but they made no sense. Had they discovered that the wall by the doorway was still soft? Had they already broken the other end of the wall?

Someone ... something ... screamed outside. More voices, laughter, another scream. Suddenly the world was cold, even the scrap of light was growing black, blacker even than the night.

No, thought Sui. She wouldn't faint. She couldn't faint. This was just the beginning. She must stand still.

Another voice yelled in the distance — then no more voices, and just the sound of hooves.

The speck of light grew dull, then dark, but this was normal darkness — night. The wall grew cold. Sui stood there, in the darkness, knowing her family stood beside her, even though no-one could see one another.

The thunder of the hoof beats slowly ceased. There were men's voices again and laughter, hard and horrid laughter, and the smell of meat and fire. Her stomach gurgled at the smell. She tried to will it into silence and hoped the noise outside was too loud for anyone to hear.

The noise of feasting men grew less and less, and finally the army slept, with only the whinny of horses and the shuffle of their hooves to break the silence.

The speck of light grew bright once more, a flickering light now. Again, horse after horse went past. The noise grew louder and louder still. There was a strange smell too, like rotten milk, and Sui remembered Timur telling her: 'They grease their bodies with the fat, to keep out the cold. Sometimes I think I smell them coming from a hundred miles away.'

Timur ... it was good to think of Timur. If she thought of Timur she didn't have to think of what was outside. She would think of South Wind too, galloping across the hills, away from noise and armies and away from air so thick it choked your throat ...

If she had gone with Timur they ... no, she couldn't think about that now. Just think of Timur free, of him riding with the wind.

The day passed. The hole grew dark again. This time the night was broken by the sound of snores, next to the wall. Sui would have laughed, if laughter had been possible. If her bones weren't screaming with the pain ...

The next day was easier. The next day she was hardly there at all. She floated somewhere else and only dimly realised where she was when her body began to fall. The ropes cut into her flesh. Deep in her mind she heard Auntie Fai say, 'You're a good girl, a good girl, a good girl ...'

Thank you Auntie Fai, she said, and wondered why there was no noise. She tried again and this time there *was* noise, horse noises, thunder noises, hooves across the plain, and she remembered that she must make no sound at all.

Another night, then light again. Was the noise less now? But the noise didn't matter. Only one thing mattered — just to stand — stand and not to move, not to fall because if she fell, they all would die.

Sound roared in her ears. But it wasn't the noise of horses. It was a wind noise, but in her head, not outside. But that was good, because while her mind-wind played she could hear nothing from outside: nothing, nothing, nothing at all.

Someone beat fists against the wall. For a moment Sui panicked, thinking one of the small children or animals had broken free. Then she realised — the beating came from the outside!

She hadn't thought her body had the strength to freeze.

'Sui!'

How did the soldiers know her name? How ...?

Suddenly her mind cleared. For the first time in three days she moved ... or tried to move. The pain shrieked down her arms as she forced them up enough to slide the ropes down from her wrists. Her legs screamed at her as she slowly lifted each foot and shuffled the bonds off. She tried to kick at the wall, but her legs wouldn't move enough. She tried to move her hands, but they refused to lift.

The battering had become a scraping now.

Suddenly there was light; light so white her eyes refused to accept it. The world grew dark again, but there were arms around her, gentle arms and firm. They lowered her to the ground; they held water to her lips. Sui drank, then let the darkness come.

Did she sleep or was she unconscious? Somehow she had the impression a long time had passed. She woke as someone stroked her hair.

'Sui?'

This time the world was steady when she opened her eyes.

'Timur?'

'I came back,' he said simply. 'I rode back, but you were already in the wall. I told Great Uncle I would circle round the army and ride back here when they were gone.'

Sui tried to sit up. The world swam again. 'How ... how ...' She wanted to ask, how many of us survived? but her throat was too raw to talk.

'It's alright, Sui. No-one died in the wall. Even little Dalan — he's weak, but he's alive.'

'Goa ...?' she choked.

'The goats? The billy goat is dead, and one of the kids. But you still have enough to breed from. The pigs survived and most of the hens. The seed is safe and everything else.'

It was impossible. It was too much to believe. She had to see, she had to look at them to be sure ...

'Sit up ...' she whispered.

Timur lifted her, so she rested against his knee. She looked around.

Mama, leaning against the wall ... she sensed Sui's gaze and smiled faintly at her, then closed her eyes again. There were the small shapes of the children, their bonds still on the ground around them. Timur had covered them with blankets. There were the aunts, the uncles ... Sui blinked, and looked again. 'Auntie Fai! Where is Auntie Fai? And Great Uncle?'

'Sui.'

'Where are they! You said no-one died!'

Timur hesitated. 'No-one died in the wall. Your Auntie Fai and Great Uncle, they chose to stay outside.'

'But ... but why?'

'To close the wall up, to make sure nothing could be seen outside. I said ... I offered to do that instead, so they could hide as well, but Great Uncle said no. He said ride, ride and escape and then come back. He said there must be someone here when the soldiers come, someone to tell the soldiers everyone had fled down south into the city. Someone for them to kill.'

The scream, thought Sui. Which one of them screamed?

She blinked again in the fresh harsh light. The world was clearer now. The rooves were off the huts. The soldiers must have burnt the thatch in their fires, but rooves could be built again. The apricot trees had been chopped down, but the roots would sprout. There was no grass on the plain, no millet or tall green wheat.

Instead there was endless churned up dust and horse droppings and ...

'What's that?' she breathed.

Timur turned. 'Where?'

'Over there!'

'It's just a horse, lying down. No, no, don't worry, it's not South Wind, he's behind the wall. It must be injured ...' His voice broke off.

'No, it isn't!' insisted Sui. 'Look! Timur, look!'

It wasn't one horse. It was two. One large brown horse who staggered to her feet, another tiny one that staggered on legs too thin and frail to ever hold it upright, and yet they did, splayed apart and trembling.

Timur ran over and grabbed the mother's bridle. She tossed her head and snorted, then seemed to accept him; relieved, perhaps, to have a human take charge again in a world suddenly empty of all the men and horses she had known before.

Sui pushed herself to her feet. The pain almost made her faint again, but she forced herself to take a step and then another ... Timur caught her again as she staggered.

'Careful!'

Sui reached out to stroke the horse's sweaty neck. The big teeth snapped at her and she drew back.

'Better not get too close till she's used to you,' said Timur. 'She's only known men before. I'm surprised she let me so close with her foal. But the army trains its horses well.' He bent, and slipped a rope around the mare's front legs.

'A hobble,' he explained. 'That means she can't go far and the foal won't go any distance from its mother.' He smiled suddenly. It was the deepest smile, Sui realised, that she had ever seen him give.

'You know what this foal means?' he asked.

'What?'

'Milk. Milk for the children as well as the foal. Look! There are clouds on the horizon too — real clouds, not dust and armies. It will rain soon. The grass will grow and we can plant more millet, more than you have ever grown before! We'll harness the horses to the plough. We'll breed more horses too.'

'But ... but none of us knows how to make a horse plough the ground. Or how to breed horses, or ...'

'I do,' said Timur. 'And I'm staying here. Look, you sit down again. I need to help the others drink some more, and make a fire to keep us warm before night comes. It should be safe to light a fire inside the walls. No-one will see its light from there.'

'But ... but you said you had to warn people that the army was coming ...'

'I warned the city,' said Timur. 'And they had horses too. Other riders can take my place. Sit here, I'll be back soon.'

Sui watched him stride off towards the others. She looked at the plain — dirt-coloured instead of green — the mud walls streaked black from soldiers' fires, her huddled family and her horses.

Horses had taken Great Uncle and Auntie Fai and the last of her childhood, but they were giving her a future too.

'Sleep well, Great Uncle, Auntie Fai,' she whispered. 'The family is safe now. Timur and I will take care of them. I promise.'

Behind her the tiny foal nuzzled at its mother and began to drink.

Sir Grey Nose

Two knights on two great chargers faced each other across the forest clearing. Through the trees a lake shimmered and next to that a castle's turrets rose against the sky, their black banners flying in the wind. Green leaf shadows fluttered on the shields and on the silks that their great horses wore.

One horse was brown, with a darker mane. The silk it wore was black; no coat of arms lightened its drabness. Its knight's shield was made of black wood and the knight's leathers and helmet feathers were black too.

The other horse was grey. Its silks were royal blue, with a gold border and white swans. This knight's helmet feather was white and the cloak over his chain mail was royal blue.

The grey horse's rider lifted the iron visor of his combat helmet. His eyes were young, and green as the forest. 'Do you yield, Sir Knight?' he cried.

The black knight laughed. He lifted his lance in answer and slowly, deliberately, scraped off the coronel that covered its razor-sharp tip on the grass.

This would be no courtesy match where the winner took only the horse, arms and saddle of the loser. This would be a joust to the death.

The white knight's face was expressionless as he lowered his helmet and removed the coronel from his lance too, though it was possible that the sadness in the green eyes deepened just a little. He lifted the lance, so that it balanced along his arm and hefted the shield and reins that he held in his other hand higher.

'Easy, Grey Nose, old man,' he whispered.

There was no need to say anything — a good war horse like this one was trained for years; his rider knew that the movements of his body — the shifts in the saddle, the press of the spurs, the tug on the bit — would tell the horse what to do more effectively than spoken orders. But sometimes humans need to hear words.

The grey horse bent his head. The thick neck arched above the blue silk. The grey horse charged. The hooves thundered across the soft grass. Now the brown horse was charging too. The ground vibrated in the clearing.

Closer … closer … The power behind a knight's lance depends on the speed of his horse, and how accurately the knight places the point of his spear on the shield of the knight before him, as the great horses pound the ground beneath. It took years of training to learn to meet the target, not to slide the lance too high or low, or to one side, and allow your enemy's lance to thump into your shield instead and send you spinning from your horse.

Once unhorsed you lost the joust. You usually survived, perhaps with a broken collar-bone, or bruised and dazed, but you would live to fight again. But if a sharp lance with its coronel removed pierced your shield and chain mail or helmet, with the power of a charging horse behind it, you would die.

Nearer ... nearer ... The white knight made a small adjustment to his lance, his eyes fixed on the exact spot it had to hit on his opponent. Nearer ... nearer ...

Then suddenly the black knight swerved. His lance shot down. Instead of aiming for his opponent's shield he now aimed at the heart of the grey horse.

The lances struck.

The black knight's lance hit first, biting deep into the horse. The grey horse screamed. But unbelievably he held his stride for two more paces till he fell, the lance still thrust into his flesh. Enough time for the white knight's lance to strike its victim, though most of its power was lost.

The black knight tumbled backwards, while his horse cantered onwards, slowly stopping at the edge of the clearing. It stood there, shaking its head.

The grey horse lay upon the grass. Blood stained the blue silk and dyed the white swans red. He screamed, once, twice, then appeared to go into shock. He shuddered and lay silent.

The white knight struggled to his feet. Even in his agony the great grey horse had fallen so that his rider wasn't trapped beneath him. The white knight was dazed, that's all.

The black knight stood too. He drew his sword, long and grey and massive. The white knight drew his sword as well. It was a slimmer, longer sword than the black knight's. Its pommel and haft were all of precious stones, blue and white like the white knight's silks, and red like the blood of his horse. On one side of the blade was written 'Take me' and on the other 'Throw me away'.

The knights approached each other, circling round and round the glade, each trying to tempt the other to attack with the afternoon sun in his eyes. Suddenly the black knight leapt, his sword in both hands. The sword plunged down just as the white knight raised his shield and took the blow.

Now the white knight struck. The two swords met. Iron struck iron, and sparks flashed into the clearing's shadows.

The white knight lunged again. This time his sword met the black knight's shield, but with such strength that the shield was rent in two.

The black knight struck wildly now. He had one chance before the white knight struck him undefended. But the white knight's sword met his and cast it off.

Now the white knight struck. The first blow hit the black knight's sword arm. The bone cracked and the sword fell to the ground. The white knight's sword struck again. This time it crashed through the black knight's helmet and through the skull as well, splitting it in two. The black knight fell.

The white knight stood there panting, his sword by his side. He pushed his visor up and gazed at the black knight. 'If you had been a knight of honour, I would have begged thee yield,' he said. 'But no honourable knight strikes at a horse.'

Suddenly there was a commotion at the edge of the clearing, cheering and applause. The white knight looked up. Unnoticed, his retinue had followed him during the fight. One man ran forward, and knelt before him. 'Pardon, Your Majesty,' he said. 'You outpaced us!'

'No matter,' said the king wearily. 'Where is Sir Kay?'

'He is coming directly,' said the man. 'A damsel wished to have words with him.'

King Arthur almost smiled. Damsels were always wishing a word with Sir Kay. The man saw the almost smile, and shook his head. 'Nay, Sire,' he said. 'This is a very young damsel. She saw the joust and said it was most urgent ...'

The king shrugged. 'It always is,' he said. His gaze was on his horse, lying still and silent now in the clearing, no longer on the man-at-arms. 'Perhaps she needs saving from a dragon,' he added, though the look in his eyes didn't match the lightness of his tone.

'Stand back, good man, if you will. I must do this alone.'

King Arthur stepped across the clearing and knelt before his horse. His eyes were open, but not in the unseeing stare of death. Blood still pulsed from the wound on to the flattened grass. The grey horse was still alive.

Arthur took his knife from his belt and slit the bloody silk, exposing the wound. The lance had pierced right through the shoulder, and out the other side. The edges gaped raw and bleeding around the metal.

The king laid his hand on his horse's neck. 'I'm sorry, my friend,' he whispered. 'Thank you for many years.' He laid a cloth over the horse's eyes, so he wouldn't see the final blow, and raised his knife over the horse's throat.

'Arthur! No!'

The king halted. Only one man in England called him Arthur, and that was his foster brother.

'Sir Kay?'

Sir Kay ran across the clearing, his blue cloak flapping against his chain mail. A girl ran after him.

'This child ...' panted Sir Kay.

'I'm not a child,' stated the girl firmly. 'I'm simply small for my age.' Suddenly she remembered, and dipped a deep curtsy. 'I mean, Your Majesty.'

The king stared at her. She spoke as a gentlewoman, and her green linen dress and surcoat were good, if worn, but her hands were red and callused, not fine and white as a lady's should be. 'What do you want?' he demanded briefly, with more weariness than rudeness.

'Sire ... your horse. Can I have a look at him?'

'He's dying,' said the king bluntly. 'Let him die in peace.'

'No,' said the girl stubbornly then, as Sir Kay cleared his throat, 'I mean, no, Sire. Perhaps he doesn't have to die.'

'Child, I have seen many wounded horses,' said King Arthur. 'And too many wounded men as well. I know when they will die.'

The girl lifted her chin. 'I have seen wounded men too,' she insisted. 'And horses. My mother was a healer, as well as daughter to a farrier. My father was my late lord's hearth brother, before the black knight killed them. My father knew horses as well, Sire. He was seneschal of the castle, but he had charge of my lord's horses too. Perhaps ... perhaps I can heal your horse, Sire, but I won't know unless I look at him.'

King Arthur hesitated. But the horse was in shock; another few minutes would mean nothing to him. And the girl — well, she'd seen trouble enough. It would do no harm to grant her this.

'You may look,' he said.

The girl knelt beside the horse. Her hands moved the silk gently away from the great wound. She studied it for a moment, then dipped her finger in the blood.

'What ...' began the king.

The girl looked up at him briefly. 'I am seeing how thick the blood is,' she explained. 'That way I can tell how deep the wound is.'

'Well?' asked the king.

The girl didn't reply. She put her hand on the horse's neck, as though feeling for the beat of his veins. She opened the horse's mouth and sniffed.

'Well?' demanded the king again. He was tired, and the world about him was beginning to spin.

'I don't know,' said the girl honestly. 'But there is a chance, my lord, I mean, Sire.'

'A chance for me to ride him again? I think not,' said the king.

'No. But a chance for him to live,' said the girl.

The king hesitated. To him the wound looked hopeless. To agree to the girl's wishes would mean more pain for the horse, and time wasted for him. He could not in honour leave his horse while he lived, and the defeat of the black knight had been just one task that a weary king needed to perform in this corner of his country.

'Please,' said the girl quietly. 'He deserves a chance.'

The king shut his eyes. It was a long moment before he opened them again and said, 'Yes, he deserves a chance. More than you know, perhaps. What do you need?'

The girl stood, wiping her bloody hands on her skirt. 'A fire, two kettles, clean cloths, two bunches of dried rosemary and two of lavender; you'll find such things in the lower kitchen of the castle yonder. Mouldy bread — there is a basket of it kept under a napkin in the stillroom — and leather bandages, they are in the still room too. Oh, and a handful of boiled wool, too, and the dried herbs next to the bread basket — comfrey root and camomile — and brandy, a pot of honey, and good wine and fresh bread to sop it in.'

'You intend to feed my horse sops in wine?' asked the king, almost amused.

'No, Sire. They're for you. Sit down before you fall down. I mean, Sire, if you would be pleased to sit.'

The king did smile this time. He nodded to Sir Kay. 'Have all she asked for fetched.'

'I will need a shelter too,' said the girl slowly. 'Four poles, and a covering. We need to keep him warm; a fire won't be enough, and the dew will fall soon. And blankets and a brazier, no, two braziers and coal to burn in them.'

'Do it,' said the king.

'Arthur, are you sure …?' began Sir Kay.

'No,' said the king. 'But what does it matter? We can go no further tonight as it is. If the horse is no better by tomorrow, then … well, then there'll be an ending. Establish order in the castle, will you? I will need three guards here tonight, no more.'

'I will return,' said Sir Kay.

'No,' said the king. 'You are more use at the castle. Besides …' he shrugged, 'I will be better by myself.'

'You need not remain here,' began the girl, 'I will stay with the horse.'

'I'll stay,' said King Arthur.

He lifted the helmet from his head and laid it on the ground, and removed his hauberk as well. He looked younger than he had with his helmet on. The king pulled off the chain mail from his upper body, leaving just his quilted leather undergarment. He drew his cloak around him and sat down beside the horse.

The girl pulled a small silver knife from the pouch at her belt and began to cut at the bloody silk around the wound.

'What is your name?' asked the king suddenly.

'Suzanne, Sire,' she said.

'Well, my lady Suzanne ...'

'Not my lady. Just Suzanne.'

The king raised an eyebrow. 'It is usually not done,' he said, 'to contradict a king.'

The girl didn't look up. 'I'm sorry, Sire. I have never met a king before.'

'So I gather,' said King Arthur.

There was a commotion behind them. Two men-at-arms laid firewood on the ground and began to prepare the fire.

The horse gasped suddenly and began to breathe in short, ragged gasps.

'He's dying,' said the king gently.

'No, Sire. He's in shock. He may still live if we can keep him warm.'

The fires were lit. A man-at-arms returned on horseback from the castle with baskets and kettles and laid them on the ground before the king and Suzanne. Servants began to set up the braziers on each side of the grey horse, and erect the poles and covering. Suzanne laid the blankets over him and tucked them as far beneath the great grey body as she could as well.

'What first?' asked the king. 'Shall I pull the lance out?'

'No!' cried Suzanne. 'That's the worst thing you can do! I beg your pardon, Sire. I mean we have to push it through, not pull it, or we'll cause even more damage.'

Arthur nodded. 'I see. Like an arrow. If a man is to live, an arrow must be pushed, not pulled, as well. Very well.' He took out his knife and began to saw through the wood of the lance. The horse shuddered, and showed the whites of his eyes.

'Gently, Sire,' ordered Suzanne.

The king raised an eyebrow. 'I'm trying to,' was all he said.

The lance fell back onto the grass. Only the metal tip now protruded from the horse's flesh. The blood still dripped onto the grass.

'Should I push the tip through?' asked the king.

'Not yet,' said Suzanne quickly.

The kettles were steaming on the fire. Suzanne added the lavender and camomile flowers, the rosemary leaves, and the comfrey root to one kettle, then poured boiling water from the second into a pewter goblet and added wine and bread and honey. She handed this to the king.

'Drink,' she said. 'You'll do no-one any good if you collapse.'

The servants stared at her back as though they expected lightning to strike, at this discourtesy to the king. The king waved them away, back to the edge of the clearing.

'You're bossy,' he observed, sipping his hot sops in wine.

'So are you,' said Suzanne. She was checking the bandages now, long wide strips of leather, pounded till soft.

'But I'm king,' Arthur pointed out.

Suzanne flushed. 'I'm sorry, Sire,' she said. 'I … since my uncle's death, you see, there has been no-one else to command the castle. Sir Baris, the black knight was rarely at home, and when he was he was drunk. He preferred tournaments to tending his lands, and for that at least we were grateful. Sir Baris away was better than Sir Baris at home — hold this will you?'

The king held one end of the bandage as she measured it against the horse.

'How old are you?' asked the king.

'Fourteen.' She flushed again. 'You thought I was younger.'

'And now you seem older. It was a great responsibility for a fourteen-year-old girl.'

'I managed,' said Suzanne shortly. The king noticed she did not claim it had been easy.

The kettle had boiled enough now. Suzanne tipped the bandages and the wool into the simmering water, then poured some of the herb water into another goblet. The water steamed, green and fragrant as she washed her hands. Slowly, very slowly, she pushed at the remains of the lance. At first it didn't move, then suddenly the exit wound gaped large. The lance head slipped out, followed by a gush of blood.

Suzanne looked apologetically at the king. 'I know it looks as though I have made it worse,' she said. 'But the bleeding helps to clean the wound, and having two holes is better than one, though you may not think it. It means the wound can drain instead of going bad inside.'

'I understand,' said Arthur abruptly. 'I too have seen wounds before.'

Suzanne grasped the brandy bottle. 'This will hurt him,' she whispered, 'but it has to be cleaned.'

The king nodded. He pressed his hands to the great grey neck as Suzanne poured brandy into the wound. The horse groaned and shuddered, then lay still, his breathing long and laboured. The blood ran dark from the exit wound, then slowly lightened as it mixed with the brandy.

Suzanne lifted the lump of wool out of the kettle with the silver knife, then pressed half of it deep into the exit wound. The other half poked out. 'That will keep the wound open,' she said. 'So that the badness can drain out. I'll have to change it every day if he lives.'

'If he lives,' said Arthur softly.

Suzanne nodded. She lifted the bandages now, spread honey on one square and held it to the larger wound where the lance had gone in. 'Now to stop the bleeding. Hold this,' she commanded the king. Arthur nodded and stretched out his hands.

Suzanne took the longest bandage, tied it across the square one, round the horse's shoulders and over his back and tied it tightly. This she repeated with the others, so the larger wound was covered tightly in all directions. 'They'll tighten as they dry,' she said, 'and hold the edges of the wound together. At least I hope so. It will heal quicker that way.'

'If it heals at all,' said the king, his glance going to the bloody lance on the grass.

'I made no promises,' said Suzanne. 'I just said there was a chance.'

'What do you think now?'

'I think there is a chance.' She picked up a piece of bread and began to nibble it.

'Now what?' asked the king.

'We wait. If he gets to his feet, he will recover. If he doesn't … but there is no need for you to stay, Sire.'

'No, I will stay,' said the king. 'I owe him that.'

The fires flickered. The shadows were thickening now in the forest. A frog began to beep. At the edge of the clearing the servants and men at arms wrapped themselves in their cloaks and began to get comfortable.

Neither the king nor Suzanne spoke for a while. The horse panted on the ground beside them, as King Arthur stroked his neck. 'I'm here, old man,' he whispered.

'Sire?'

'Yes,' said the king absently. He was watching the horse.

'Would you ... would you stay like this for any of your ... your dependents?'

'What? No,' said the king slowly. 'I have had men under my command injured and have left them to die, while I went on to other battles — knights of my own Round Table too. But Grey Nose is different, he is my friend.'

Suzanne blinked. 'What did you call him?'

'Eh? Oh, he has some long French name; I never used it. I always called him Grey Nose from the moment I first met him.'

The king smiled. His eyes were far away. 'Fifteen years ago it was,' he said, 'I was only two years older than you are now. I was small for my age, like you. There was a tournament, you see. My brother — my foster brother, Sir Kay, had forgotten his sword. I was too young to compete, so I rode back to get it, and there was this other sword in the Churchyard, a sword in a stone.'

The king shrugged. 'So I pulled it out. It seemed easier than riding all the way back, that's all. And they asked me to do it again, so I put the sword back, and pulled it out ...' The king shook his head. 'And when I turned round they were kneeling to me, my foster father and my brother. I had to do it again, at Candlemas, pull that sword from the stone with the barons watching and all the common people, and then they knelt to me as well, and suddenly I was king of England.'

Suzanne snorted. 'It doesn't seem a very good way to choose a king.'

The king laughed for the first time since his horse had fallen. The first time in many months, he realised. Or maybe years. 'No, it wasn't a good test, I agree. But it turned out that I was King Uther Pendragon's son too, given to my foster father at birth to keep me safe. But you are right. Neither of those is enough to make a good king.

'I knew nothing about being king, good or otherwise. I was just a lad in too-short leggings, because I was finally starting to grow. But they gave me a crown and they gave me a horse; this great grey horse with a long French name, and he looked down his long grey nose at me and I tell you, he laughed at me.' The king smiled at the memory. 'We were friends from then on. Who else would have the courage to laugh at a king, even if that king knew nothing of kingship?' The king paused. 'He has been my only friend for fifteen years.'

'But ...' began Suzanne hesitantly. 'Sir Kay, your foster brother ... he called you Arthur, not "your Majesty".'

'No,' said the king softly. 'Sir Kay is not my friend. When a man has knelt to you in the dust of a churchyard, he can never be your friend again. I would trust Sir Kay with my life, but that is not the same thing as a friend. When you are king, you have no friends. A man must be your equal to be your friend. I am responsible for all of England, and until a man has felt that burden he can never really be my friend.'

'But Grey Nose has never felt the burden of all England,' pointed out Suzanne.

The king laughed again. 'He has felt the burden of me on his back, and I am England. No, they chose well when they gave me Grey Nose.

'He wasn't a young horse, even then. He was eight, perhaps, or nine. He was trained, as I was not. He knew how to step proudly at the front of a procession, which I had never done. He knew how to charge straight and true in the joust, whereas I was just a beginner. He would rear to defend me when knights slashed at me with their swords. He would strike them with his fore hooves and kick with his hind hooves. Whenever I wondered what to do in those early years of my reign, I looked at Grey Nose and he looked down his great nose at me and grinned and showed me how.'

The king stroked the horse again, but Grey Nose made no sign that he felt his touch. Arthur sighed, but he left his hand on the grey neck.

They sat silently for a while. It was quite dark now. The braziers glowed red. The king stood and threw more wood on the fire, then sat next to the horse again. At the edge of the clearing the servants had built a fire too, larger than the one that warmed the king and Suzanne and Grey Nose.

'There have been many battles in those fifteen years,' said the king at last. 'I had to fight King Lot of Lothian and Orkney and his five hundred knights, and the Kings of Scotland and Carados too, and the man they called the King of a Hundred Knights. They would have no beardless boy as king, they said. I could never hold the country, I thought. How could I even have time to raise an army, with so many against me?

'But I looked at Grey Nose and he looked at me, and I remembered where he had come from. So I sent Sir Kay to France to beg assistance, and two French kings, King Ban and King Bors, brought their men to aid me. Their men fought for me, and the common people fought for me as well, but there have been too many battles. I have had fifteen years of it, and sometimes they feel like a thousand. And there will be more battles still to come ...'

'How do you know?' whispered Suzanne.

'Because there are always men like your Sir Baris who take what they want and have no honour. One day, perhaps, there will be another way to stop them. But for now ...' he shrugged. 'What is the duty of a knight? To fight against treachery, to fend off injustice for the poor, to make peace in your own province, to shed blood for your brethren and, if needs must be, to lay down your life. That is the duty of a king as well. And of a horse, I suppose.'

Arthur stroked the grey neck again. 'I think they expected Grey Nose to turn white, you know, as we both grew older. A white horse for a good king. But he's stubborn. He was a grey horse then, and he's a grey horse now. And I have never been a perfect king, so we fit together well. A grey horse for a less than perfect king. But I have done my best, as he has done.'

'Why weren't you a perfect king, Sire?' asked Suzanne.

King Arthur smiled at her. 'If you were older, or a king, you wouldn't ask that question. No man can be perfect. There have been … incidents,' he added shortly, and Suzanne remembered a tale whispered in the kitchens when she was small, about how the king had ordered all the babies in the kingdom killed, in order to destroy the one that Merlin had prophesied would take his throne.

'People die,' whispered the king in the darkness, 'and sometimes they are the evil ones, like your Sir Baris. But sometimes they are innocent, killed so that good might triumph in the end. Men caught up in battle, families whose good men have died in my cause. If it is right that innocent men die, that families starve because they are gone, surely it is right that babies may die too?'

'No,' said Suzanne.

'No?' asked the king.

'No, it could never be right to kill babies. Your soldiers chose to fight, the babies had no choice at all.'

'Not even to save the kingdom from a war? A war in which many, many more will die who are as innocent as those babies?'

Suzanne looked up as though to say more, then caught the king's gaze and was silent.

Arthur shook his head. 'I do not know. I am just a king. My job is to fight, not answer questions. But sometimes in the darkness their voices whisper — the men who have died, the innocents who have suffered — and I do not know. No, I have not been a perfect king.'

Suzanne shivered. The night seemed to have closed in on them now.

'Take my cloak,' said the king.

'No, Sire ...'

The king removed his cloak and put it round her shoulders. It was warm from his body. 'Take it,' he said roughly. 'I have sat by many camp fires and through many nights without a fire too. I no longer feel the cold.' His hands stroked the horse again. 'Besides, Grey Nose will keep me warm, even if this is the last night he will do so.'

Suzanne's eyes closed. She must have slept, for when she opened them again the stars had shifted across the sky and the moon had risen too, a short sickle of a moon. The king's hand still rested on the grey horse's neck, but he no longer stroked it.

For a moment Suzanne wondered if perhaps the horse had died while she slept. She struggled upright. 'How is he?' she whispered urgently.

'Still breathing,' said the king tiredly. He stood, and threw more wood on the fire. It was only red coals now, but the wood caught and sparked into the night. 'I didn't want to disturb you by throwing wood on before,' explained the king. 'It will be morning soon.'

Suzanne rubbed her eyes. She wanted to ask, what will happen to our castle now and the people and the lands around? But the king was looking at the horse, and she felt she couldn't speak.

The fire at the edge of the clearing had died down too. The men-at-arms were asleep. Through the darkness Suzanne could see the castle, beyond the mist that shimmered above the lake. She hoped that Sir Kay was treating the people there well.

'Sir Kay is a good man,' said the king, as though reading her thoughts. 'All the Knights of the Round Table have given their oath. Over and above the oaths all knights must take.'

'What does the oath say?'

'To give mercy when mercy is asked. To protect women and children and enforce their rights, and never to enforce lust upon them. Never to fight in an unjust cause or fight for personal gain. Every year at the High Feast of Pentecost they renew their oath.'

'It is a hard oath to take,' said Suzanne sleepily. 'Especially not to fight for gain.'

'If it was easy to keep, there would be no use taking an oath,' said the king, sitting down again by Grey Nose.

Suzanne wondered if he had slept at all. She thought not.

She bent forward and felt the bandages. They felt dry, the blood crusted at the edges. The wound had stopped bleeding, though fluid still seeped through the wool at the other side. She felt the pulse on the great grey neck. 'He should have got to his feet by now,' she said worriedly. 'I'm afraid ...'

'He's had his chance,' said King Arthur gently. 'We'll give him a little longer. Better a swift death than a lingering one. That's all any one of us asks who expects to die in battle. We'll wait till the sun has risen. Then you will go back to the castle, and I ... I will do what I have to do.'

He meant he would kill the horse, thought Suzanne, as he had been going to do before she interrupted. 'No,' she said. 'If that's what needs to be done, I'll stay with you till it's over.'

'So very young to give orders to the king,' murmured Arthur.

'Nonetheless,' said Suzanne stubbornly. 'I'll stay. England is your duty. This horse is mine.'

A cuckoo sang softly in the forest. The stars faded to silver and then to grey, then mingled with the greying sky and were gone. It would be a bright clear day, thought Suzanne.

'Please get up, Grey Nose,' she pleaded in her mind.

The men stirred at the edge of the clearing. There were sounds of voices and splintering firewood for the first time since the quietness of the night.

Behind the castle the sky turned pink, then red, then gold as the sun slipped above the horizon. The mist shivered above the lake and vanished with the last shadows of the night.

The king gazed at the grey horse. 'Well, my friend,' he began softly.

Suddenly the great horse moved. Slowly he raised his neck and head, his whole front braced on his extended front legs. He paused for a long moment, and the eyes above the long grey nose seemed to meet the king's. Finally, with enormous effort, the horse heaved himself up from his haunches. For a moment Suzanne thought that he might fall again, but although he kept his weight off his forefoot, he stayed steady.

Suzanne stood too, almost as shakily as the horse. Her legs were cold and stiff. She stepped over to Grey Nose and felt the bandages. They were still tight, but not too tight. The bleeding hadn't started again, and the wool at the drainage hole was still in place. She gestured to one of the men-at-arms seated on the edge of the clearing. He ran over with a clank of chain mail. 'Fetch fresh water,' she ordered.

The man looked at King Arthur. Arthur nodded wearily. The man ran off.

'He'll live then?' the king asked softly.

'He'll live,' said Suzanne. She hesitated. 'But he will not fight again, Your Majesty. Nor will he carry you long distances.'

The old horse butted the king's shoulder. For the first time since she had met him there were tears in the king's eyes. He reached into his pouch, and pulled out a jagged lump of something hard and brown. He held it out on the palm of his hand, and the grey horse nuzzled it up.

'Sugar,' explained the king. 'It comes from the Holy Land.'

'I've heard of sugar,' said Suzanne. 'My mother used it in medicines, but it has been too expensive since my uncle died. Is it good for horses then?'

The king smiled wearily. 'I don't know about that,' he said, 'but Grey Nose seems to like it.' He stroked the horse's long grey neck, as the man-at-arms ran up with a wooden bucket filled with spring water. The king held it up and the horse drank, slowly and deeply.

'Well, old boy,' said the king. 'It seems this is the end of our friendship. For I must keep fighting until, like you, I can battle no longer.' The old horse butted him again and whickered softly.

King Arthur hesitated. He drew Excalibur from its scabbard. The sword was stained dark brown with the black knight's blood.

King Arthur shook his head. 'I would have a clean sword for this,' he said. He drew a cloth from his pouch and dipped it in the water that Suzanne had used to wash the bandages, and scrubbed the sword clean of blood. He held it high. The iron gleamed like silver in the morning light.

Suzanne gasped.

Then King Arthur brought the sword flat side down upon the horse's head, then another tap upon each shoulder. 'Rise, Sir Grey Nose,' said the king, then smiled, as the horse was already on his feet, though shakily. 'And from this hour thy name shall be Grey Nose of ...' The king looked around. 'Sir Grey Nose of Green Grass, most worshipful and loyal Knight of my Round Table.'

Sir Grey Nose of Green Grass whickered softly again and nuzzled the king's waist, hoping for more sugar.

Suzanne hesitated. Then she curtsied deep and low to Sir Grey Nose, as she would to any knight. Then she put her arms around his neck and hugged him.

The horse tolerated it, glancing over at the king as though to say: 'They're so emotional, these girls.'

Finally she looked back at the king.

'Your Majesty?' she asked.

'Yes,' said the king.

'What ... what of us ... and the castle ... and the Black Knight's lands?'

The king smiled. 'They are Sir Grey Nose's,' he said. 'But you shall care for the lands and castle for him, my Lady Suzanne, and your children shall care for his children.'

'I ...' began Suzanne. Then she curtsied deeply again. 'Thank you, Your Majesty. I vow to do my duty, according to your will.'

'Rise,' said King Arthur tiredly, for the second time that morning.

'Your Majesty?'

'Yes?' said Arthur.

'I hope you find a friend. Another friend, some day.'

Arthur smiled, but the smile was sad. 'Perhaps,' he said, 'but I suspect my truest friends will always be here.'

There was a slight commotion at the edge of the clearing. A new knight had arrived, leading a fresh great horse — a fine black horse, dressed in blue silk with gold borders and an emblem of white swans. Sir Grey Nose whinnied and looked at the king.

The king stroked the long grey nose. 'The black horse may carry me well and swiftly,' said Arthur softly to Sir

Grey Nose, 'but he will never take your place. Goodbye my friend.'

And so King Arthur rode away on the black horse, and Sir Grey Nose of Green Grass stayed in the clearing by the lake. A fence was built around it, so that Sir Grey Nose could not stray too far, and a proper stable was erected to keep him warm if he chose. Sweet grass was cut for him each summer, that he might have the best hay in winter, and hot oat mash was brought to him and the best mares as well, and turnips and apples and sugar lumps each morning, and his children roamed the forest near the castle.

King Arthur faced many battles after that. There was little peace for the king, but there was for his great horse, Sir Grey Nose of Green Grass, in his quiet lands by the lake.

The Black Kid

WARNING

This is a story about racism, so some of the words in it are racist, like 'black kid' and 'piccaninny'. If you write about racism you need to use racist words.

In fact the greatest piece of racism in this story isn't a word at all. It is the absence of a word. This is a story about a racism so strong that a child might not even be given a name ...

It was winter when the black kid appeared. The sky was high and blue and the air so dry and cold it felt like it would crack if you moved too fast, thought Alf McWhirty, as he leant over the raw posts of the horse yards and watched the men struggle with the stallion. Frozen spiders' webs clung between the gum leaves. Even the wombat droppings were frozen.

No-one noticed the black kid at first. All eyes were on the stallion, rearing in terror in the yards. The horse was sweating in spite of the cold; his nostrils wide and his eyes staring white as his hooves kicked and reared above the men who tried to hold him.

'What the ...?' Young Mike ducked, tripped and rolled in the dust till he was safely out of the yard and away from the hooves. Flash Jack made another leap for the rope then ducked out of the way as the horse reared again.

'No use,' said McWhirty quietly to Colonel Gloucester.

Colonel Gloucester ignored him. Colonel Gloucester only heard what he wanted to hear.

'Try again,' he ordered.

The horse's head came down then. He cantered over to the rails where the Colonel stood with Alf McWhirty, as though he knew who his chief tormentor was. He turned. The hard black hooves kicked out towards the Colonel.

The Colonel leapt back. So did McWhirty.

McWhirty glanced at the Colonel. 'Give it a rest then,' he called to the man still in the horse yard. 'We'll give him a day or two to calm himself down.'

The Colonel glared at McWhirty. 'Shouldn't have to,' he barked. 'Paid good money for that horse. Two thousand pounds! That horse is supposed to be broken to the saddle! Major O'Leary swore to me ...' He stopped, then stomped back across the yard and up the wide stone steps to the back door of the main house.

McWhirty stayed where he was, and watched the horse. He was still cantering roughly around the horse yards, as though the only way he could express his agitation was through action. McWhirty knew his horses. Even the Colonel listened to McWhirty some times.

Anger ... or terror, thought McWhirty, as the horse shook his long black mane. He reckoned that horse had been broken to the saddle all right. But something had frightened him, so he reared with terror at the touch of a rope around his neck.

He was a good horse, a fine horse — pure Arab, the Colonel claimed. Colonel Gloucester had an old army acquaintance ship him out from Calcutta.

It must have been a terrifying journey for a horse, thought McWhirty, the shaking and the shuddering of the boat, and hay that smelt of mould and salt maybe, and who knows what ropes the stallion had been confined with? No wonder he couldn't abide the touch of anything on his skin again.

Ah, a pity it was that horses couldn't speak, thought McWhirty, and understand you too. If the horse could just understand his words, he could explain his journey was over now; that the horse was safe. McWhirty gave a half smile. Though to be sure, that would only be half the truth. The horse's journey might be over but he didn't envy any horse that had to carry the Colonel. The Colonel was used to every order being carried out and he used his temper and his whip against any human or animal that didn't obey.

The stallion was quieter now. He looked at McWhirty suspiciously, as though waiting for the attack to begin again.

'No, don't you be worrying, fellow,' said McWhirty. 'Sure, I'll do what I can to make them leave you alone for a time.'

At least the horse could be used for breeding, he thought as he turned to go, even if no-one could climb on his back. A colt from the stallion would be worth a lot. There were still precious few good horses in the colony. The Colonel might make a fortune from his horse yet, even if he could never make a show, riding high and fine on his black stallion.

That's when McWhirty saw the black kid.

He was behind a tree, or almost. Just his wide brown eyes were peering round, and a flash of black hair and the dark fingers of one hand brown against the white of the bark. He was gazing at the stallion like he'd never seen anything like it before.

Which he hadn't, like enough, thought McWhirty. There were few enough quality horses in the district and nothing in this stallion's league.

It had been a while since McWhirty had seen any kid, black or white. The Colonel's were all grown — the girl in Sydney, the boy at Sandhurst military college in England.

Alf McWhirty had a kid of his own once. He'd had to leave the child behind with his wife when he'd been transported ten years ago for burning down an English landlord's house; though, as McWhirty said, it wasn't like the landlord had been in it at the time. He'd been far away in England where the rent money kept him wealthy.

McWhirty looked at the black child. Maybe he recognised something in the black kid's gaze, the joy and excitement he'd felt the day he'd seen his first great horse. Or maybe ... maybe it was just good to see a child again.

'Hey, boyo! Catch!' he called.

The black kid couldn't have understood the words. But his gaze tore from the horse just as McWhirty tossed him the apple from his pocket. It was meant for the horse, but there was no way the stallion would take an apple from anybody's hand today.

The black kid caught the apple. He met McWhirty's gaze and laughed.

Then he was gone.

McWhirty shoved his hands in his pockets and strolled down to the paddock behind the big house to saddle up Barney. There were fences to repair and gates to check.

But somehow the black kid stayed in his mind. The look in those brown eyes as he watched that horse ... Sure, it was a good thing the Colonel hadn't seen him. The Colonel wouldn't have blacks on his property.

There was a camp way down the river, well off the Colonel's land. That's where the kid had come from, most like. Well, no harm done. The boy had gone and that was the end of it.

The black kid was back next day. He was standing at the rails gazing at the stallion when McWhirty came out.

McWhirty shook his head at him. 'Don't you be getting too close there, sonny boy.'

The kid just stared. He didn't speak English, of course, and McWhirty didn't speak an Aboriginal language. None of the men did, though they'd lived in Australia all or most of their lives. (Colonel Gloucester had lived twenty years in India without learning more than half a dozen words of any Indian language either.)

McWhirty crossed over to the rail. 'The Colonel's been writing to that friend of his, the one who sold him this animal here,' McWhirty said to the boy, just as though he could understand him. He nodded towards the stallion. The horse tossed his head, as though he knew he was being discussed. 'He's asking for his money back. Don't think he'll be getting it, but.'

The black kid glanced at him, then stared again at the stallion.

'Dhadhi?' he asked.

'His name's Trumpeter,' said McWhirty. He spoke slowly and gestured to the horse as he repeated the name. 'Trumpeter.'

The boy shot him another look. 'Muurruubarraay!' he declared.

'Well, what's that mean when it's at home?' inquired McWhirty.

'Muurruubarraay!' repeated the boy stubbornly, staring at the horse.

'Is that your name for him then? Well, if you say so,' said McWhirty easily. He dug down in his pocket for another apple. The Colonel had a good orchard of apple trees; a dozen varieties sent out from England. The stone storeroom was full of barrels of apples, all stored in sawdust to keep through the winter. Even now they were hardly withered.

The boy took the apple, but this time he didn't run away. He just grinned his thanks then stared back at the stallion. He said something softly that McWhirty didn't understand.

Or maybe he did, even though it was in another language. Sometimes it was like that with horses, McWhirty thought, if there was bond enough between you. Sometimes you didn't have to speak each other's language to understand.

'No, he's wild, that one,' said McWhirty. 'Can't be doing anything with him. Don't suppose anyone ever will. Sometimes when a horse has been badly treated, they never forget, no matter how gentle you are with them after.'

Not that Colonel Gloucester's ways were gentle with anything and nor, for the most part, were the ways of the men above him either.

The boy said something else, almost too low to hear. He could have been speaking to either McWhirty or the horse. Then he was gone again, his bare feet padding through the cold dust of the yard, taking his apple with him.

It was Colonel Gloucester who saw the kid the next day. He'd been inspecting the stables and came out to the yards with McWhirty and three of the other men behind him. And there was the black kid, but he wasn't at the rails today.

The black kid was in the horse yards with the stallion. The five men pulled up and stood still.

McWhirty opened his mouth to yell 'Get out!', but something stopped him.

Even the Colonel was silent.

The black kid was looking at the stallion.

Slowly, very slowly, he stepped forward, one step, another, bare feet edging forward softly on the sand. The stallion watched him, his eyes just slightly wide, his curved ears swivelling, his nostrils flared and breathing in deeply.

One small hand crept towards the stallion. It held the apple that McWhirty had given him the day before.

And slowly, very slowly, with a single whicker of acceptance, the stallion bent his head and took the apple from the child.

Suddenly the black kid laughed. It was a gurgle of pure delight, of total joy. The stallion reared back, but the hooves were nowhere near the child. The stallion bucked and plunged and kicked his heels, but this time, thought McWhirty, it looked like the stallion was simply showing off for the child.

'Catch him,' ordered the Colonel.

'The stallion? But ... but no-one can catch him,' stammered McWhirty, startled.

'Not the horse, you fool. The piccaninny,' said the Colonel. 'I want him kept here.'

'But ... but what ... What will you be doing with him?'

'Isn't it obvious, man? Give the piccaninny some clothes, a decent feed. I want him here tomorrow morning.'

'But you can't ...' began McWhirty.

'Don't be an idiot,' said the Colonel. 'He's got the right hands. You're either born with them or you're not. That child understands horses or the horse understands him, what difference does it make? Saw something like that in India once. Horse made friends with a goat. No-one could do anything with him if that goat wasn't in his stable when he returned. I want that kid here tomorrow.'

The Colonel marched off. McWhirty didn't move. The child laughed suddenly, as the black horse whinnied near his ear.

One of the men, Young Mike, ran towards the rails. The black kid looked up, as though aware of them for the first time. He backed away.

'Round the other side, someone!' yelled Young Mike.

Still McWhirty didn't move.

Flash Jack sprinted around the other side of the horse yard. The black kid glanced from Young Mike to Flash Jack, then ducked under the rails between them. Young Mike leapt, and landed on him in a flying tackle.

'Got you!' yelled Young Mike. 'Arrrk!' he screamed, as the black kid bit his hand.

Flash Jack hauled the black kid to his feet. The boy was dusty and there was blood at the corner of his mouth. 'You try that again and I'll give you the back of my hand,' swore Flash Jack. He shook the kid roughly then dragged him across the yard, the thin brown arm held tightly in his hand.

McWhirty came out of his trance. 'Where are you taking him?' he demanded.

Flash Jack glanced over his shoulder. 'You heard the Colonel,' he said. 'The storeroom. He'll run off, else. Let's see the kid get out of there.'

'Why not the kitchen?' demanded McWhirty.

Flash Jack grinned. He looked down at the child. 'Better get some clothes on him before Mrs Connolly sees him. She'd have a fit.'

Mrs Connolly's seen more than that before, McWhirty thought. But he said nothing. It paid most times, he'd found, to keep your thoughts to yourself.

The storeroom was past the stables, next to what had been the dairy when the Colonel's lady was alive, and the Colonel had bothered with a milking cow. The big rusty hinge creaked as the storeroom door opened. Flash Jack thrust the black kid inside. He turned back to McWhirty.

'You got any clothes that'll fit him?' he asked.

'Why should the likes of me have children's clothes?' inquired McWhirty. He shrugged. 'I'll find him something.'

Flash Jack nodded as he turned the big key in the lock, then pulled it out. 'I'll put this safe by the back door,' he said, holding up the key, and headed off towards the house.

McWhirty hesitated. He stared at the locked door. There was no sound from inside.

It was late afternoon when McWhirty came back to the storeroom. He unlocked the door and stepped inside.

It was dark in the storeroom. A little light from the high barred window shone on the barrels of apples, the honey set to strain over a wooden bucket, the late pears shrivelling on their shelves.

The more valuable stores — the chests of tea, the sugar and flour and treacle — were in the storeroom by the kitchen. That room was kept locked as well. Mrs Connolly kept that key with her and the Colonel himself kept the key to 'the cellar', which was not a cellar at all, but yet another room with thick stone walls where he kept his port and his brandy and the rum he sold to the men.

There was no sign of the child.

McWhirty stepped quietly. 'It's alright,' he said softly. 'There's no call to be afraid.' It was a lie, he knew —

there was every reason in the world for the child to be afraid — but the kid wouldn't understand anyway, he reasoned, so perhaps it wasn't a lie at all.

He peered between a pair of barrels. The black child starred up at him, huddled against a barrel, his eyes as white and scared as the stallion's had been the day before.

'I've brought you some clothes,' said McWhirty. 'Sure, it's half frozen you must be in here.' It was cold enough outside; in here the chill seeped into your bones.

The child inched slowly around the barrel.

'It's no use trying to run,' said McWhirty. He held out the clothes. The child glanced at them, then up at him.

'Look,' said McWhirty. 'It's one of my shirts.' He held it up and pantomimed how to put it on. The child watched him, silent. 'And I cut down a pair of my trousers for you too,' said McWhirty. 'You'll swim in them, I know, but it's the best I can do. I'll see if the Colonel will get you some proper clothes next time someone goes in to town.'

The boy still said nothing.

'We can roll the sleeves up on the shirt,' said McWhirty.

Still the kid said nothing. McWhirty looked more closely.

The kid was crying.

'I'll help you then,' said McWhirty softly, with a gentleness he hadn't used on another human in twenty years. He knelt beside the boy and draped the shirt around his shoulders, then lifted his arms into the sleeves.

The boy let him, his eyes on McWhirty's face.

McWhirty rolled the sleeves up. 'Now the trousers,' he said. He lifted the boy and showed him how to put one leg into each hole, then belted it all with a piece of rope from the stables. 'Not too bad,' he judged.

Suddenly the boy wriggled from his grasp. He ran to the door before McWhirty could catch him, struggled with the handle for a moment, then flung the door open. He was almost through the door when the too-long trousers tripped him, and he fell.

McWhirty ran to him and picked him up. He carried him back inside, holding his arms firmly so he couldn't struggle. He locked the door behind him before he put the boy down.

The boy backed away from him. McWhirty sat down on a barrel of apples and crossed his arms and stared at him. 'Well,' he said, 'what are we to do with you now?'

'Gaja!' yelled the boy, then a long stream of something McWhirty couldn't catch.

'Well, yes,' said McWhirty slowly. 'I can follow what you're telling me clear enough. You're saying why don't I unlock that door and let you out? What call has any man to lock away a child like he was a goat in a stable? Why don't I just be giving you your freedom and let you run away?'

He stared at the boy some more. 'They locked me up once,' he told the boy. 'Sure, I was a good few years older than you but not that old, all the same, for all I had a wife and a child. They threw me in a stone room, but not like this. There were fourteen of us in that room, and the straw stank and not of apples, and at night you could hear the cries of grieving from the women on the other side.'

The boy backed over to the wall. 'It was months I spent in there,' said McWhirty slowly. 'Then they put me in a cart with four others, and they chained us at the wrists and ankles and the carts dragged us down to Cork and then to Cobh, to the boats that would take us here. They tried to follow the carts a while, the women like my Mary, but she had to turn back in the end, and that was the last I saw of her, her and my Michael.

'They dressed us in new clothes for the boats, just like I dressed you. We heard their boots beat against the decking like the clang of chains above. There was only one way out for us, into the sea, but for that we'd burn in the fires of hell as a suicide.'

The boy was listening now, his eyes wide.

'So now I'm wondering,' said McWhirty. 'Why I don't free you, having longed for my freedom all those years. Well, I'll tell you boyo; my Mary sent her petition over and over to the Governor, to let her join me here and I petitioned the magistrate here too. But she never came, because it's only a convict ship that will take her for nothing, and none of those are sailing now, and nor can I go back, and the Colonel pays well if you've got a skill that he can use. So that's why I stay here, and that's why I'll do what he says, because one sweet day I'll have the money to bring my Mary over here and my Michael too, and enough for us to have a farm to live on.'

McWhirty stood up. 'I'll bring you some food later on,' he said, 'and some straw and a blanket for sleeping. And my advice to you is to be as useless as you can, because once the Colonel takes a dislike to you he'll send you away and that's the only chance you've got, boy, to be of no use to the Colonel at all.'

'Minyang?' whispered the boy.

'You don't understand me, do you?' asked McWhirty. 'Well, that makes two of us, because I'm not understanding myself sometimes.'

He left the boy in the darkness.

They came looking for the black kid, of course.

A bloke came up from the camp by the river that evening. He may have been the kid's father, though he was getting on in years, and his beard was grey — the boy's grandfather, perhaps, or uncle.

He didn't knock at the back door of the Colonel's house, or the front. He called from the trees behind the horse yards and the black kid called back to him, urgently from his prison in the storeroom.

The Colonel ran down the stairs, his shotgun in his hand.

'Off with you!' he yelled, and fired once into the air. The Colonel had been at his dinner. The scent of steak and kidney pudding and madeira was still thick around him, and he was angry at being disturbed. 'Off with you! The boy stays here!'

McWhirty reckoned the old man didn't speak English, but he understood the shotgun. The boy cried out once more from the storeroom, but the old man had gone away.

The Colonel nodded at McWhirty. 'Keep watch,' he ordered. 'I want two men on guard there all night.'

McWhirty and Young Mike took the first watch, then Young Mike changed places with Flash Jack. McWhirty stayed on. He could have let Chookie Neilson relieve him but for some reason he felt he should stay with the black kid, even if it was as his guard by the door.

Three men came just before dawn. McWhirty saw them first, darker shadows among the trees. For a moment he hesitated, but some noise must have woken Flash Jack, who had been dozing with his back against the wall. Flash Jack raised his shotgun and fired into the night.

One of the shadows fell. The child cried out in the storeroom. The two men still standing knelt by their companion and half lifted him off the ground. He staggered between them, then the three were lost among the shadows.

At least he isn't dead, thought McWhirty. Maybe it was just a scratch — Flash Jack's aim was never very good. McWhirty hoped it was only that.

The Colonel came to let the black kid out next morning. The frost clung to the grass and the smoke from the house chimneys hung in a haze over the roof in the still air. Even the gum leaves were motionless.

The Colonel nodded at McWhirty. 'Unlock the door.'

McWhirty shoved the key into the lock, and turned it. The door swung open. McWhirty half expected the boy to try to run again, but either he'd understood the shots in the night or he judged there were too many hands to grab him if he tried to escape.

The black kid walked forward slowly. He looked even smaller this morning in McWhirty's too-big clothes. McWhirty glanced at the plate on the floor. He was relieved to see the boy had eaten the meat and the bread too. At least there was always food in plenty at the Colonel's.

'Get some rope,' ordered the Colonel suddenly.

McWhirty blinked.

'Tie it round the piccaninny,' explained the Colonel. 'That way he can't try to run. Ah, that's the ticket,' he said, as Young Mike brought over a length of rope from the stable and tied it round the boy's waist. 'From now on I want that rope on whenever the child is outdoors. You understand?'

'Yes, sir,' said McWhirty.

The Colonel took the rope in his leather-gloved hand and led the boy over to the horse yards. The stallion tossed his head. His hooves thumped on the ground.

'Better stand back, sir,' said McWhirty quietly. 'We're upsetting him.' He nodded at the rope around the child. 'I'd take that off of him too. Don't think the horse likes rope much.'

The Colonel hesitated. Then he nodded at McWhirty. 'Take it off then. But put it on as soon as he's out again. I don't want him running off.'

McWhirty untied the rope, then pushed the boy lightly towards the horse. The Colonel smiled.

'Let's see what happens, then,' he said.

McWhirty nodded. He gazed at the horse, hoping that if he thought hard enough the horse might hear him: don't be going near the boy, lash out at him maybe, just a little, not to hurt him mind, just to let the Colonel think the boy is useless to him, so he'll let him go …

The black kid looked back at the Colonel, at McWhirty and Flash Jack. Then he looked at the stallion.

It was as though they recognised each other, the boy and the horse. The terror of the journey from Calcutta, the horrors of the night in the storeroom all vanished in the sunlight. The boy slipped through the rails and pulled an apple from his pocket.

'The boy has some sense in him,' thought McWhirty sadly. 'He must have taken that apple from the barrels in the storeroom. He learns fast.'

The boy held the apple out to the horse. The stallion took a step closer, then another. He bent his head down and, once again, took the apple delicately from the outstretched hand.

'There now,' said the Colonel with satisfaction. 'Was I not right? Look at that now.'

McWhirty looked.

The horse whinnied softly into the boy's face. This time the boy didn't laugh. But he pulled the long, bony head down towards him and whispered in the horse's ear.

It was enough to break the heart in you, thought Alf McWhirty.

'Keep the boy out here till tonight,' ordered the Colonel. 'So the horse gets used to him, but keep an eye on him at all times. You,' he said to McWhirty, 'I hold you responsible if anything happens to him. I want the boy to bring his feed, his water, muck out the yard — everything. Let's see if that will calm him down.'

'Yes, sir,' said McWhirty.

'And put the rope back on him whenever he's not with the horse. Understand?'

In the horse yards the boy ran his hand along the horse's side.

They kept the black kid prisoner.

Each night McWhirty took him back to the storeroom, with its straw and its blanket and its small barred window, and locked him in. Every morning the Colonel supervised his release, and led him on the rope over to the stallion. And every day the mighty horse grew quieter.

No-one came again from the camp down by the river.

Sometimes McWhirty thought he saw a woman, eyes wide and shiny with tears, watching the black kid from the trees, but when he looked again it was shadows, just the shadows and the wind.

He said nothing about the woman to the others. Perhaps, anyway, she was never really there. And if sometimes at night someone whispered up through the tiny window of the storeroom — perhaps that never happened either.

Perhaps it WAS only the wind.

Every day the Colonel watched as the black kid fed the stallion, stroked him and patted him. No-one else was even able to touch the stallion, or even come near him, except the boy.

The black kid never spoke after that first day, except to the horse. He was always whispering to him, and sometimes it almost seemed that the horse was whispering back. Of course no-one knew his language — unless the horse understood — but McWhirty thought it was something more than that.

Alf McWhirty was good at not talking too, except to horses, though he still talked to the black kid sometimes. It seemed easier, somehow, when the person you talked to didn't know your language.

After a week the black kid was able to place a rope around the horse's neck and lead him slowly round the yard. A week after that he put a bridle on him too, though the horse tossed his head at the bridle and never seemed happy when it was on.

The boy looked almost happy when he was with the horse, decided McWhirty, as he tried to shove away the guilt that rose when he saw the rope hanging on the fence that he would have to replace around the child's waist when his session in the yard had finished.

You got good money when you worked with horses, so the kid was learning a trade, McWhirty told himself just a bit too firmly. And it wouldn't be forever, surely. One day either the Colonel would let the boy go, or maybe one day the child would decide he wanted to stay …

And the Colonel watched and dreamt of riding tall and straight on the great horse, and of the whole town watching him controlling the stallion's power.

Three weeks after the black kid came the Colonel ordered McWhirty to get the child onto the horse's back.

'And how am I supposed to do that, you great bosthoon,' thought McWhirty, 'when neither of us speaks the other's language.'

But he gestured to the boy nonetheless, with the Colonel and the men looking on, safely behind the rails.

The boy's eyes gleamed. He patted the great neck until the horse drew close to the rails — the side furthest way from the Colonel and the men. McWhirty slid into the yards then, and slipped the reins and bridle on. The stallion tossed his head, but quietened again when the boy touched him.

Then the boy climbed the rails and let himself gently down onto the horse's back.

The black horse froze. His eyes rolled and he tossed his head again, then seemed to settle.

'He's had a rider before,' thought McWhirty, as he gazed at the boy and the horse. 'The bloke who sold him to the Colonel was right then. That horse has been broken, he was just too scared to remember.'

The black kid sat there half surprised, with a look of joy dawning on his face. It was the look he had had that first day when he peered at the stallion from the trees.

Colonel Gloucester rubbed his hands. He gestured to McWhirty. 'Lead him around the yard,' he ordered. 'Let's see his paces.'

McWhirty nodded.

The parrots peeped in the trees above them, waiting for the humans to leave so they could feed on the corn in the stallion's droppings. The horse came quietly, one step, two, three. Then suddenly he reared, forelegs high, then crashed down, so McWhirty had to roll under the railings to avoid being struck.

When he looked up there was no sign of the black kid.

The horse was careering round and round the horse yards. The black kid lay by the gate. He looked ... crumpled ... somehow. McWhirty leapt to his feet and ran over.

The boy was conscious. But one leg was twisted awkwardly and one arm looked out of shape as well.

The Colonel swore and stamped inside, as McWhirty knelt by the black child. The boy looked up at him. McWhirty hadn't known a dark face could look so pale.

'Someone ride to town! Fetch a doctor!' yelled McWhirty.

Young Mike blinked. 'Not sure the Colonel would like ...' he began.

'I'll pay the man if the Colonel won't!' roared McWhirty. 'But you fetch him. Now!'

McWhirty and Flash Jack rolled the boy onto a blanket. Then the men lifted the blanket carefully, each hand holding one corner, so the blanket stayed taut and gave the child some support.

'We'll take him to my hut,' stated McWhirty.

'But ...' began Flash Jack.

'The boy isn't going to escape like this,' said McWhirty shortly. The way he felt at the moment, McWhirty didn't care if he did.

The kid made no noise, though he must have been in pain.

McWhirty kicked the door open. It was just a dirt floor and no glass at the windows and bark for a roof, but it kept the rain out and there was a fireplace and there was a proper bed, with a straw mattress and blankets and a pillow too.

They rolled the boy carefully off the blanket and onto the bed. The child winced with pain, but didn't say anything. It was only then that McWhirty realised the boy had probably never seen a bed before.

'It's alright,' said McWhirty, then realised how silly that sounded. But maybe the boy didn't understand anyway, though his eyes were wide and steady every time McWhirty spoke to him.

Doctor Miller arrived late that afternoon. McWhirty heard the hoof beats outside his hut and went to meet him. He glanced at the sun behind the trees, sending their shadows stretching across the dust. The doctor would never get back to town in daylight now; he'd have to spend the night at the Colonel's. He'd probably planned that all along, thought McWhirty. The two would drink the Colonel's port late into the night. Well, at least it would keep the Colonel away from the black kid, and the doctor would be on hand if he was needed in the night.

'Got a patient for me, I hear?' said Doctor Miller, as he dismounted and tied the reins to the verandah post.

'A boy,' said McWhirty.

'What's his name?' asked the doctor, pulling his case out of his saddle bag.

McWhirty blinked. Somehow he'd never even thought the kid had a name. 'Don't know,' he admitted. 'Some native name, I expect.'

'Well, what do you call him, then?' asked the doctor impatiently.

McWhirty shrugged. 'We don't,' he said.

Doctor Miller looked him up and down. 'I see,' he said shortly. He stepped into the hut. 'I'm Doc Miller,' he said to the black kid. 'Now, let's be having a look at you.'

The black child lay quiet while the doctor examined him, pressed his stomach and smelt his breath, held his wrist to feel his pulse and looked into his eyes. He cried out only once when the doctor touched his leg.

'Bad break there,' said Doctor Miller finally. 'The arm is broken too, but that'll set alright. Don't know about the leg. Don't seem to be any other injuries.'

'Can you set them?' asked McWhirty.

'I can try. I'll need some branches — straight ones, about this long. Trim them smooth as you can.' The doctor took a tall brown bottle filled with a thick white liquid and a long silver spoon out of his bag.

'Now I'm going to give you a spoonful of this, young fellow me lad,' he said to the black kid. 'It'll make you feel sleepy but it'll keep the worst of the pain away. Understand?'

The black kid said nothing but he opened his mouth, McWhirty noticed, when the doctor poured the medicine into the spoon.

McWhirty found the branches while the doctor sat with the black kid, and then whittled them smooth with his pocketknife. He held the black kid down too, while Doctor Miller straightened the broken leg, fitted the branches on either side, and tied bandages dipped in water and plaster of Paris around them to keep them firm. Then he set the arm too.

The kid was pale and sweating at the end but he hadn't cried out again. McWhirty reckoned the medicine hadn't done much good, as there was blood on the kid's lips where he'd bitten them, but at least the kid fell asleep soon after, from shock and pain perhaps, as much as the medicine.

'What do I owe you?' asked McWhirty finally.

'The Colonel will pay me,' said the doctor easily.

'If he doesn't, I will,' said McWhirty. 'Will you look in on him again tomorrow before you leave?'

'I'll do that. Fond of the boy, are you?'

'Me? Of course not. I've got a boy of my own back home ...'McWhirty hesitated. Michael would no longer be a child ...

'Well, you look after the lad,' said the doctor. 'Keep him warm. He might run a fever in the next few days; make sure he gets enough to drink and keep the blanket on. Try to keep him as quiet as possible, so he doesn't move around. The medicine will help. I'll leave you the bottle. A spoonful whenever he gets restless, but not more than six spoonfuls a day. And keep his bowels open too.'

'How in Hades do I do that?' demanded McWhirty.

'Prune juice,' said Doctor Miller, taking out another bottle — a clear glass one this time, with a black liquid inside. 'One dose in the morning. Have you got a bedpan?'

'A what?'

'A bedpan. He won't be able to go outside. I'll see one gets sent down to you from the main house. He'd better have his food sent down too.'

McWhirty gazed at the sleeping kid as the doctor left. 'Bedpans,' he muttered.

The black kid woke up twice in the night, muttering with pain. Or perhaps he wasn't quite awake, thought McWhirty. Maybe the medicine was finally doing its job.

'Easy boy, easy,' said McWhirty. The boy looked at him with unseeing eyes as he drank the water McWhirty held to his lips and spoke to him in a language that McWhirty didn't understand.

It was the first time since the boy had been captured that he had heard him talk, apart from a word or two. 'Well, that makes something clear,' he muttered. 'At least you've not been struck dumb.'

McWhirty slept wrapped in a blanket on the floor that night, when he slept at all. It was harder than the bed, but McWhirty was used to it. It was the way he'd slept every night for the two years he'd spent droving, before the Colonel hired him.

He gave the boy more medicine in the morning and his prune juice too. It obviously hurt the kid too much to sit, so McWhirty soaked bread in tea and fed that to him with the spoon instead.

It was a long day after that.

McWhirty sat and watched the sleeping boy and thought. It had been a long time since he'd had a whole day of doing nothing, just him and his thoughts. Finally after lunch, when he reckoned the kid would keep sleeping, he went out to the stables to oversee the chores.

The boy was still asleep when he came back. He slept until sunset. He was still asleep when the mopokes began to call from the trees, and the moon was beginning to sink in the sky.

McWhirty was worried by now. Perhaps the medicine was too strong for a boy his age, or he'd given him too much.

The boy opened his eyes.

'Well, you're awake then,' said McWhirty.

The fire was out, and he couldn't make more tea, so he spread the bread with jam — it was fresh and soft enough — and fed it to the kid in tiny bites. Then he held the bedpan under him. The boy seemed to get the hang of the bedpan faster than McWhirty.

The kid was still awake when he came back from emptying it among the trees.

'Well,' said McWhirty again, sitting on the hut's single chair.

The boy said nothing.

'I made you something,' said McWhirty. 'It's nothing much. Don't suppose you'll like it.'

The boy looked at him solemnly. McWhirty reached under his chair then held the object out.

It was a horse, carved from a piece of casuarina from down the river. The Colonel had made his men cut one down and split it into shingles for the house, and McWhirty had kept a couple of branches for carving. The wood was softer than gum tree wood, and didn't split so much when it dried.

It was a pretty good horse, the front legs bent as though it galloped across the hills.

The boy looked at it.

'Sorry it's not black,' said McWhirty. 'I rubbed some oil into it to darken it a piece, but that's the best I can do with it.'

The boy reached out and took the horse with his good arm. His fingers traced the back, the neck, the legs. He looked back up at McWhirty and, for the first time ever, McWhirty saw him smile.

'Doc Miller wanted to know your name,' said McWhirty. 'I had to say I didn't know.'

The kid was silent, still stroking his horse.

'What is your name then?' asked McWhirty.

For a moment he thought the boy wasn't going to answer. Then he said softly something that sounded like 'Wallaamaala.'

'Don't think I quite got that,' said McWhirty. 'Wal something or other. If that IS your name, and you're not just asking for another drink of water.' He held the mug up to the boy's lips. He drank and closed his eyes.

McWhirty touched him lightly on the shoulder, and the boy opened his eyes again. 'One thing I have to tell you,' said McWhirty. 'And it's sorry I am to have to do it. Those people of yours — the camp down by the river. They've gone.'

The kid's eyes opened wider. 'Dhaguu?' he asked.

'No, I don't know where they've gone either,' said McWhirty. 'It was the Colonel's doing, you can be sure of that. But if you're thinking of escaping, dragging that broken leg of yours about, well, you won't be finding your people, and you'll cripple yourself into the bargain. Understood?'

No answer. The dark eyes shut again. When McWhirty looked again there were tears on the kid's cheeks, but that might just have been pain. There was no way to tell if he had understood or not.

The black kid recovered slowly.

The cicadas sizzled in the trees. The only smoke now rose from the kitchen chimney, where Mrs Connolly sweated at the wood stove and tried to have the bread cooked before the worst heat of the day.

McWhirty took to leaving the kid in the hut while he was working most of the day, looking in on him every hour or two in case he needed a drink or the bedpan that both of them had come to hate. McWhirty reckoned there was little danger of the kid running off now. For a start he couldn't run and even if he hobbled, where could he hobble to?

Doctor Miller called out every week or so. He said the child was healing well and to feed him up a bit and keep his bowels open.

McWhirty looked guilty at that. The prune juice sat almost unused next to the fly safe. McWhirty hadn't bothered with it after the first two days.

McWhirty took to flattering Mrs Connolly after that, so she'd give him some of the delicacies she made for the Colonel — slices of cold apple pudding left over from dinner the night before, and egg and bacon pie.

The boy seemed to enjoy the new foods. He ate them all anyway and sometimes he even smiled when McWhirty came in after work.

It was good, McWhirty found, to have someone smile at you when you came in from work.

The boy was out of doors for the first time the day the letter came. It was a Sunday, a quiet day at the Colonel's. There was no church nearer than town for the men to go to, and Mrs Connolly took the buggy into town most Sundays, and sometimes Young Mike joined her.

McWhirty had fixed a chair for the black kid in the shade of the verandah. He begged a cushion from Mrs Connolly and fixed up a footstool from a block of wood for the kid to rest his leg on. The kid could see the mares and foals in the house paddock from there. It'd be more interesting for him, McWhirty reckoned, than just lying on the bed indoors. He found another hunk of wood for himself to sit on too, beside the boy.

It was while they were sitting there that Young Mike brought the letter. Young Mike's boots were freshly oiled and shining black and his spurs were polished too, and he wore his good red shirt and his cummerbund and the green handkerchief at his neck as well, like a blooming parrot, thought McWhirty, but he said nothing as the young man walked up.

'A letter,' he said, holding it out. 'It was waiting at the Post Office for you.'

McWhirty nodded. He tried to keep his face calm and his hands from trembling. There was only one reason anybody would be writing to him.

'How's the boy?' asked Young Mike, with a grin towards the black kid. The black kid smiled back.

'Him? Oh, he's alright,' said McWhirty.

He waited till Young Mike had left before he ripped the letter open.

He read it once and then a second time, and then a third. Then he let the sheet of paper settle in his lap while he looked out at the horse paddock, and the blue green trees beyond.

'Minyang?' asked the boy softly.

'It's a letter from home,' said McWhirty quietly, not looking at the boy. 'It's from Father Feehan. He'd heard from the Bishop that I'd petitioned to have Mary and Michael sent out to join me. He thought I should know … that I should know …' McWhirty took a deep breath as though the next words were hard to say. 'They died three years ago,' said McWhirty. 'And I never knew.

It was the typhoid, Father Feehan said it was bad that year. And I never knew.'

McWhirty folded the letter carefully and placed it in his pocket. 'I'll be back by dinner time,' he said. 'Do you want to go back inside, or stay out here?'

The boy glanced back at the hut and shook his head. McWhirty nodded.

The boy watched him stride across the yard. A few minutes later he was back with Barney, the horse he usually used to check the fences or the mares when they were foaling in the paddock. He mounted the horse, cantered across the yard and was gone.

As soon as the kid was able to use his arm again, McWhirty made him rough crutches out of wattle branches and showed him how to use them. He tried to tell the kid that he wouldn't have to use the crutches forever; that one day his leg would heal, but there was no way to tell if he understood or not.

The boy worked out how to use the crutches almost at once, swinging himself between the crutches round and round the hut.

'You be careful now,' warned McWhirty. 'No tiring yourself out mind and no going outside either! There's no call for you to be falling and hurting your leg further. I'll be checking the fences in the top paddock all day, so

I'll bring some food over for you before I go, and I'll be back tonight. You understand?'

The boy nodded, still balanced on his crutches.

It was hot that day. The bush was quiet, even the birds sheltered in the shade till the cool of dusk brought them out to feed again. The storm hit almost without warning, the black and purple clouds spreading thick and ominous from the horizon.

It was too far back to the main house. McWhirty led Barney into the trees, where the lightning had a good choice if it decided to strike, and tethered him to a sturdy branch. 'Sorry, old boy,' said McWhirty. 'If I could find shelter for the both of us I'd take it. But you're hairier than I am and bigger into the bargain.'

Barney whinnied softly as McWhirty hauled off his saddle, then made himself comfortable in the relative dryness underneath the horse's wide body, stroking the horse's underside soothingly each time the thunder yelled above them. It was a trick he'd learnt years ago, mostly to show off to men who'd exclaim, 'That McWhirty! Got that horse so well trained he can shelter under it when it rains!' But sometimes it was useful too.

It was late afternoon when the rain eased, a soft fluff of mist drifting over the distant hills. McWhirty saddled up Barney again, and rode back to the house. He brushed Barney down and gave him extra corn for warmth before heading to his hut.

The black kid was gone.

McWhirty ran from the hut. He didn't even think what the Colonel might say when he found the boy had left. He was worried that the kid might fall, might hurt himself again, might starve even, unable to hunt with his broken leg.

He was wondering frantically whether to saddle up Barney again and search himself or call the others out to hunt as well, when he looked down towards the horse yards.

The kid was down at the horse yard, his crutches leaning against the rails, watching the stallion.

It was the first time the boy and horse had met since his accident.

There were no apples left now, in mid-summer, but the boy had saved some bread from dinner and he held it out now to the horse.

The horse stepped over quietly. He bent his great neck and nuzzled the boy's cheek almost, thought McWhirty, as though he were apologising for having hurt the boy.

The boy murmured something. The horse bent his head further and took the bread, then stayed there as the boy stroked his neck.

McWhirty waited till his heart had stopped pounding in his chest, then walked over to the horse yards. A faint burst of thunder growled up in the hills. The boy turned to him. 'Muurruubarraay!' he said.

'What's that? That's what you called Trumpeter, isn't it?'

The boy shook his head. He pointed to the hills as the thunder muttered even more faintly. 'Muurruubarraay!'

'Thunder? Is that what you're saying? Ah, now I'm understanding you — is that what you call the horse then? Thunder? How do you say it? Mowbray was it then?'

'Muurruubarraay,' agreed the boy, stroking the horse's neck.

'A good name for him,' agreed McWhirty. 'Better than Trumpeter. Black like thunder clouds and his hooves sound like thunder too. But it's time you had a rest, then.' He helped the boy gently onto his crutches again. 'Come on, back to the house, and I'll see what Mrs Connolly has got to feed us.'

So the days continued. The boy grew stronger. There was no need for the crutches now. He still limped, but his arm was as good as ever. He fed the stallion (McWhirty found he thought of the horse as Thunder now as well) and watered him, just as he'd done before.

He still refused to speak English, though McWhirty reckoned he must have picked up a fair bit by now. Kids are quick at picking up languages. He obeyed if he was spoken to, but otherwise he spoke only to the horse.

He was always whispering to the stallion, softly, secretly as though afraid the men might hear, afraid they'd understand him if they heard. But of course none of them spoke any language except English and if Alf McWhirty was finally learning another language than his own, he didn't say.

Sometimes, when his work was done, McWhirty took Barney over to the hut and led him round and round and through the trees while the black kid perched up on his back. The boy rode like he had ridden all his life. Had a knack with horses, as the Colonel said.

But people are good with horses in different ways, thought McWhirty, as he listened to the clop of Barney's hooves behind him, the crack of leaves and twigs and the soft breathing of the boy. The Colonel loved horses because he could control them, like the men he had once commanded in the army. And McWhirty — well for him, the horse was his partner, someone who worked with him, who he could trust and who didn't demand too much.

But the boy — well, that was something different. For the boy the black horse was just an animal of beauty, more beautiful and powerful than any animal he'd known before. What would it be like, thought McWhirty, to live your life with animals like 'roos and wombats, and then see your first horse? And that a horse like Thunder, or Mowbray (as McWhirty pronounced the boy's name for the horse).

Ah, McWhirty understood the beauty of a horse, the way it flowed with the wind, its muscles bunching, its head held high, the fine legs and the arch of the neck, the lift of the proud feet and the angle of its eyes. But he knew he'd never felt for any horse what the boy felt towards the stallion.

The boy enjoyed the rides and patted Barney afterwards. But he saved his love for the black stallion.

'Time to get him up on Trumpeter again,' said the Colonel thoughtfully one day, after watching the black kid ride Barney across the yard. It was autumn and the shadows were blue under the trees. The English trees the Colonel's wife had planted had turned red and gold, but their colours were still diminished by the gum trees up on the hills.

'Not yet, sir,' said McWhirty. 'Let him get a bit more strength up first.'

'Nonsense,' said the Colonel. 'Boy looks strong as an ox. Give him one more go up on the horse, eh? And if that doesn't work,' the Colonel shrugged, 'we'll just put him out in the paddock with the mares. At least he'll earn his keep that way. Time that boy was doing a bit more work around the place anyway, with the other horses. He been behaving himself?'

'Yes, sir,' said McWhirty. 'He's been behaving himself.'

McWhirty walked over to the horse yards with the Colonel. The boy looked up from his seat in the dust in the corner of the horse yards. He stood up awkwardly, steadying himself against the rails. He rarely used the crutches any more.

'Try putting the bridle on him again,' ordered the Colonel.

The boy looked at McWhirty. McWhirty hesitated. 'Look, sir, how about we try it without the bridle? It's the reins that seem to scare him. See if the boy can stay on his back without them.'

The Colonel considered. 'Might work,' he admitted. 'Get the horse used to the weight on his back, eh, before we try any more? It might work at that. Go ahead and try it.'

McWhirty gestured 'up' to the black kid, though he had a feeling the boy had understood everything they'd said. McWhirty's face was tight with worry.

The black kid grinned. It was a reassuring grin, but there was something else there too.

The other men had realised something was happening now. They drifted over: Young Mike and Flash Jack and Chookie Neilson, and a couple of the stockmen in from the hills. McWhirty even caught a glimpse of Mrs Connolly peering through the kitchen window.

He held his breath.

The black kid rested his hands on the horse's neck. Then he linked his hands over the horse's neck, and dropped his left shoulder and simultaneously swung his right leg up and over the animal's back. It was a smooth leap, despite the crippled leg. The black kid sat straight and proud on the stallion's back and grinned at the men below him.

One hand held the horse's mane now. The other stroked the smooth black coat, while he bent and whispered in the horse's ear.

The stallion began to move, one step, two steps ... It was impossible, thought McWhirty, staring at the boy. He had never ridden the stallion before. The only time he had ever been on his back he had been thrown down into the dust. But this time the boy was in control.

The boy had watched, thought McWhirty. And he had understood.

Maybe the horse understood something too.

Slowly, slowly, the great black horse walked around the horse yard, lifting his feet proudly and steadily, step by step. It was almost as though they were showing off, thought McWhirty, the black kid and the stallion both.

The boy bent down to the horse's ear again. He whispered something and patted the muscled neck.

The stallion began to trot and then to canter around the yard, round and round and round, the black kid clinging to his mane, his raggy-trousered knees clinging to his back.

The black kid laughed. He glanced just once at Alf McWhirty, then looked away. He leant forward, close to the animal's neck, and held even more tightly to the mane. The knees in their dusty, baggy moleskins clung tightly too.

And then the stallion swerved across the yard. The massive haunches crouched, then he was rising up and up and up.

The stallion leapt the fence, the black kid still upon his back, and galloped away across the paddock and through the trees, and all that was left was the echo of laughter and the thunder of hooves.

That was the last anyone ever saw of the stallion or the black kid either.

Colonel Gloucester gave chase of course. The Colonel was at his best in an emergency when he could take command. He had the horses saddled up in minutes with all the men, including himself, ready for the chase. They went in all directions, the Colonel down towards the river where the camp had been, McWhirty high into the hills, Flash Jack down the track to town and Young Mike along the flats.

By late afternoon, half the district was looking for the black kid and the stallion. But a horse like that stallion can gallop faster than the wind. A horse like that can gallop an entire day and be ready to gallop again all the next.

There was no horse in the district that could catch a horse like that.

The Colonel sent word to the magistrate, and the magistrate sent messages around the colony. But the colony was large, and there were many black horses and many, many places where a horse and boy could hide.

The magistrate sent troopers to all the camps too. But there was no black horse, and no black child who walked with a limp that they could find.

A week later Alf McWhirty quit the Colonel's employment and left the farm. The Colonel's temper was still high and there was no shortage of places for a man who knew horses like McWhirty, even if the pay wasn't as high. And besides, he had his savings, and no fares that needed paying now.

Five years later the Colonel gave up horse breeding and moved back to Sydney.

That's the end of the story. Or is it? ... Maybe, just maybe, there's another chapter still to tell.

It was ten years after Colonel Gloucester went back to Sydney, twenty years after the black kid leapt the fence and galloped laughing back into the bush. A bloke named Jim Kearney was out fencing, repairing the boundary between his place and the Mossops'.

Old Mossop had sold his place about six months before. Jim and his wife hadn't met the new owners yet. They seemed to keep to themselves.

It wasn't much of a fence, the one Jim was repairing, just two strands of wire strung between the trees, but it kept the cattle in alright. But there'd been a storm the week before and there were branches down over the wire and once cattle get the idea they can walk through fences, no fence will hold them.

Jim was down off his horse for the fifth time that day, chopping at a fallen tree with his axe, when he heard the hoof beats. He put the axe down and wiped the sweat from his eyes and, as he told his wife that night, there it was: this great black horse cantering through the trees on the other side of the fence. Even at first glance you could see it was no ordinary horse. This horse knew that it was king.

The rider pulled the horse to a stop. Jim stepped forward and now he could see that the horse was much older than he'd thought. There was grey around his eyes and down his muzzle, and his teeth, when he bent to snatch some grass under the trees, were long and yellow.

The horse's rider slipped down off his back and held out his hand and stepped over to Jim. He limped a bit, Jim noticed, but not too bad.

'G'day,' said the rider. 'Wal Mowbray.'

The rider's hand was black, not white, though of course neither man was white or black: the rider's skin was brownish, the colour of the soil along the river bank, and Jim's was brown as well, a different colour brown from a year's work in the sun.

Jim hesitated. But he'd spent years droving before he married Jean and bought the farm; it'd been black stockmen who'd taught him most of what he knew, so he took the hand, even though the colour was a bit of a shock. As far as he knew there were no Aboriginal stockmen around here, and the local tribe had been moved down to the coast years before.

'Jim Kearney,' said Jim.

The rider nodded. 'Need a hand?' he asked. There was a bit of an accent, but not that you'd notice thought Jim.

'Wouldn't mind,' said Jim.

It was easier with two. Jim finished cutting through the tree. They hauled it off the fence together, and repaired the broken strands of wire, then rode along the fence line in silence, down towards the river.

The sun was high above them when they reached the river that formed the far boundary for both farms and stopped to let their horses drink.

'Good horse,' said Jim, breaking the silence. 'What's he called?'

'Thunder,' said Wal. He looked at Jim's horse with an experienced eye. No-one could call Billy Boy a good horse, so he said, 'Looks like he's got a good bit of work in him,' instead.

Jim snorted. 'The only time he gets a move on is when he's heading home to a feed.'

'You a stockman on the Mossop place then?' asked Jim. He'd half a notion that the rider might be looking for a job, might have lent him a hand hoping he'd take him on.

Wal shook his head. 'It's the Mowbray place now. I'm the owner. Me and me Uncle Alf. Well, I call him uncle. He married my aunt, at any road.'

'Cattle?' asked Jim.

'Yeah. And horses. Got a contract with a buyer for the East India Company.'

Jim nodded, slightly envious. There was good money in quality horses, and by the look of the black stallion the Mowbray horses should be good.

'You married then?' asked Jim.

'Yeah. You?'

'Yeah,' said Jim. 'Her name's Jean.'

'Mine's Sue,' said Wal, and with that they went to finish the fence.

The afternoon was only half done when they had finished the last bit up the hill. It was good to work with someone else again, thought Jim. The work was done in less than half the time.

They could see the Mossop–Mowbray place on the rise above the river. There'd been changes since Jim had seen it last. The old house was still there, but there was a new house standing next to it, connected to the old house by a passage.

The new house had stone chimneys and a wide verandah. The old bark roof was gone from the old house too, and a new corrugated iron one shone in its place.

There were rows of cabbages and turnips and fruit-tree saplings nearer the house and hens strutting between the fruit trees and dogs asleep in the shade under the verandah.

And there were horses — mostly black, but there were chestnut ones as well — in the newly fenced paddocks next to the corn and in the new yards by the house.

'Looks good,' said Jim, a little enviously. He and Jean were still at the slab hut and bark roof stage, but he planned to get her a proper iron stove next cattle sale.

The black rider hesitated. 'You want to come down to the house then?' he offered. 'We killed a beast yesterday. Let you have a hindquarter if you want.'

'Wouldn't mind,' said Jim gratefully. 'The missus would be glad of it.'

The two men rode down the hill together. The mutton was hanging in a fly-proof meat safe in the shed. Wal unhooked it and chopped off a hindquarter with an axe.

'Good bit of meat on that,' said Jim appreciatively. He paused. 'Might see if the missus would like to come over tomorrow,' he offered. 'She can meet your missus and all. Bring you over some cheese if you want; Jean's good with cheese.'

He'd have to talk hard to convince her, he thought, what with them being black and all. But he thought that she'd come round. Wal and the Mowbrays looked like being good neighbours to have, and besides, it had been six months since Jean had talked to anyone except him and the cockatoo, and sometimes she said the cockatoo had more conversation than Jim did.

'The wife'd like that,' said Wal. He spoke with an accent, Jim realised, though it was hard to say what it was. 'Bought her some china last time I was in town, teacups and that. That thin stuff, all roses and gold paint. She'll be glad to show it off.'

Jim mounted Billy Boy again. The horse sensed it was heading home now and stepped more briskly up the hill.

That was when he saw the kid. He was on a black horse, a younger version of the stallion that Wal had ridden today. Wal's son, Jim reckoned, and the horse would be Thunder's son or even great grandson perhaps.

The boy saw him, laughed and waved his hat high above his head. Then he was gone, and only the echo of the hoof beats sang across the hill.

So that is the end of the story of a family called Mowbray (or Muurruubarraay perhaps) and a horse called Thunder, and their farm by the river.

Or is it?

Stories never really end. There are still black horses by the river and their riders still urge them through the trees and laugh as they gallop across the hills.

The Baker's Horse

Winters were the worst — dark streets and a cold wind bringing the smells of garbage bins and dunny cans. The bakery was all warmth behind us, its golden light and the hot smell of bread spilling out into the night.

I had to be careful where I trod in winter. The streets were rutted and the gloom sucked all the goodness from the street lights. Old Sam wore his checked coat in winter and Young Bob's nose ran all the time. Sometimes it rained. The cart had a roof that kept the bread dry, and a sort of verandah roof where Old Sam and Bob sat behind me, but the cold drops would run miserably down my back and legs. Mrs Sam used to make a hot mash for me when it rained.

Summer was easier. The horizon was pale pink even before Old Sam had finished loading the loaves onto the cart. We clip-clopped down the street in the soft dawn light, carrying the hot bread, the loaves in the cart warm and fragrant behind us.

It was good bread we carried in those days — long white loaves or brown, flat tops and charcoaled high tops, malt loaves, round milk loaves and fruit bread on Thursdays — not so much variety as we had carried before The War, though why The War should stop us carrying fancy breads, I never understood.

Young Bob leapt on and off the wagon, poking the loaves wrapped in their tissue paper into the letter boxes, or resting them between the box and the fence, or placing them in the box put there on purpose because the owner had a dog who liked fresh bread. Old Sam's bones creaked too much to jump on and off the wagon himself now, and Young Sam was at The War.

I wasn't sure where The War was. It was a place a long way off at any rate, I thought, near Sydney maybe, or even Melbourne.

Early mornings it was just us and sleepless dogs, who'd bark at us just for the pleasure of it, even though we passed that way each night. Dogs have no intelligence in my opinion. They've more bark than brains.

Sometimes a cat would stalk across the road, and glance at us indignantly. Cats think they own the world. Sometimes a possum would grunt up in the tree tops, or a baby would cry as we passed a house, and the light would flick on as its mother got up to nurse it.

But mostly it was just the clip-clop of my hooves, Old Sam's soft 'gee up, boy' and the sniffles of Bob wiping his nose on his sleeve. Young Bob's feet were always cold in winter. None of the kids wore shoes back then. I saw Bob wriggle his toes in my droppings to warm them more than once.

The evening star would fade in the night sky, the stars would lose their gleam. There'd be early morning shift-workers, off up to the tram with their lunch bags in their hands. They'd tip their hats to Sam and the politest would greet me too. 'How you going, Snowy Boy? Alright? Been a long night, old man?'

Sometimes we'd hear the clink of the milkman's cart a few streets away from us, but his route and times were different from ours and we never met.

Dawn would come with magpies and kookaburras yelling their heads off for no good reason at all, if you ask me, and housewives in dressing gowns and scarves around their curlers would watch from their windows till we'd passed, so they could duck out and get their bread without Old Sam seeing them in their nightdresses.

More often there'd be kids waiting at the gate. They'd take the loaf from Bob and tear the crusts off before they were halfway up the garden paths, to get their teeth into the soft warm bread.

'A mouse must have got it!' we'd hear them yelling as they ran in the door, but we reckoned their mothers knew the mice had two long legs and no fur.

We had to have our run finished early so the women got the bread in time to make the lunches for the men off to work and the children off to school, then they could settle down with another cup of tea and a slice or two of toast or fresh bread maybe, with plum jam or maybe strawberry or melon. (I got to know the jams from the crusts that Young Bob fed me sometimes; melon was my favourite, I believe.)

Mr Gordon's was the last house on our round. He'd be waiting at the front gate for us, and every morning he would say, 'Thought you'd never get here. Reckon I can have my breakfast now.'

He'd take the loaf from Young Bob and every Friday, regular, would slip a threepence in his hand. Mr Gordon's wife had died two years before, and both boys and his daughter too were at The War, like our Young Sam.

And then we'd wander homeward more slowly than before, although the cart wasn't as heavy, and halfway back Mrs Jamieson would come to join us, pushing her pram with the baby in one end and a couple of buckets behind and a small spade to shovel up my droppings as we went.

'It's an outing for me and an outing for baby too,' she'd say. She was someone for Old Sam to talk to as well, because once the deliveries were over Young Bob ran off home to get his lunch for school. Mrs Jamieson said my droppings made the best rose food she'd ever had.

Mrs Jamieson had the best garden in the district. Sometimes she'd bring a giant cabbage for Old Sam and a carrot or two for me, still with their green tops on them. In spring sometimes, just after the wattle trees had finished blooming, she'd hand Old Sam up a bunch of roses for Mrs Sam, and Old Sam would say to me,

'You see old Snowy Boy? You see what your doings have gone and done? Never thought they'd smell as good as this, would you?' as he breathed the deep scent of the roses.

Then we'd be home and Sam would lead me round the back and brush me down, give me my oats and maybe a biscuit of hay (if it was winter when the grass lost its goodness) and put me out in the paddock next door. I would munch and doze and watch the children coming home and then the men, and wait for it all again tomorrow.

We worked six days a week and on Sunday we rested. Families, all dressed-up, would pass by on their way to church, and there would be tennis in the afternoons with everyone done up in white, and children on their billycarts flying down the street or double-dinking on their bicycles.

And so it went, till one day Young Sam came home from The War.

Even I heard the uproar in my paddock then — the yelling and the screaming then a party with balloons, and Mrs Sam so happy she came out under the clothes line to cry.

But things were different the next morning.

We delivered our bread as usual, me and Old Sam and Bob, and when we got home there was Young Sam and Mrs Sam to greet us. Young Sam held the brush this time, and it was him who brushed me down, all the while talking to his father.

'You see it's like this, Dad,' he said, 'no need to push yourself now I'm back. You take it easy and tend the garden maybe. Mum says there's a million things want doing round the house. And as for this old boy here —' he gave my neck a pat, 'well, I've got the offer of a van, been up on blocks all war it has, a real beauty, it's a steal ...'

That was the last day I carried the bread. The last day for Old Sam too.

They put me in my paddock, and that was where I stayed. It wasn't easy, I confess, those first few days. The fence around my paddock was like a prison wall, barring me from the streets I'd called my own.

What is a horse to do when his whole life has been with a man, helping him, working with him, then suddenly the work goes on, but you are left behind?

No, those first few days weren't easy.

It wasn't that I was lonely; I had company enough. There was Old Sam beyond the fence, working in his garden, and sometimes he'd hold a carrot out over the fence. There was Mrs Sam hanging out the washing too, and the people passing, just as they'd done before.

No, I wasn't lonely. It was the work I missed. What is a horse worth when the heart of his life has gone?

I'd been in that paddock two weeks, munching grass and staring at the air, when I met Susan.

She hadn't been among the children tramping home from school before. (I found out later her family had only just moved to our street.) She was carrying a school bag, and she saw me standing there. She stopped and stared across the fence.

'Hey, horse!' she called.

One of the other girls came up beside her. 'That's the baker's horse,' she said. 'They used to do deliveries up our street.'

Susan held out her hand. There was nothing in it, but I wandered up anyway. I had nothing else to do.

'Look out,' said the friend. 'He might bite.'

'No, he won't,' said Susan confidently.

I mumbled at her empty hand, just to be polite, and also to show the other girl that though some horses might bite, I didn't — not Susan, at any rate.

Susan laughed. 'His mouth feels soft! Wait a minute.'

She reached down and unclicked the fastenings of her school bag. It looked like brown cardboard, all worn at the corners. There was a book in there, and something wrapped up in greaseproof paper, and a round thing, orange, like a ball.

Susan held the orange ball thing out to me. 'Here,' she said. 'Do horses like oranges?'

I sniffed at the ball, just in case it smelt more interesting close up, then dropped it at her feet. I knickered softly, just to tell her no hard feelings, but horses didn't like oranges very much.

Susan bent down again, and unwrapped the greaseproof paper. 'There's just crusts left,' she apologised. She held them out to me. 'How about bread and honey, horse?'

It was sweet and it was wonderful. I ate them from her hand, then mumbled round her fingers just to see if any more was left, then swished my nose around the ground in case I'd dropped some crumbs.

I've never seen a girl smile so wide. 'Isn't he beautiful?' she said to her friend.

Her friend shrugged. 'He's alright,' she said.

So that was the start of it.

Susan came the next afternoon, with a whole honey sandwich for me this time.

I munched it and then I grinned at her. She thought that I was laughing, but I wasn't — the honey had made my teeth ache, though it was worth it. But she laughed right back and Old Sam looked up at the noise from where he was mending the chicken run, and came on over.

'You like horses, missy?' he asked.

Susan nodded. 'I've never seen a white one before though,' she said. 'Is he yours?'

Old Sam nodded. 'Me and Snowy go way back,' he said, stroking my side. A thought seemed to strike him. 'Would you like a ride on him?'

'On Snowy? Really?' Susan danced up on tiptoes like she was trying to reach the moon. 'Really? Really?'

'You stay there a minute,' said Old Sam, and he hopped over the fence again and came back with my bridle.

You know, it had been ten years or so since I'd had someone on my back — not since Young Sam was a little boy. But I suppose you don't forget. It's a different weight from pulling a cart, and Susan — why she was no weight at all.

There was no saddle, of course. Old Sam had never had one. But there was no need. Like Old Sam said, my back was as solid and broad as Susan's bed at home.

She held on to my mane while Old Sam led me round and round the paddock. Two or three of her friends passed too and they stopped to watch, and Susan waved at them as proud as a queen.

There were four children waiting for a ride next afternoon.

I grew to know them all: Joy from down the road and Sharon from the market gardens and Cheryl-Anne, and there were others too. But Susan was my favourite.

I think she was Old Sam's favourite as well. Susan had the first ride every day, no matter how many of the others were waiting. It was only right, as she'd been the first one to say hello.

And as for me, I was working again. It's a great responsibility having children on your back, as important as delivering the bread. I was steady. I did it well.

Every day Susan had a honey sandwich for me. The others had offerings too sometimes: carrots and apples and Vegemite crusts, or long tender grass they'd pulled up over the fence line where I couldn't reach, but I liked Susan's sandwiches best.

School holidays and weekends she took to coming down in the early afternoons, and Old Sam would show her how to brush me down. She'd hold me and watch while the farrier trimmed my hooves as well. My feet needed trimming often now that they were no longer worn down on the road. Sometimes she'd plait my mane, a silly job, I thought. What was the point of it? But I stood it patiently, for Susan.

Susan got taller and I got slower, and Old Sam grew slower too. It was Susan, now, who led me round and round the paddock in the afternoons, and when she couldn't come the children had to do without their ride, and they fed and patted me instead.

Ten more years I lived in that paddock. One morning I heard an engine mutter in the early morning instead of the clip-clop of the milkman's cart. The milkman's horse was the last of us delivery horses; I don't know where they put him out to grass.

A few years after Young Sam came home, they built houses on the market gardens then on the paddock where the Mortimers had kept their sheep. One afternoon I saw Young Sam standing with a smart man in a suit and briefcase. They were staring at my paddock, as though wondering how many houses they'd fit there.

Then Young Sam shook his head. The smart man shrugged, and drove away.

Young Sam brought me out a carrot that night. A few weeks later he brought a baby to meet me, wrapped up in a blanket. He had three children by the end. On

Saturday afternoons he'd lead me round and round the paddock with all three of them on my back.

They put black stuff down on the road one week, a noisy beast of a machine rolling it over and over till it was flat. The road wasn't rutted any more now, and the rain ran off the road into the gutter instead of carving channels down the middle, and there were concrete gutters soon too. It wasn't my road after that, not the dusty or muddy or frosty road I'd travelled up and down.

Things change as you get older. I overheard Old Sam tell someone that.

It was Susan who found me that Christmas morning, lying by the fence. I'd been watching for her, dozing on and off before she came, and I suppose one doze grew longer than the rest.

She'd brought me a honey sandwich for my Christmas dinner, and she cried, and Old Sam cried as well, but kept his face straight so Susan wouldn't notice, and Young Sam fetched Johnny Rogers and his tractor over, and he dug a good deep hole.

It took Johnny two hours to dig the hole and then to fill it in, but he said he didn't mind, even though it was Christmas Day. I'd given his children rides, and he remembered. They buried me there in that paddock where I'd lived the last years of my life, and Susan and Old Sam and Mrs Sam and Young Sam and his children watched it all, but it was Susan who cried the most.

I wanted to say, 'Don't cry, Susan. I'm still here.' When the body dies, the heart stays with what it loves.

Look down the streets in the early morning, Susan, when the world is grey and only the stars are bright. Listen and you'll hear the clip-clop of my hooves, and sometimes the dogs will bark. The dogs hear me, even if their owners can't.

I am the horse that pulled the baker's cart. I am the horse that brought the mail. I carried shearers and drove cattle through the dust.

Where trucks and cars now drive, I bore my loads with love and duty. Trucks are more powerful than I was, but you won't get love from motors. I was humankind's partner for six thousand years.

Look along the roads I travelled, where trucks and cars rush now. My heart is with you, Susan. Wherever you go from here, I'm with you still.

Notes on the stories

The Golden Pony

The first people to tame horses (instead of just spearing them and roasting them then chewing the bones) may have been the ancient Ukranians, about 4,000 BCE.

Horses and humans have been partners, then, for about 6,000 years. It's unlikely that we could have been as successful a species, and wandered so fast or achieved so much so quickly without them.

In this story, Sunlight the Golden Pony is a cross between a Tarpan or 'wild horse', and an Asiatic Wild Horse, sometimes called Przewalski's horse. These wild horse types are probably the ancestors of modern horses in Northern Europe and Asia.

The Golden Pony would have looked different from most modern horses. He was much smaller for a start, about 1.3 metres high, which was why Zushan's feet touched the ground when she rode him. His mane would have stood straight up, his back would have been straight, and his ears dropped, instead of upright. He would also have had stripes when he was young that faded as he grew older. Like many wild animals, he would have grown a white coat in winter.

Strangers on Horseback

This story is set in ancient Greece, about 600 BCE. Early Greek horses were small — in Homer's time battles were fought in two-horse chariots, and the horses were probably too small for men to ride in battle. At the time this story is set, small ponies were still common, and large horses like Simon comparatively rare and valuable.

The strangers

Zanna and her family were either Scythians or Sauromatians from around the Black Sea. According to legend — and the ancient Greek historian Herodotus — the Scythians intermarried with the Amazons, a fierce tribe of warrior women. It is difficult to know how much of that legend is true, but there is archaeological evidence that at the time this story is set, the Scythians had women warriors who rode horses.

The family's trade goods came from China. Although what we now know as 'the Silk Road' was only established in Roman times (long after this story is set), gold, cloth, fruits and herbs were traded from east to west and back again for hundreds, if not thousands, of years before that.

Half a Million Horses

Many years ago an elderly woman told me how she and her younger sister stood without moving or speaking for three days inside the paper walls of their house in China, as the soldiers of the Boxer rebellion marched through their garden. If either child spoke or moved the soldiers would find them and kill them ... and also kill the loyal servants who had hidden them.

I've taken that story and moved it 700 years into the past to about 1215, when Genghis Khan led his army in a vicious, pitiless sweep across most of Asia and parts of Europe, conquering and killing as he went. He even conquered China, the most advanced and wealthy nation in the world at that time. By the end of the thirteenth century the Mongol empire stretched from Hong Kong to southern Russia and the Danube, up to the Arctic circle and as far west as Persia and Turkey.

Every soldier in the Mongol army was a horseman and each had at least two, and often up to five, horses. The army travelled up to 124 kilometres a day and lived on what they could capture, and the meat, milk and blood their horses provided.

Half a million horses

Neither Timur nor the family at the farm would probably have been able to count to 'half a million'. They'd have used a phrase that meant 'an incredibly large number', but I have used the term 'half a million' because it sounds more familiar to us today.

Sir Grey Nose
Glossary
Hauberk: a metal neck and torso that protects a knight from sword blows.

Hearth brother: Younger sons did not inherit family property. A younger son could either take arms with another lord, and hope to win reputation and fortune in battle or in tournaments, or he might become a 'hearth son' of his older brother, renouncing any claim to inheritance. Most hearth sons never married. A few did marry, however, usually to women far below them in rank. Daughters inherited only if there were no sons or other male heirs. This usually needed the king's consent.

The Black Kid
Aboriginal words in 'The Black Kid'
These words are all from the Wiradjuri language, which was one of the largest language groupings over central and southern New South Wales.

By 1900 most Aboriginal kids in the Wiradjuri area had learnt English as their first language, and theirs was probably the last generation to speak the language every day.

Sometimes whole Aboriginal communities were killed or died of new diseases, or were moved many miles away to new reserves with people who spoke other languages and so they had only English in common. Children in government settlements were separated from their parents, and put into dormitories, and only allowed to see their parents at weekends. If the children were heard to speak anything but English they were punished. But even today many Wiradjuri people still use Wiradjuri words in everyday speech.

When white people came here there were about 250 languages spoken in Australia, but for many years most Europeans either paid no attention at all to Aboriginal languages (even white people who worked with Aboriginal people every day expected them to learn English, while the white people didn't learn even basic Aboriginal terms) or assumed there was only one Aboriginal language — the one spoken around Sydney where most of the early translations were made.

This is a bit like thinking that all white people speak 'European', a mix of every language in Europe: Good tag, haben vous uno bon giorno?

Some Wiradjuri words from the text

Dhadi?: Where's it from?
Dhaguu?: Where to?
Gaja!: Get away!
Garria!: Don't!
Minyang?: What?
Muurruubarraay: Thunder
Wallaamaala: A boy's name

The Baker's Horse

There really was a baker's horse when I was young. His paddock was four houses down from ours.

I never knew the baker's horse in the days when he pulled the baker's cart, but every afternoon as I passed his paddock on my way home from school, I fed him my lunch crusts or the soft grass from my side of the fence and he mumbled at my hands and sometimes his owner gave us rides.

I grew up in the 1950s and 1960s when, one by one, the last of the work horses were retired. When I was a baby, horses still pulled the milkman's cart and the dunny cart, the water cart and the fruitman's wagon. There were no supermarkets in those days. The baker came every day and so did the milkman; the dunny man emptied out the smelly cans under the dunny twice a week; the iceman brought ice for the ice chest in the days before refrigerators (he came on Tuesdays, I think), and the butcher and grocer delivered too.

The first story I ever wrote was about a horse called Tresses, who was haunted by a ghost. Tresses was based on the baker's horse. I was six years old when I wrote that story, and forty-two years later I am finally writing about him again, with love and with gratitude.

The Book of
Unicorns

To Noel and Fabia and their horses
(and to Geoff, too) with love

Contents

Warts

It was a bad summer the Christmas the unicorn was born. The grasshoppers leapt across the hills, the trees drooped hot and limp. The creek was dry and Sam's warts had spread all down his thumbs.

Mum turned the steering wheel too sharply onto the gravel drive that led to Gramma's. The car lurched, then bounced on the stones.

'Watch out!' cried Dad. 'At least I know how to drive on gravel roads.'

'I am watching,' muttered Mum. 'What there is to watch for I don't know. Dry stones and dry hills. They look like skulls all gathered together.'

'Only a week,' said Dad. 'Just one week in the whole year, that's all I ask.'

'I agreed to come, didn't I?' asked Mum. 'So stop complaining.'

'You're the one that's complaining,' argued Dad. 'You're the one who ...'

Sam looked out the window and scratched his warts. It all looked the same as last year. Just drier, and the fences drooped a little more, and the creek was bald white rocks instead of water. Last year Gramma had taken him eeling, just like Dad used to do, said Gramma. Gramma's knee had hurt too much for her to leap across the rocks, but she sat on the bank and told him where to throw the line and how to stop the eels snapping at his fingers ...

The car lurched into a pothole. 'You should have let me drive,' said Dad.

'It's impossible to avoid every pothole on this road,' said Mum.

'All right, all right. I'll put the blade on the tractor tomorrow and give it a grade.'

'And half a million other things your mother's got for you to do. Which leaves me in the kitchen and Sam ...'

'You leave Sam out of it. Sam likes it here.'

'You'd rather have gone to the beach, wouldn't you, Sam?'

'I ...' said Sam. The car bounced round the final corner. 'Hey, there's Gramma!'

Gramma was sitting on the verandah. She looked like she'd been sitting there for a while. She looked up in surprise at the car and its attendant dust.

'Gramma!' yelled Sam.

'Why ... Sam,' said Gramma. She looked like she was pleased to have the name right. 'What a lovely surprise.'

'It's not a surprise, Gramma! You knew we were coming!'

'Yes. Of course,' said Gramma. She stepped down the stairs carefully, holding onto the rail. 'It's lovely to see you. Lovely.'

'Mother, I rang last night. Don't you remember?'

'Of course I remember,' said Gramma, holding up her cheek for a kiss. 'You come on in. I'll get some lunch ready.'

'I'll get some lunch ready,' said Gramma for the fourth time, as they wandered round the dusty garden.

Mum sighed and cast Dad a look. 'I'll get it,' she said.

'Oh will you, dear? That'd be nice,' said Gramma absently. She picked a grasshopper off what was left of a rose bush, and wandered over to the apple tree. She fingered the apples.

There were a lot of apples this year, thought Sam, but they'd drop off before they were ripe. They always did.

'Now tell me, Sam,' said Gramma vaguely. 'How is school going?'

Sam sighed. Gramma had asked how school was going twice already. He'd told her 'fine' before. Suddenly he decided to tell the truth.

'Lousy,' said Sam.

Gramma blinked.

'The kids laugh at me because of my warts,' said Sam. Dad shifted uncomfortably.

'They're all over my hands,' said Sam. 'Elspeth Motrell said she wouldn't share a desk with me last term, in case I touched her with my warts.'

'The doctor burnt them off but they just grow again,' said Dad.

Gramma looked confused. 'Who wouldn't sit next to you?' she asked.

'Elspeth,' said Sam.

'You don't know her, Mother,' said Dad.

'No, that's right,' said Gramma. 'Is she a nice girl? She doesn't sound very nice.' Gramma paused. 'I'll just go and make some lunch.'

'It's okay,' said Sam. 'Mum's getting it.'

'That's nice of her,' said Gramma.

Sam grew bored. He wandered into the kitchen after Mum.

'What's for lunch?' he asked.

Mum slammed the fridge door. 'Slimey lettuce, stale Jatz crackers, a chop that should have been thrown out a week ago. And two thousand eggs.'

'Guess the chooks are laying well,' said Sam.

'What's for lunch?' Dad peered through the screen door.

'Scrambled eggs,' said Mum, grabbing a saucepan with so much force the cupboard shook. 'That's what we're having for dinner too. That's all there is in the house. Look, isn't it time you faced it? Your mother can't cope out here by herself. You have to do something.'

Dad nodded slowly.

'Don't just nod,' said Mum. 'I'm sick of it! We come down here for what's supposed to be a holiday and you spend all your time trying to catch up on a year's worth of repairs, and half the time at home you're feeling guilty because she's down here alone. It's time we put a stop to it!'

'We'll talk about it after dinner,' said Dad. 'I think Mother realises now she's not coping. Look, do you mind scrambled eggs tonight, too? I'll pop into town tomorrow and stock up.'

'We'll manage,' said Mum.

Sam sneaked off outside.

That was before the unicorn was born.

No one knew the foal was coming, except maybe its mother, the old white mare down by the fence near the creek. Mum and Dad didn't know, and Sam didn't know. He didn't even know Gramma had a horse. She hadn't had one last Christmas or the one before, much less one that was in foal.

Even Gramma couldn't have known. She was too confused to remember things like horses giving birth. But somehow she did know, because she was hobbling down to the fence to this big, old, hungry looking horse just lying there in the dust, and suddenly she was yelling.

'Sam! Sam!'

Sam ran. 'What is it, Gramma? Is it a snake? Have you hurt yourself?'

'Look,' said Gramma. 'Just look.'

Sam looked.

The foal had skinny legs. All foals had skinny legs, but not like this. These legs were thin like chopsticks. Even without knowing much about horses Sam could see they weren't made right. The head was too small too with this funny bony thing pointing out of its forehead, and the eyes looked blank and blue, not like proper horse eyes at all. Even the body looked lopsided.

'It's a unicorn,' said Gramma proudly, batting a grasshopper out of her eye.

'There's no such thing as unicorns, Gramma,' said Sam. She'd be telling him about the tooth fairy next. Sometimes Sam thought that Gramma still believed that he was three years old.

The foal tried to stand. Its legs were still too weak. It stumbled and gave a bleating cry, then just lay there, panting.

The mare sniffed it. She whinnied, a funny crazy sound. She struggled to her feet, then walked slowly down the fence line.

'Where's she going?' cried Sam. 'Why's she leaving her baby?'

Gramma blinked. 'I don't know,' she said slowly. 'Maybe ... well, I don't know.'

'Is it 'cause it's different?' whispered Sam. He reached out and stroked the creature's head. It felt damp, but very warm.

'Maybe,' said Gramma. She sat beside Sam and pulled the whimpering foal onto her lap. It came easily, like it had no bones. Its head drooped onto Gramma's dress as she stroked its too-long neck.

'What do we do now, Gramma?' asked Sam.

Gramma seemed to look into the distance for a while. She didn't speak. She just stroked and stroked till finally Sam couldn't wait any more.

'Gramma?' he asked again. 'What are we going to do?'

Gramma blinked, like she'd been a long way off. She looked at Sam like she was surprised to see him there. 'Sam ...' said Gramma. She looked down at the ugly foal. 'Well, I reckon we'll take him back to the house,' she said slowly. 'Put him in a box by the stove like the poddy lambs. We used to have lots of poddy lambs ...'

'But what'll he eat?' demanded Sam.

Something seemed to seep back into Gramma, something strong and sure. 'Why, I reckon I'll have to milk the old girl if she won't feed her foal,' said Gramma. 'I used to milk cows often enough.'

'But this is a horse, Gramma!'

'I reckon I can milk a horse,' said Gramma, even more firmly now.

'And feed the baby with a bottle?'

'And feed him with a bottle,' agreed Gramma. 'Here, help me to my feet. It's my knees. They don't work like they used to. Nothing works much like it did before.'

Gramma settled the limp foal into a big cardboard fruit box by the stove. It could hold its head up now, but still didn't look like it could ever stand. Its blue blank eyes stared unblinking at the world.

'It's a freak. It's deformed,' said Mum flatly. 'It should be put down.' She turned to Dad. 'Don't you think so ...'

'I agree,' said Dad. 'Look Mother, I'll take it out the back and ...'

'It stays here,' said Gramma firmly.

'But ...'

'I said no,' said Gramma. Dad looked rattled and Mum just stared. 'And while we're at it,' said Gramma, 'there'll be no more talk about me going to a nursing home. Not while I've still got my strength. Now, what's for dinner?'

'Scrambled eggs,' said Mum. 'Just like for lunch. That's all there was in the fridge. Just eggs and stuff that should have been thrown out. We'll go into town tomorrow and buy some ...'

Gramma snorted. 'Scrambled eggs is no fit food for a growing boy. Is that what you feed Sam at home? Sam, you get my axe. It's down the back of the shed. We're having roast chook for tea.'

Gramma stuffed the chook with stale bread, and a chopped onion from the back of the cupboard and herbs from the dusty garden out the back. Then she hobbled down to the fence by the creek with a bucket. Sam carried her stool.

Gramma lowered herself down onto the stool slowly. She stretched out her legs. 'Used to be my knees only ached when it rained,' she said. 'Then they ached in winter too. Now they ache all the time. And most of the rest of me.'

'What's wrong with them, Gramma?' asked Sam.

'Arthritis, the doctor says,' said Gramma. 'But I reckon it's just I'm getting old.' She reached for the mare's udder. The mare just stood there, gazing out at the bare paddock, indifferent.

The first squirt of milk battered at the edges of the bucket and ran down the side. It pooled in a small blue puddle at the bottom. 'Firm but gentle, see?' said Gramma, as she alternated strokes from teat to teat.

Sam nodded. 'Can I have a go?'

'Maybe tomorrow,' said Gramma. 'Or the next day, when she's used to being milked. You remind me to get some hay in town tomorrow, and a bag of stud mix too. We need to feed her up.'

Sam watched, fascinated. 'Does it feel different from a cow?' he asked.

'Cow or horse, it's all the same,' said Gramma, watching the thin blue milk squirt into the bucket. 'I suppose you could milk an elephant too if you had to. I knew a bloke once who milked an echidna.'

'Yuk. What did he do with the milk?'

'Sent it to the uni. Someone was going to analyse it, see what the echidna had been eating. But he drank a bit first, just to see what it tasted like.'

'What did it taste like?'

'Ants,' said Gramma. 'There we are. I reckon that's enough for now. Can you carry the bucket as well as the stool, Sam? My hands are shaky. I'd hate to spill it now.'

It took the foal a few minutes to work out how to suck from a bottle. It drank slowly, as though it hurt to swallow. It shivered, even though the kitchen was warm.

'Hot-water bottle,' said Gramma. 'It's in the drawer under the sink. Yes, that's the one. Thanks, Sam. Now if you'd just fill the kettle we'll boil it up ...'

Gramma wrapped the hot-water bottle in an old towel and tucked it next to the unicorn, and covered them both with a blanket. The foal rested its head against the side of the box and closed its pale blue blank eyes.

'Gramma?'

'Yes, Sam.'

'Is it going to live?'

'It'll live,' said Gramma.

Dad insisted on driving into town next day, even though Gramma said she was quite capable.

'I've been driving into town for fifty years. It's still the same way in it's always been. It hasn't changed,' Gramma complained from the front seat beside Dad.

Dad veered around another pothole. 'The way into town hasn't changed, but I think you have, Mother,' he said warily. 'The back tyre was flat this morning. And the battery was flat too. I bet you haven't driven the car for months.'

'It's been a while since I drove,' admitted Gramma. 'I haven't been feeling the best. But I'm better now.'

'How have you been getting groceries?' asked Sam.

'The postman brings them down,' said Gramma. 'You know, Len McIntyre, your father was at school with his brother. He brings my groceries out. When I remember to let him know what to bring.'

'Look Mother ...' said Dad.

'No,' said Gramma. 'I'm not going into a nursing home. I'm not coming down to the city to live with you either. But thank you anyway. Now stop here ... no, to the right. You pop in to the baker's and get the bread while I pick up some stud mix for the mare.'

The foal was sleeping when they got home, but it lifted its head when they came in.

'See, it's getting stronger,' said Gramma.

'I still think ...' said Dad, and then he stopped. He sighed and began to put away the groceries instead.

'Where's Mum?' asked Sam.

'Off in a snit somewhere,' said Dad. 'All I ask is a few days down here once a year, but ...'

'Hey, Gramma! The grasshoppers have gone!'

Dad peered out the window. 'My word, they have too. I reckon they've decided they've eaten everything they could round here and just moved on.'

''Bout time too,' said Gramma.

Sam and Gramma took a bucket of stud mix down to the mare after lunch. Sam carried the bucket.

Gramma seemed to walk straighter today. 'Arthritis always gets better in dry weather,' she said. 'I reckon this is about as dry as it comes.'

The mare thrust her nose into the stud mix and ate gratefully.

'I'm sorry old thing,' said Gramma. 'I should have been feeding you long before this. You get stuck into it.'

'Where did she come from, Gramma?' asked Sam.

'Sale up at town,' said Gramma. 'No one wanted her. She was going to be bought for dog meat when I bought her. Didn't cost me much. Didn't know she was in foal till later.'

'Poor old thing,' said Sam, stroking her nose. 'I wish she'd liked her baby though.'

Darkness seemed to sit on the house, squeezing out all sound. It was too quiet, thought Sam, lying in the narrow bed that used to be Dad's, watching the trees droop against the stars. You kept thinking that a car would go by or a dog would bark or someone yell. But no one did.

Something squeaked, so suddenly the silence almost cracked. Sam sat up. What was it?

The sound came again.

Sam pulled the sheet up around his chest. Should he get up and investigate? But it was probably just a mouse, or Gramma going down to the bathroom or ...

... or a rat — a great big rat. Rats attacked baby animals didn't they? Maybe it would hurt the foal.

Maybe it was the foal crying in its sleep ...

The noise stopped. Sam waited for it to start again. But it didn't. A possum screamed out in the trees, then there was silence.

Sam dozed. Suddenly his eyes opened again. A different noise ...

Sam slid out of bed and felt for his slippers. The moonlight washed gently through the room. He was glad there was no need to turn on the light. The light might wake up Mum and Dad.

The passageway was quiet too. His slippers flopped gently on the old linoleum.

Mum sat by the foal's box. Its head rested tiredly in her lap. She looked up as he came in. For a horrible moment Sam thought the foal was dead, then he realised its eyes were open, pale as old glass in the moonlight. Mum stroked its head.

'It was whimpering,' she explained.

'I know. I heard it.' Sam squatted down beside them. 'I thought you didn't like the foal,' said Sam.

'I didn't like it,' said Mum. 'But it looks different tonight. Sort of sweet.'

It looked the same to Sam. Floppy and weak and that strange almost glowing white. Its head lolled back onto the edge of the box. Mum shifted a bit of blanket under it like a pillow.

'Have you been here long?' asked Sam.

'A while,' said Mum. 'It's been peaceful, just sitting here. You forget what silence is like at home.'

The possum shrieked again, nearer this time.

Something ran across the roof. Mum smiled. 'Not that it's really silent,' she said. 'There're all sorts of noises if you listen to them. I heard an owl a little while ago. Maybe it's hunting the possum. And there was a funny bird call, like something running down the scales but not quite getting there. I don't know what it was.'

'Dad'd know,' said Sam.

'I'll ask him later,' said Mum.

They sat quietly for a while. The foal managed to lift its head. It whinnied again, softly, but this time it didn't sound in pain.

'Is there any more milk?' whispered Mum. 'I'll heat up a bottle for it.'

'Gramma left some in the fridge,' said Sam.

Mum put the kettle on, then tiptoed to the fridge. 'You pop back to bed,' she said to Sam. 'You're getting cold.'

'You don't need a hand?' asked Sam.

'No,' said Mum. 'I'm fine.'

Gramma made baked-bean jaffles for breakfast. The foal lifted its head and watched for a moment before sinking back into its box. Mum ate her jaffle slowly. Sam knew she didn't like baked beans.

'Elva?' she said to Gramma.

'Yes?'

'Is there someone around who does odd jobs? Someone who could grade the road for you, fix the fences, stuff like that?'

Gramma paused with the dish mop in her hand. 'Willie McRae,' she said. 'He's always after a job of work.'

'Do you think he'd come down today? Gary and I would pay him of course,' said Mum quickly. 'I know it's hard to afford help on your pension. But if he could grade the road ...'

'I was going to grade the road,' said Dad. 'I'll stick the blade on the tractor this morning. I'd have done it yesterday but we had to go into town ...'

'I know. But I was thinking ...'

'What?'

'Maybe we could go for a walk instead. Up to the old hut by the waterfall.'

'The waterfall'll be dry,' warned Gramma.

'I know. But it'd be interesting anyway. I've never been there. You've told me about that hut so many times, how you used to go up there and camp when you were a kid. I'd like to see it.'

Dad hesitated.

'I'll ring Willie after breakfast,' said Gramma. 'You pack up some lunch. It's a long walk up to the hut.'

Dad grinned. 'The old hut,' he said. 'I haven't thought about it for years. You coming, Sam?'

'Sam and I are going to strain the fence down by the creek,' said Gramma. 'And we have to feed the mare and give the foal its bottles. Off you go. We'll expect you when we see you.'

It had been a good holiday, thought Sam, as the car drove down the newly graded track. He turned back for a final look. Gramma was still waving, the ugly foal in her lap. It could hold its head up now, though it still couldn't stand.

'And so it's all sorted out with Willie,' Mum was saying in the front. 'He'll finish re-straining the fences this week, then after that he'll come every Thursday.'

Dad nodded.

'And you'll send him a cheque once a month. I mean, it's not like we can't afford it,' said Mum.

Dad nodded again. 'And he's getting Matt Godwin at the hardware store to get someone to paint the house.

It'll be good to see the old place looking good again.' He glanced back at the house. 'It's a long time to Christmas,' he said to himself.

'There's always Easter,' said Mum offhandedly 'Why don't we come down then? It's a long drive, but we've both got some leave up our sleeves ...'

'But we always go to the beach at Easter,' said Dad. 'You said it's not fair to Sam to come back here so soon.'

He looked back at Sam. 'Do you mind coming down here again, instead of the beach?' he asked.

'I don't mind,' said Sam. 'Besides, I want to see the foal.'

'How's the foal?' asked Sam. It was the same question he always asked, every Sunday night when Dad rang Gramma.

'It's fine,' said Gramma. 'It almost stood up by itself yesterday. I'm getting Willie to rig something up for it. You'll see when you come down. How's school?'

'Okay,' said Sam. 'I'm in the basketball team. Hey! Guess what, Gramma?'

'What?'

'My warts are gone. Just like that. I woke up yesterday and they were gone.'

'Gone where?'

'I dunno. They must've dropped off. I looked in the bed but I couldn't see them.'

'They must've flown away,' said Gramma. 'Warts do that sometimes.'

'How's the old mare?' asked Sam.

'She's getting fat,' said Gramma. 'All this grass. It's green as a new carpet after all this rain. You wouldn't think she was the same horse. Look, I have to go. I've got a cake in the oven. I promised to take it to the tennis club tomorrow. You take care won't you? Love you, Sam.'

'Love you, Gramma,' said Sam. 'Give my love to the foal.'

'I will,' said Gramma.

Gramma's house looked different as they drove down the drive that Easter. Someone had painted it pale blue and there was grass now instead of dust. The hills looked like green balls waiting for someone to play.

Gramma was in the vegie garden. She waved as they came over. 'Just picking corn for lunch,' she said. 'It's a good garden this year, isn't it? I had Willie put it in just after you left.'

'I've never seen corn that big!' said Sam. 'Those cobs are as long as a cricket bat, almost.'

'Unicorn dung,' grinned Gramma. 'I bring a bagful down every morning.'

'Gramma, there's no such things as unicorns.'

'Sure there is. There's such a thing as unicorn's dung fertiliser there is. Come on up to the house and I'll show you the foal. You won't believe how he's grown.'

The ugly foal had grown, thought Sam, but not much. It looked like it'd never be a full-sized horse. It was like it didn't have the energy to grow. As though it was saving all its energy — for what? Sam thought. The foal gazed slightly to one side of them with its milky eyes.

'Looking good, isn't he?' demanded Gramma.

'Yes,' said Sam doubtfully. 'Is that what you had rigged up, Gramma?' He pointed to the cage structure around the foal.

'That's it,' said Gramma proudly. 'You see the sling goes round its body and holds it up so its feet can touch the ground without any weight on them. Then the cage supports the sling. When the foal tries to walk the wheels go round and the foal can move along ... well, it moves a bit anyway. That way it can graze for a couple of hours all by itself. I keep moving the sling so it doesn't get too sore. How's school?'

'It's great,' said Sam. And it was, sort of.

Gramma grinned. 'Let's see your hands.'

Sam held them out. 'No warts,' he said. 'Not a single one.'

'I bet they don't come back either,' said Gramma. 'You're immune to warts now. There's something else I want to show you too.'

'What, Gramma?'

'You wait and see,' said Gramma. She led the way to the shed. It looked better now, thought Sam, with the broken palings replaced and new posts put in on one side. Gramma pulled one of the doors aside. 'Look,' she said.

Sam looked. 'Gramma! It's a farm bike!'

'Good as new,' said Gramma. 'Except it isn't. I got it from Bob Braddon up in town, who got it from … well, never mind that. Point is it still goes. Willie uses it when he's out fencing, but I thought you'd like to have a go while you're here.'

'Gramma!'

'Now you ask your parents first. And make sure you wear a helmet and long sleeves and jeans and boots … and no haring off at a hundred miles an hour either. You be careful.'

'I'll be careful,' promised Sam, staring at the machine. 'Wow!'

Gramma laughed.

Paddocks were made for farm bikes, thought Sam, feeling the tussocks bump beneath him. You felt like you could ride forever — over the ford in the creek, the water spraying in your face, down the track to the fence and up the fence line. You could see the highway from here through the thin barrier of trees along the fence, cars and trucks and the odd motorbike looking hard to one side then beetling off to who knows where.

Sam paused, as a semi slowed, then drew off the road a little way ahead. Sam accelerated to catch up with it.

'Is anything wrong?' he called out through the open window. 'I could ride back to the house if you like and ring the garage.'

The truckie leant out of the window and grinned. 'No worries, kid. I'm just stopping for a snack. Most of us stop along here now.' He gestured out the window.

Sam looked around. The truckie must be right. There was a clear track now beside the gum trees, long enough for a semi to park and be quite off the road.

'Why here?' asked Sam. 'I mean, no one used to stop here.'

The truckie shrugged and looked embarrassed. 'Dunno,' he said. 'Started last Christmas I reckon. This bloke broke down here, or so he thought. But when he tried to start her up again she ran like a dream. Since then people just stop here.'

'Why not down the road though?' said Sam. 'There's a proper rest stop there with a toilet and everything.'

The truckie looked even more embarrassed. 'This spot's different,' he said. 'Most of the blokes'll tell you that. You stop for ten minutes here and shut your eyes and it'll seem like you've slept the whole night through. You don't get accidents if you stop for a bit of a break here. Least that's what they say.' He passed a thermos out to Sam. 'You like a drink, kid?'

'No thanks.' Sam shook his head. 'I need to get back for lunch.'

'You live round here?' asked the truckie.

'No. Just staying with my gramma.'

'You're lucky,' said the truckie. He paused. 'I've got a kid your age. It makes my heart break sometimes thinking of him cramped in the city in the holidays.' The truckie grinned. 'Not that he seems to mind. The only thing that bothers him are these great plantar warts on his foot. Says it stops him playing soccer.'

The bike began to mutter. Sam gave it more accelerator. 'You should bring him out with you some time,' said Sam. He hesitated. 'I'd better get back,' he said. 'Gramma'll be expecting me. We have to feed the ...' He stopped.

'See you,' said the truckie. 'It's got a good feel to it, this place. Feels like ... well, I dunno what it feels like. But it does you good. You must love it down here.'

'It's a good place,' said Sam.

'I reckon,' said the truckie.

Gramma was picking apples when Sam rode up. He parked the bike in the shed and fetched another box to help her.

'Thanks, Sam,' said Gramma, piling another armful of apples into the new box. 'That's six boxes full so far. I'll be making apple jelly till the cows come home with this lot. You'd better take some back with you.'

Sam nodded, though he didn't like apple jelly much. 'I thought the apples all fell off this tree before they ripened.'

'Always have before,' said Gramma. 'I've been feeding it this year though. Couple of buckets of unicorn manure every week. I reckon that's all it needed, just a bit of feeding.' She looked at her watch. 'Time for lunch,' she said. 'I have to go into town later. It's my line dancing afternoon.'

'Your what?' asked Sam.

'Texas line dancing. It's the latest thing. We all get into these two lines and do the same steps. It's twice a week now at the Returned Services Club. Don't you have Texas line dancing up in the city?'

'I don't know,' said Sam. 'It sounds sort of ... energetic. Can you manage it okay, Gramma?'

'Of course I can,' said Gramma. 'I was a bit stiff at first, that's all. But it's done me the world of good. I just needed some more exercise, that's all. How about you come with me? Lots of kids round here do line dancing.'

'No thanks, Gramma,' said Sam politely. 'I'll just stay here. Maybe I'll take the foal for a walk.'

Gramma looked at him sharply. 'It doesn't walk much,' she reminded him.

'Well, a sort of a push then. Maybe down to the creek — the grass looks all soft there. Maybe it'll like it.'

'It probably will,' said Gramma. 'Probably tastes different from the grass up here. Things like that must mean something to a horse.'

'Is the old mare still down there, Gramma?' Sam wondered what the horse thought of her foal now.

Gramma shook her head. 'I gave her away,' she said. 'You don't mind do you? Funny thing, these people were just driving past and this girl saw her and fell in love with her.'

Sam snorted. 'Girls always fall in love with horses,' he said. 'She probably thinks she's going to win a ribbon at the Easter show with the poor old thing.'

'Not this kid,' said Gramma. 'She didn't even want to ride her. I told her the mare was too old to do much with, but it didn't matter to her. She had some sort of palsy I reckon. Her hands were shaking like mad. I think she just wanted a pet — her parents asked if they could buy her. I said she hadn't cost me much, they could have her if they promised to take good care of her. I think they will. They looked that type.'

'I hope they had a decent paddock to put her in,' said Sam.

'They said there was a paddock just down the road from their place,' said Gramma. 'Hired a horse float for her and everything. You know, it's funny, but I could have sworn she was in foal again. Impossible. I mean at her age, and there hasn't been another horse around for donkey's years. I warned them she might be, but they didn't seem to mind. I hope there wasn't anything too bad wrong with the kid. Maybe she's better now.'

'Maybe she is,' said Sam.

It was peaceful in the house with everyone gone, Gramma off to her whatsit dancing up in town, and Dad had hauled Mum off to meet some old friends of his. They had a property the other side of town, but no kids his age, so it sounded pretty boring to Sam.

The foal was lying under the old apple tree. It didn't even try to struggle as Sam approached, just looked at him sort of sideways with its milky eyes. Sam wondered how much it could see. Maybe it just saw differently, that was all.

He stroked its head. The hair felt smooth, not like a horse's at all, sort of moist and flat. Like a seal's fur, thought Sam, who'd never felt a seal.

'Come on, boy,' he said. 'Let's go for a walk.'

The foal leant against his arm as he fixed its harness, limp and impassive. Like it was waiting, thought Sam, but waiting for what? Its feet pulled tentatively at the harness, far too slow and delicate to move it much, so Sam had to push it all the way.

The creek was thick with autumn shadows and the faint smell of cooling rocks and water. Sam unstrapped the foal, and made sure it was settled comfortably on the grass. The foal sniffed and whinnied once, a short sharp cry like a small baby's, then tore a mouthful of grass. It chewed it slowly then seemed to go to sleep.

Sam lay down as well. The grass was soft and thin on the sandy ground. He could see the casuarina needles toss against the sky, still faintly red tinged from autumn pollen. He thought he heard the foal whimper again. He listened for a moment more, but it was silent.

Sam closed his eyes.

It was a funny dream. He was by the creek, but the casuarinas were dark green now. The creek looked sort of different too, as though the rocks had shifted in a flood ... or two ... or three ... but things always looked different in a dream.

He wasn't alone. There were other people too. Two men, a woman. They were important people. Somehow in the background of his dream he knew they were important. They had problems to discuss. Important problems. They couldn't agree. So he'd said, 'Let's take the whole day off. I'll take you down and show you Gramma's unicorn.'

They'd laughed. 'There's no such thing as unicorns,' one of the men had said. But still they'd come down to Gramma's, down to the creek, down to see the unicorn ...

The men had taken their jackets off. The woman's shoes lay by the bank. Now they sat on the soft grass ... but it was thicker now, thought Sam, and there were tiny orchid heads among the green and the problems seemed to dissolve into the flash of water ...

The unicorn whinnied softly and Sam woke up.

Sam walked slowly back up the track to the house, pulling the unicorn behind him.

A Present for Aunt Addie

'You're old enough,' said Dad thoughtfully.

Harry looked up from the TV. 'Old enough for what?' he demanded warily.

Dad was silent for a moment. Harry expected him to say to clean out the chook shed. To bring the steers down from the back paddock by yourself. To make sure your room is tidy without telling you all the time. But he didn't. He looked out the window instead.

'To visit Aunt Addie,' said Dad at last. 'There's something that she needs.'

Harry looked out the window too. There was nothing to see. Or nothing special anyway. Just the hills beyond the lucerne paddock, hazy in the blue green heat.

'Who's Aunt Addie?' he asked. 'Hey, she must be your sister if she's my aunt. I didn't know you had a sister.'

'I don't,' said Dad.

'Mum's sister then,' said Harry. 'But I thought her only sisters were Aunt Sue and Auntie Sheila.'

'Not your mother's sister,' said Dad.

'Well, what then?' asked Harry, exasperated. This wasn't like Dad at all. 'You mean she's not really an aunt. Just a friend I'm supposed to call Auntie but she isn't really related to us.'

'She's related to us,' said Dad. 'Oh my word, she's related to us.'

'Well, what then?' demanded Harry.

Dad reached over and turned off the TV. The chooks out the back clucked in the sudden silence.

'She's my great-great-aunt,' said Dad slowly. 'Your great-great-great-aunt that'd make her. I think that's right. I get confused with all these greats.'

'But that'd make her ...' Harry stared. 'She can't be that old.'

'Well, she is,' said Dad softly. 'Aunt Addie's very old.'

'Where is she then? In town? In the nursing home? Or the hospital? Heck, she should be in the papers if she's as old as that.'

'No. She's not in the nursing home. Or in the hospital for that matter either. She lives here. On the farm.'

'But I've never seen her.'

'No,' said Dad. 'You haven't seen her yet. She lives up in a hut up past the hills.'

'By herself! Dad she can't! Not an old woman like that! She shouldn't be living by herself.'

'She wants to live by herself,' said Dad.

'But …' Harry stood up. 'It isn't right. We should visit her at least. See if she's all right. Take her food and stuff.'

'She doesn't need food,' said Dad. 'Aunt Addie grows all she needs. Or gets it somehow, anyway. All she needs is … well, you'll find out.'

'But … but someone should at least keep her company! What if she breaks her leg? Old people's bones are fragile. We learnt that at school …'

Dad held up a hand. 'All right. All right. I said it's time you visited her.'

Harry nodded. 'Well, sure.' He blinked. 'How long is it since you've seen her?'

'Fifteen years,' said Dad. 'It's been fifteen years since I last saw Aunt Addie.'

'What? You haven't seen her since before I was born? Why not?'

'That's the way it turned out,' said Dad.

The hills glared gold in the morning light, as though the sun shone from them as well. Not much feed, thought Harry automatically. It had all dried up since last month's rain. The sheep lay like sleeping boulders under the scattered stringybarks.

Harry pulled his hat down lower. He wondered if he should have brought some water. It was too dangerous to drink from any of the streams nowadays, what with hydatids and giardia and sheep droppings, but Dad said there was no need to take anything.

It seemed wrong not to take anything though. You always took something when you went to visit people — a cake or jam or a leg of lamb. He'd thought of taking flowers, but they'd have wilted by the time he got there, and if anyone saw him he'd look a burk carrying flowers across a paddock.

Surely there was something Aunt Addie needed. Maybe she was really independent, like Saul's grandma. Saul's grandma just lived on sardines and bread and powdered milk and what she grew in the garden. She didn't even need lights because she went to bed when it got dark. Saul's mum wanted her to go down to the nursing home in town, but Saul's gran wouldn't budge. But even she needed to buy the sardines and milk and flour ...

Maybe it was just company Aunt Addie needed. Or some repairs maybe? Or digging in the garden? But how would Dad know if he hadn't seen her for fifteen years?

Harry shooed the flies from the back of his neck. They were probably thirsty too, but let them find their own water and leave his sweat alone.

Why hadn't Dad let him take his motorbike? It was a Honda 110, he'd only got it last Christmas, only two thousand and twenty k's when he got it from Phil up in town, though he'd put a lot more on it since then. Phil was moving down the coast and couldn't use a motorbike down there. But Dad had said he'd never find

Aunt Addie on a motorbike, which was crazy, 'cause a bike could carry you anywhere, just about.

Walking was crazy in this heat. Dad was crazy. The whole thing was crazy too.

How could he have an aunt living at the back of the property that no one ever saw? He'd explored the whole place hundreds of times, and he'd never even seen a hint of someone living there.

It was impossible. A woman that old. It had to be a joke. But Dad wasn't one for joking much.

Aunt Addie needed something, Dad had said. But what?

Harry looked around him. Which way had Dad said? Back of the hill paddock, up the gully between the second and third hills. Then just keep going till you find it. It'd be even hotter up there, no breeze at all. Who'd want to live up there?

Had he ever come this way before? He couldn't remember. Surely he must have. He'd come up into the hills lots of times. He must have come this way before ...

The sheep looked at him curiously, then looked away, bored by the heat. Humans were only interesting if they carried hay or were followed by dogs.

Gold grass gave way to rocks, leaning out of the hill like they'd fallen backwards and hadn't managed to rise again. The gully rose in wide sharp lips of stone, ascending in what would be cascades of water when it rained. The rock was dry now, grey instead of brown. A frog creaked hopefully behind a boulder, then was still.

There must be damp spots somewhere, thought Harry, looking at the green fringes round the rocks. The musky scent of black snake floated up from the hot rocks. If that frog didn't watch out it'd be a snake's dinner, thought Harry.

Up, up, up the rocks. Surely no one could live up here. Dad must be mad.

Maybe that was it. Maybe Dad was going bonkers. You heard of people going bonkers with stress and worry when it wouldn't rain and the cattle prices were down. Except that cattle prices weren't bad at the moment, thought Harry, and there was still enough feed. Dad was a good farmer. Even in the bad drought the paddocks weren't overstocked. There'd still been hay in the shed at the end of the drought, thought Harry proudly. And their pasture was coming back, now that it had finally rained, almost as good as it had been four years before.

More rocks. The gully closed around him. Crikey, you couldn't even build a hut up here it was so steep, much less live here. What would you do for water? You'd break your ankle every time you went outside.

Suddenly the gully forked. Harry hesitated, wondering which way to go. It was all right for Dad to say, 'Just keep going till you get there.' What if he'd forgotten the way? It had been fifteen years since he'd been to Aunt Addie's, after all.

Straight up or to the left ... well, not straight up. No one lived on the top of the hill, you'd see the house miles away. It must be to the left.

Harry turned and began to clamber up again.

It was more level going now, as though this gully ran between the first hill and a higher one above. It was almost flat, but even hotter. Incredibly hot ...

The air swam round him. The rock seemed to swim as well. Heat, heat, heat ... The hills rose steeply on either side, almost too steep for grass now. It was thinner, longer, almost like hair, ungrazed by sheep or wallaby.

Round a corner, round another — the gully seemed to flatten even further. For the first time water seeped between the rocks, pooling at the lips. The smell of moisture almost overcame the scent of rock.

Another corner and another. Sweat stung his eyes and the world blurred even more. Surely it wouldn't hurt to have a drink up here, so far from the sheep and roos. He'd bet even the wombats didn't come up here. No animals at all ... He'd only drink a little where it seeped out cool from the crevices, not from the pools. Surely the water wouldn't be too bad straight from underground.

Harry knelt and touched his fingers to the water. It was colder than he'd expected, like frozen aluminium on your skin. Now if he could catch some water as it seeped down from the rock ...

Something flickered in the pool. It was white and large. A cloud, thought Harry dreamily. A cloud reflected in the pool. Then the white thing moved and he saw it wasn't a cloud at all.

It was an animal. A large animal.

Harry stood up slowly.

The animal looked at him. It was a little shorter than he was, so the green eyes looked almost into his. It was white, pure white, not like a cloud at all. Clouds always had shades of grey and blue. Its tail hung almost to the ground. Its teeth were yellow, stained with grass. Its horn was whiter than its body, twisted round into a straight sharp point.

The unicorn whinnied and bent its head to drink.

Harry wiped his wet hands across his face. He had sunstroke, that's what it was. He was hallucinating, dreaming in the heat.

Maybe he wasn't dreaming. Dreams weren't as real as this. Maybe someone was making a movie. That was it. A movie with a unicorn. You could do all sorts of things with make-up and special effects and computers nowadays. They were making a unicorn movie in the gully and that's why Dad had sent him here ...

It still didn't make sense.

The unicorn lifted its wet muzzle from the water and looked at Harry. Its gaze was straight and clear. It tossed its mane, as though to say, 'come on', and trotted up the gully. Its hooves clicked sharply on the rock. Harry followed.

Around another bend, and then another. The air was fresher somehow. The gully smelt ... strange. Not just the scents of horse and water, but something more, like that stuff Mum squirted in the bathroom sometimes, but different from that, too.

Suddenly the unicorn stopped. Harry stopped as well. The world was shimmering as though it wasn't real. But it was real. It was.

The gully had opened slightly, so creek flats spread on each side. They were green, impossibly green, the grass like a green blanket spread between the hills. Cliffs rose steeply on three sides, too steep for grass, tufted with ferns about the crevices. A miniature waterfall tumbled from a dark hole halfway up the cliff, dropping to a small dark pool below. The spray drifted through the clearing like tiny specks of sun so the clearing seemed to shiver as they danced.

A hut sat at the far end of the clearing. It was old, like sketches he'd seen in a book at school. The roof was made from wood as well, square slabs like bits of greyish toast, overlapped together. The hut itself was small and square and made from long fat slabs of wood, like they'd been cut from the tree and nailed together willy-nilly. Some sort of vine clambered over every wall, dotted with flowers, like roses, but too fat to be roses, thought Harry. Surely roses didn't droop and glow like that.

There was no verandah, no windows, no TV aerial or power lines. Just wooden shutters over what must be gaps in the wall, a chimney that smoked small puffs of white, and — the garden.

Why hadn't he seen the smoke from down below? thought Harry. It didn't make sense. But nothing here made sense.

Especially not the garden.

Half the clearing was a garden, but a funny garden, not like any that he'd ever seen. It shivered in the sunlight, as though the colours melted with the waterspray.

There were no garden beds, no patches of dark soil, no lawn unless you counted the brilliant green around. Just flowers ... and flowers ... and more flowers — bursting from the ground in spires of red and blue and yellow, carpets of blues and golds and pinks stretching at their feet. Their colours seemed to float up to the waterspray and merge into the sunlight, so it was hard to see what was garden or sun. A path ran crazily round and through and in between.

A woman stood in the middle of the garden, a basket of peaches tucked under one arm. Her dress was long, almost to her ankles, a sort of straw colour flecked with pink and white. Her hair was brown and curled round her shoulders. Her skin was very clear and white. Her eyes were the same colour as the unicorn's.

She took a step towards him. 'Ron,' she said. She smiled, took a peach out of her basket and before Harry could react she'd thrown it to him. He caught it automatically.

'It's the first of the season,' said the woman. The unicorn whinnied softly. The woman smiled again. 'One for you as well,' she said. She tossed another peach to the unicorn. It caught it with its yellow teeth and crunched it carefully, spitting the stone out at its feet. The woman looked at Harry again. 'Ron?' she said uncertainly.

Harry shook his head. 'My name's Harry,' he said. 'My father's name is Ron.'

'Then you're Ron's son!' The woman clapped her hands delightedly. 'I'm so very pleased! It's years since Ron was here! So many years ... I lose track of time, I think. And here you are, Ron's son!'

'Aunt Addie?' said Harry uncertainly.

'Yes. I am your Aunt Addie.' The woman's smile was clear as the blue flowers.

'But you can't be Aunt Addie! Aunt Addie's old! Dad said ...'

Aunt Addie seemed amused. 'I am Aunt Addie. Come!'

Harry stepped into the shimmering garden.

It was the softness that struck him first. The ground felt soft. The air felt soft, as though it stroked his cheek. Even the sounds seemed softer, muted by the hum of bees, the ripple of the water, as though the flowers whispered in the breeze.

The unicorn stepped after him. Harry glanced up at Aunt Addie, expecting her to shoo it from the garden, before it ate the flowers or trod on something. But the woman simply held out her hand. The unicorn stepped neatly between the flowers and nuzzled at her fingers, then trotted to a bank of green. It began to graze.

Aunt Addie gestured to a seat. It was made of twisted wood, old but not rotted-looking either. 'Sit you down, sit down,' she insisted. 'I'll bring you a drink. It's of my own making, and very good this year. You'll see.' Her skirts whispered against the flowers as she went into the hut.

Harry craned his head to look inside. A glimpse of a table spread with cloth much the same colour as Aunt Addie's dress, a bed of pink and white as well, a wooden floor with coloured mats. The door swung shut, then opened as Aunt Addie came out.

She carried an enamelled jug and a thick brown stumpy glass. She handed the glass to Harry, then poured the liquid from the jug. She looked at him expectantly. 'Try it,' she said.

He supposed it was all right to drink. Surely Dad would have told him if Aunt Addie was dangerous. It smelt all right.

Harry sipped.

The liquid tasted like flowers, warm and just a little oversweet. A bird sang deep among the trees. A strange bird. He'd never heard a song like that before. Harry blinked. The trees. Why hadn't he noticed them before? Spreading trees in different shades of green, with broad soft leaves that seemed to welcome sunlight, suck it down.

Harry sipped the drink again. 'It's good,' he said. 'What is it?'

Aunt Addie looked pleased. 'Violet cordial,' she said. 'I just yesterday uncorked it. Will you have some more?'

Harry shook his head. He felt like he'd swallowed sunlight — and like it might be alcoholic too. 'Maybe just some water,' he said.

Aunt Addie nodded at the pool under the waterfall. 'It's coolest there,' she said.

Harry went slowly over to the waterfall and dipped his cup. The water was colder than the cordial. Harry dipped his cup again, then stared back. 'Hey ...'

'What is it?' For a moment Aunt Addie looked alarmed.

'Something's down there. An eel maybe. Or a snake.'

Aunt Addie laughed. It was a bit like a horse laughing, thought Harry. Maybe if you lived with a unicorn you started to sound a bit like one, too.

'That be the water sprite.'

'The what? But they're just in books!'

'You read books? It's good to read books,' said Aunt Addie. 'Once I read books all the time. I have no books here though.'

'Maybe I could bring you some,' offered Harry.

Aunt Addie seemed to consider. Then she shook her head. 'They may not be the same,' she said finally. 'It's better not.'

'But why not?' began Harry. He stopped. There was something about Aunt Addie that stopped you asking questions. As though what Aunt Addie decided simply was.

'Dad said you needed something,' said Harry finally. 'But he didn't tell me what. Do you need a hand with something? I'm strong for my age,' he offered. 'Do you need firewood? Or something nailed up? I made a new chook house these holidays.'

'Chook house?' asked Aunt Addie doubtfully.

'Yeah, you know. Chooks. Hens,' said Harry.

'Ah, hens,' said Aunt Addie. She seemed to choke down a smile. 'I have no hens here.'

'No chooks? What do you do for eggs then?'

'My friends bring me what I need,' said Aunt Addie. 'And I grow what they need in return.'

'Friends?' Harry blinked doubtfully. What friends would she have up here? 'What things do you grow?' he asked politely.

Aunt Addie's smile was as bright as the tall golden flowers. 'Divers things,' she offered. She gestured at a spire edged with cup-shaped red flowers. 'Hollyhocks for them to drink from. And foxgloves for them to sleep in. And fairies' fishing rods to fish with, and clover for their ale.'

'Hold on a sec,' said Harry. 'What are you talking about? Foxgloves to sleep in? What are foxgloves?'

Aunt Addie gestured at some tall pale pinkish purple flowers. 'These are foxgloves,' she said.

'To sleep on? You mean they dry them and make mattresses from them ...'

'They sleep in the flowers!' laughed Aunt Addie.

'They what? But no one can sleep in flowers.'

'Fairies do,' said Aunt Addie.

Fairies! For a moment Harry thought she meant something else ... but she didn't, he realised. She meant real fairies. 'Fairies with wings and wands?' he asked cautiously.

'Sometimes,' said Aunt Addie matter-of-factly. 'Betimes they bring their wands.'

She was barmy. She had to be. Thinking she had fairies in her garden and water sprites ...

The unicorn snickered from the grassy bank and tossed its bright horn at the sky.

... and unicorns. She really did have a unicorn. This was *real*, really real.

'Do the fairies come often?' he asked hesitantly.

Aunt Addie looked amused. 'They're here all the time,' she said. 'Look! You see! There they are!'

Something fluttered round the spire of a — what had Aunt Addie called them? Hollyhocks. But it was just a bee. A bee with shimmering wings that glistened blue and silver as they caught the sun.

Harry blinked. The glistening thing was gone.

Aunt Addie's smile was serene, as though of course he'd seen the fairy, as though unicorns and water sprites were perfectly natural, just like a garden like this was something you saw every day too. She looked at him consideringly. 'Belike you *can* help me.'

Harry nodded. 'Sure. How?'

'You can help me pick the raspberries.' Aunt Addie lifted her skirts a little as she brushed past the flowers down the path. Harry followed her uncertainly.

'Raspberries? I'm not sure. I mean ...'

'You've never picked raspberries? For shame.'

'I don't think they'd grow down at our place,' said Harry.

'There's no skill to picking raspberries,' said Aunt Addie kindly. 'You pick them and you eat them, and what don't be eaten you put in the basket. You line the basket with leaves first. Raspberries are easily bruised.'

'I guess they would be,' said Harry. 'I mean, I have eaten them. You can buy them frozen at the supermarket in town.'

'The supermarket?' said Aunt Addie vaguely. She picked a basket off a branch as they passed under the trees. It was a funny looking basket, thought Harry, a bit lopsided. It looked like it was made of twisted branches instead of cane.

Aunt Addie reached up and picked the broad green leaves. 'Soft leaves,' she said to Harry. 'See how soft they are?'

Harry nodded.

'Leaves should be soft,' said Aunt Addie dreamily. 'Soft and browning when they fall. Don't you love the leaves when they fall?'

'Er ...' said Harry.

'Raspberries,' said Aunt Addie more matter-of-factly. 'You take that side and I'll take this. Don't be ashamed of eating them neither. That's what raspberries are for.'

The raspberries were hot and squishy sweet. It was hard to stop eating them once you started, thought Harry guiltily, as he forced himself to lay some in the basket. After all he was here to help Aunt Addie. That's what Dad had said. Aunt Addie needed something.

Surely not just help picking the raspberries.

'Tell me then,' said Aunt Addie after a while. 'Tell me about Ron. It's so strange, thinking of him as your father. Little Ron a father too. Tell me about him.'

'Er ... there's not much to tell,' said Harry. What was there to say about Dad?

'What does he look like now?' asked Aunt Addie.

'Well, he's tall.'

'He would be tall,' said Aunt Addie approvingly. 'He were tall enough back then.'

'And he farms our place.'

Aunt Addie's face clouded just a little. 'Ah yes, the farm,' she said. She shook her head. 'Tell me other things,' she said. 'He married. Who is your dear mother then?'

'Mum? She's just Mum. She works part time at the library in town. That's how Dad met her. She was new to town ...' It all seemed far away from the flowers and the clearing. 'Hey, do you really want to hear all this?'

Aunt Addie nodded solemnly. 'I want to hear,' she said. 'Sometimes I'm afeared ...'

Afeared? 'Afraid? Afraid of what, Aunt Addie?' Unicorns, fairies, water sprites. Maybe there were dragons too ... or wizards.

But Aunt Addie was laughing. 'Of nothing surely. Bless your sweet face, what is there to be afeared of here? I'm silly sometimes, that's all. I think ... but enough of that. Would you like a nuncheon?'

'A nuncheon?'

247

'Vittles, food. You must be hungry,' said Aunt Addie gently. 'Walking all that way. I'm grateful. You must tell your father so.'

'Yes, I'll tell him. Yes, I'd love something to eat,' said Harry before he thought about it. Crikey, what would she give him to eat then? Fairy bread or elves' porridge ...

Aunt Addie took the basket, half-filled with raspberries now, and floated up the path again. She gestured to the seat among the flowers. Again she didn't ask him in. Why not? thought Harry. But it didn't matter. It was beautiful here in the sun. Beautiful, that was the only word for it. As though the whole world was beauty.

He opened his eyes at the sound of Aunt Addie's step on the path. She wore funny shoes, he noticed, sort of slippers, shining and in bright colours, almost like they were made of silk.

She carried a tray filled with more of the peaches, and apples too and cherries, and some funny nuts, and some sort of bun thing and honeycomb in a blue bowl.

'They're hazelnuts,' said Aunt Addie, as he picked one up curiously. 'Your father didn't know hazelnuts either. They're plentiful up here. And that's acorn bread. The baby fairies sleep in acorn cradles and the bees rock them in the wind.'

The bird sang again, that strange sweet bird. The song twisted in his brain and carried it along. It wouldn't be so bad living up here, thought Harry. All the fruit you wanted and green grass all year round — somehow he knew this grass never dried off no matter how hot the summer. You could swim in the pool with the water sprite and the fairies would keep you company.

He tried to jerk his mind back to reality. But there were no fairies. Of course there were no fairies.

'Aunt Addie?' he said almost desperately. 'What was it you wanted me to do? The thing Dad said you needed?'

Aunt Addie's smile seemed far away. 'You brang it when you came,' she said. 'I have it here. I'll keep it safe.'

'But what was it? What do you mean?'

'Sleep,' said Aunt Addie's voice. 'It is a long walk back. Just sleep. Just sleep.'

The bird sang again. Harry shut his eyes. His dreams were filled with unicorns and silver wings and the liquid singing of the bird. And then a sheep called somewhere on the hill. A dog barked in reply. The dreams changed, and Harry dreamt of home.

The farmhouse crouched between the sheds. There was no light in the kitchen. Mum must be reading in bed.

The old sofa creaked on the verandah. Dad looked out through the darkness.

Harry said nothing as he climbed the steps.

'So, you found her,' said Dad softly.

Harry nodded. 'How did you know?'

'By your face. I felt like that, too, when I first met Aunt Addie.'

'It was real, wasn't it?' asked Harry. 'All of it was real?'

'It was real,' said Dad. 'Real enough, at any rate. Real enough to see and smell and hear.'

'Who is she, Dad?'

Dad moved over on the sofa. Harry sat next to him. The cushions felt stiff. Too much possum, Mum had said, though she'd tried to wash it out.

'I told you,' said Dad. 'Your great-something-aunt.'

'Go on,' said Harry.

Dad sighed. 'I only know what my dad told me. What his dad told him too. It's a long story. Sure you're not too tired?'

'Go on,' said Harry again.

'No, you wouldn't be too tired,' said Dad. 'I remember the first time I went to Aunt Addie's ... Anyway, it all started with your great-great-something-granddad. He settled here in the 1840s.

'It was all bush then. No paddocks. Just the trees. It was wild and isolated but he loved it. He married your great-something-gran, and she loved it too. She was the daughter of a farmer up past Black Stone Creek. She'd been born there. It never occurred to her that someone mightn't love it too.'

'Where does Aunt Addie fit in?'

'I'm coming to that,' said Dad.

'Aunt Addie was your great-something-granddad's younger sister. Twenty years younger — it happened a lot back then, a gap as big as that. Families had lots of kids in those days. They were farm kids too, almost as isolated as this probably, but different country. Very different country. Addie was only five when your great-something-granddad left to come to Australia, but she loved him, and she remembered him.

'They wrote to each other — though remember in those days it took a letter six months or so to cross the ocean. He told her about his farm, his lovely, lovely farm, about his wife, his sweet, sweet wife. They're the words Dad used to me, and his dad to him, all the way back. His lovely, lovely farm, his sweet, sweet wife.

'Then something happened to Aunt Addie. I don't know what it was. Dad just said his dad told him she'd been crossed in love. That's how they put it back in the last century.

'I don't know what it was all about. Maybe she was engaged to some bloke who ran off on her. Maybe she fell in love with someone her parents didn't like. Those sorts of things happened in those days. You had to marry someone your parents approved of.

'Who knows. But she was unhappy and she wrote to her brother, and he said, "Come out here. There's plenty of room on the farm." I suppose he thought there were many more men than women in the colony, too, she's sure to get a husband here.

'So he wrote to her, and she wrote back, and the next year she came.'

A dog muttered in its sleep down at the kennels. 'Go on,' said Harry.

'It was a long voyage out, but she was happy. It must have all been strange to a girl from the backcountry like she was, who'd never even been to a city before. But she was full of hope. She was going to a new land, a new farm, going to her beloved brother, her older brother she hadn't seen for nearly fifteen years.

'She landed at Sydney. Her brother was shearing and couldn't meet her, but he arranged for her to be met, taken to a respectable boarding house and put on the coach next morning.

'He met her up in town. He shaved specially — in those days men shaved maybe once a week. But it'd been a long shearing. His hair was shaggy. His face was brown. He wasn't the brother she remembered.

'He brought her home. His wife had made Johnny cakes and they ate them on the verandah, right where we're sitting now, though the rest of the house wasn't built back then, just this front bit with a sort of separate kitchen out the back. The flies sat on the Johnny cakes and got stuck in the treacle. And Aunt Addie sat on the verandah horrified at what she'd come to.

'Aunt Addie stuck it out, even though they killed a snake the first morning she was here, and she was scared to go down to the dunny ever after.

'She was scared of the snakes, of the bunyip howling down the creek, of the wind that tore down the hills and the heat that sent the branches cracking off the trees.

She was scared of the smoke from the bushfires in the distance. But she stuck it out.'

'Did she fall in love again?' asked Harry.

Dad shook his head. 'There were men around. Stockmen, farmers, shopkeepers up in town. Every woman in the colony had a string of suitors in those days. But she didn't fall in love again.

'She was homesick. She missed the trees, the soft green trees. She missed the bluebells in the spring. She missed the roses over the fence at home. She missed the sound of bees in the spring blossom.'

'Why didn't she go home then?' asked Harry.

'It was a long way, remember,' said Dad. 'Expensive, too. And when she got back she'd just be an old maid, unwanted ... and her parents were getting older and what would happen when they died? There were so few jobs for women in those days. Be someone's servant or nurse ... I doubt she had the education for governess. You know how she talks ... There was nothing for her at home, except the forests and the gardens that she loved. She'd sit here on the verandah and look out at the hills and she'd remember the flowers and the stories of home.

'So her brother decided they'd plant a garden for her here, something to remind her of the world she loved. She brightened up when he told her about that.

'Your great-something-grandfather wrote to Sydney and ordered plants from there. He got English catalogues and had plants and seeds sent out — a long journey for them too, remember.'

'And the garden grew?' asked Harry, looking out at Mum's tubs of petunias by the steps, the grevilleas by the front gate, the rockery where the dogs liked to sleep.

'No.' Dad looked out at the hills again. 'Most of the bulbs didn't even come up — either it was too hot or they'd been damaged in the ship or they never did get used to the change in seasons. The roses died — I reckon we've got hardier sorts now that've got used to Australia. The lily shoots shrivelled in the ground. She couldn't even get a lawn to grow. They didn't have hoses in those days, remember, or sprinkler systems. Gardens needed the rain or they died. And Aunt Addie's died.

'Aunt Addie didn't say anything. She didn't say much at all by then. Then one morning she was gone.

'Your great-something-granddad panicked. He thought she'd been bitten by a snake, drowned in the waterhole. All the blokes went looking — then that evening she turned up, cool as you please. She hadn't been bitten by a snake. She hadn't even got lost.'

'Where had she been?'

'Up at the hut. The one where she lives now. In those days it was just a shepherd's hut — a place to check the sheep when they were up that way — but it hadn't been used since the main house was built.

'Aunt Addie asked if she could grow a garden there. It was cooler up in the hills, she reckoned. She'd get water from the creek in the gully.

'Of course your great-granddad said yes. Anything to make her smile again. She spent the next year digging up the shrivelled bulbs from round the house, carefully separating the lilies from the hot soil, uprooting the roses in case there was still a spark of life.

'Years went by. Sometimes she asked her brother for seeds — grass seeds, forget-me-not seeds, hollyhock seeds. But mostly she just wandered up there in the early morning and came back late at night. Finally your great-something-granddad stopped worrying about her. She knew the way. She always came back safely.

'More years went by. Your great-something-granddad had kids — your ancestor and a few others too. Aunt Addie told the kids stories about "home" — the beech trees dappled against the sky, the fairies and the unicorns. I reckon by that time she didn't know what "home" was really like — memories of her childhood were all mixed with her stories and ... well, who knows with what else.

'She spent more and more time up at the hut.'

'Didn't anyone ever go up to see what she was doing there?' asked Harry.

Dad shook his head. 'She asked them not to. She said they could see it when it was done. Her brother and sister-in-law did what she asked. I reckon they thought that garden was probably dead, too, and Addie just wouldn't admit it, would keep on hoping that one day things would grow.'

'But surely some of the stockmen would have passed by!' objected Harry.

'You'd think so,' said Dad. 'You'd think someone would have come by. But they didn't. We can probably guess why.

'Then one day ... the first of May it was, just like today, her nephew thought he'd follow her.' Dad's voice died away. A possum shrieked out in the gum tree by the shed, and then was still.

'What happened then?' asked Harry.

'What happened to you, I reckon,' said Dad. 'What happened to me and my dad and my granddad, too. He met Aunt Addie. And he saw her garden.

Aunt Addie didn't come back to the farm that night. She never came back again. For years her brother tried to find her hut. But the only one who ever did was her nephew. Every May Day he went up there. Just like me. Now just like you.'

'But ... but you don't go there anymore,' said Harry. 'Did you have an argument? Did she ask you not to come?'

His father shook his head. 'No argument. Just one May Day I couldn't find it anymore. I hunted for hours. I was sure I'd gone the wrong way, gone up the wrong gully — but deep inside I knew what had happened.'

'I ... I don't understand ...'

'I had grown up. Aunt Addie didn't want me in her garden anymore. Not with the unicorn, the water sprite, the fairies — didn't you see the fairies, too?'

'I think I did,' said Harry.

'That's all that ever happens,' said Dad. 'You think you might have seen ... Grown ups don't fit into the world of fairies. And no man can ride the unicorn.'

'Then one day I won't be able to find Aunt Addie's either,' said Harry slowly.

'One day,' said his father. 'In a few years' time. Then one day you'll have to tell your son how he can find Aunt Addie's.'

'Dad?'

'Mmmm?' His father's eyes were on the moon, round as a golden hill, emerging from the black behind the ridge.

'Did Aunt Addie ever ask you into her house?'

'No,' said Dad.

'Why not?'

His father grinned. 'What maiden lady of last century would ask a gentleman into her bedroom? Even one as young as you.'

'Oh,' said Harry. 'I thought it might break the spell.'

'I don't think so,' said his father gently. 'I don't think the spell can be broken now.'

'You know,' said Harry after a while, 'I almost stayed there. It was so beautiful. So strange. I thought I could never leave.'

'Then you remembered home,' said his father.

'How did you know?' asked Harry.

'Because it happened to me, too,' said his father. 'Just like that. I remembered the sun on the hills and the sheep by the rocks. And I came home.'

Home, thought Harry. The bare gold hills like skulls, their shape all clean and clear under the dead grass. The hot haze of eucalypt oil around the trees that made the distance blue. The sunlight baking on corrugated iron. The hunched backs of rocks in the paddocks ...

'What was it Aunt Addie needed?' asked Harry.

'Haven't you guessed?'

Harry shook his head.

'Maybe you will next time,' said his father. 'It took me a while, too.'

'Not fair,' said Harry. 'Tell me now, Dad.'

His father shrugged. 'Reality,' he said. 'That's what she needs from us. A little bit of reality to ground that world of hers. A little bit of something that's not memories and dreams. Otherwise ... who knows ...'

The clearing had shimmered when he'd first seen it, Harry remembered. And by the time he left the shapes and colours were clear ...

'Do you think she's lonely?' asked Harry finally.

'No,' said Dad. 'She's got her unicorn, her water sprite and her fairies. I reckon she'd say we were the lonely ones. But we're not. There's another sort of magic here that Addie never learnt to see. Come on. Your mum will be waiting. It's time we went inside.'

Amfylobbsis

The hospital bed was cool, the sheets were straight and firm. You didn't need eyes to tell it was a hospital, Grandma decided. The smells, the sounds, the very feel of the air conditioning on your skin was enough to tell you where you were.

'Grandma?' The voice at the door was eager. 'Have they taken the bandages off yet?'

'Emma, is that you, pet? No, tomorrow. They'll take the bandages off tomorrow.'

'But we'll be gone tomorrow!' The voice came nearer. 'Can I come in?'

'Of course.'

'Can Amfylobbsis come in, too?'

Grandma smiled. 'I'd love to see Amfylobbsis.'

'But you can't see,' Emma pointed out. 'You won't be able to see until tomorrow.'

'Not even then, pet,' said Grandma gently. 'It'll take weeks for my eyes to get better.'

'But you'll be able to see again properly? Really properly?'

'Of course,' said Grandma.

I hope, she thought. Why do we always lie to children? Why do we always tell them everything will be all right?

'Is Amfylobbsis here yet?' she asked aloud. Emma giggled. 'No. He had to hide from the nurses.

They might be angry if they find him in their hospital.'

'But no one ever sees Amfylobbsis except you.'

'They might hear him though,' said Emma seriously. Something clattered outside — a trolley perhaps, thought Grandma. 'He's here now,' said Emma. 'Say hello to Grandma, Amfylobbsis.' She paused. 'Amfylobbsis says to say hello.'

'Hello, Amfylobbsis,' said Grandma.

Emma was silent for a moment. 'You're the only one who believes in Amfylobbsis except me,' she said finally. 'Everyone else says he's just imaginary. I'll miss you when we're in Darwin, Grandma.'

'I'll miss you too, pet,' said Grandma. 'And Amfylobbsis,' she added. 'But we'll see each other often.'

'Promise?'

'Promise,' said Grandma. She tried to sound convincing. Darwin was so far away ...

Emma was silent.

'Emma, what does Amfylobbsis look like? Is he big?'

'Really big,' said Emma. 'Almost as tall as me.'

Grandma smiled. 'It must be hard for him to hide so no one sees him, then.'

'Amfylobbsis says he's had lots of practice hiding,' said Emma matter-of-factly.

'Is he a boy? Or a dog? Or a monster? Or …?'

'Of course he's not a monster. He's sort of like a horse,' said Emma. 'Like a white horse. But he's different. Like a fairy horse maybe.'

'Has he got wings?'

'No.' Emma sounded regretful. 'Just this big horn thing in the middle of his head. It's sharp. I was scared of it at first but Amfylobbsis said …'

'Then he's a unicorn!' said Grandma.

'Is that what he is?' said Emma excitedly. 'I didn't know. Have you seen unicorns before, Grandma?'

'No, they're …' She was about to say they were imaginary. She stopped. 'They're pretty rare,' she said instead.

The nurse's voice came from the doorway. 'Visiting hours are nearly over,' she said.

Emma sat quite still. 'I don't want to go,' she whispered.

'I'll see you before you go tomorrow.'

'But everyone will be there then. It's not the same. It's hard to bring Amfylobbsis when there are so many people.'

'We'll still see each other often, pet,' said Grandma, this time to try to convince herself. If only things were different, she thought suddenly. If only this was the sort of world where hopes came true, where small girls did play with unicorns.

'Grandma?'

'Yes?'

'Amfylobbsis just said not to worry. He said everything will work out fine.'

'Thank you, Amfylobbsis,' said Grandma gently.

'He'd like to say goodbye now.'

'Goodbye Amfylobbsis,' said Grandma.

'No, goodbye properly,' said Emma. 'Because you're the only one who believes in him except me. Because he loves you too.'

Grandma smiled. 'How do I say goodbye properly?'

'Hold out your hand,' whispered Emma.

Grandma held out her hand.

Nothing happened. She half expected Emma to put a lolly in it ... a jube, maybe, she and Emma both loved jubes. Then suddenly ...

The touch was gentle, moist and very warm. The hint of hot breath, the touch of whiskers round a soft damp mouth ...

'Goodbye, Grandma,' whispered Emma.

Grandma listened to her footsteps run along the corridor, and faintly, very faintly, the light clicking of hooves.

Spots

The room smelt of sweat and old bedding. The child sat in the corner, spooning soup.

'It's a miracle,' the woman said. 'A true miracle.'

The girl shook her head. Her face was pale and thin, but not too thin. The illness had been too brief to really mark her face.

'I knew I would get better,' she said. 'The girl came.'

'What girl?'

'The girl with the unicorn,' said the child matter-of-factly. 'When she comes you get better. Everyone knows that.'

The woman shook her head. 'There are signs and portents everywhere,' she said quietly. 'They say that when the plague comes to a village the first sign is a tall man carrying an axe, his head cloaked, and shining evil eyes. No one who's seen him has ever lived to tell the tale ...'

'Then how do people know about him?' asked the child. 'I didn't see a man, though others say they did. But all of us saw the girl.'

'No one really sees him,' said the woman. 'You just had fever dream. That's what it was. But you're better now, and soon we'll be taking you home ...'

'But I did see her!' insisted the child. 'She was young and had long hair, and she was dressed all in white and the unicorn was white as well.'

'A unicorn, was it? Well, that proves it was a dream.'

'I did see her,' said the child stubbornly, laying down her spoon. Tears ran down her cheeks suddenly. 'She came riding up the path and her cloak was white and the unicorn had big blue eyes and she carried a basket. But she came too late for Ma and Da ...'

'Well, yes,' said the woman comfortingly. 'If that's what you saw, well, that's what you saw. You'll be home with us and you'll forget it all soon. There'll be kittens for you to play with and your cousins to play with too and ...'

'But I don't want to forget the unicorn!' cried the child. 'It put its face through the window and blew through its lips at me. And the girl came inside and felt my forehead and her hand was cool, so cool. And she took a sweetie out of her basket, a little white one, and she made me swallow it. Then she took Ma and Da outside.'

'Sure and sure she did,' soothed the woman. 'Or maybe it was the neighbours took them.'

'No one would touch the dead!' said the child. 'Not till the girl came on the unicorn! She gave the sweeties to everyone, two every day, and no one died after that. And she gave us water — funny sweet water and strange cakes to eat, and ...'

The woman leant over the child and wrapped another shawl around her. 'And here's your uncle with the cart,' she said. 'It's time to take you home. Your new home.'

The child nodded. 'I was asleep the last time she came,' she said. 'I just remember her pushing the last sweetie in my mouth, then I fell asleep again. So I never said goodbye. Or thank you.' She looked up at her aunt. 'Do you think if I said goodbye now she'd hear me?'

'I'm sure of it,' said her aunt, for after all it was no lie. Dreams could hear you anywhere.

'Thank you,' said the child earnestly, gazing out the door as though she expected the unicorn to appear again. 'Thank you for looking after me. Thank you for making me well. And thank Spots, too.'

'Spots?' asked the woman.

'That's what she called the unicorn,' said the child.

'But I thought it was a white unicorn!' protested the woman.

'It was,' said the child sleepily. 'But it was still called Spots.'

She lifted up her arms to be carried.

Ten minutes away, a thousand years away, another world away, the girl got off the unicorn and led it tiredly into its stable. It snickered at the horse in the next stall, then bent its head to its hay.

'Hard time?' said a voice behind the girl.

The girl turned. 'Oh, it's you,' she said. 'It's always hard. Sometimes ...'

'Sometimes what?'

'Sometimes I wonder if it's right. To interfere. To pretend to all those people.' She patted the unicorn absently.

'We have to pretend,' said her friend. 'What would people like that say if we came just like we are? They'd be terrified. No, it has to be this way. Disguised as the sort of visions they dreamt about in those days ... and the unicorn was a touch of genius. Whoever thought of the unicorn?'

'Thaddeus,' said the girl. 'It was Thaddeus of course. Just a little fiddle with the DNA, he said, and there we had a unicorn. Though it was spotty, not pure white, something went wrong there, but nothing that some hair dye wouldn't change. And its blue eyes. The blue eyes were a shock to Thaddeus too. No one quite knows where the blue eyes came from.'

The unicorn blew gently at its hay for a moment, almost as though it was laughing.

'You know, it's funny.'

'What?'

'The last village I was in and the one before — they said they'd seen another vision.'

'Another unicorn? Maybe it's a story passed about from some other village you went to.'

The girl shook her head. 'A tall man with an axe. Before the plague arrives, they said. Every time, the man appears.'

Her friend was silent. 'Who knows where the plague came from?' she said. 'All we know is why it stops. Because of us. Because of antibiotics disguised as sweeties. Because of the unicorn.'

The girl smiled suddenly. 'We're a match for anyone, aren't we, Spots?' She patted the rough back. 'You know, sometimes I wonder if you're not magic after all. Real magic.'

Her friend laughed. 'Don't let Thaddeus hear you say that. You'd be in for a long lecture. Come on. We've waited dinner for you.'

The girl patted the unicorn one last time. 'See you tomorrow, Spots,' she said.

The unicorn winked at her with one blue eye.

The Taming of the Beast

The beast had pale skin, paler than she'd ever seen before. It hovered nervously at the edge of the clearing.

It was scared. Even from here she could see that it was scared.

She started to speak to it; then stopped. Of course it wouldn't understand. One animal never understood another's words. Each creature had its own language and that was how it always was ... it was the tone of the words that animals understood, the music behind the words ...

The beast hesitated. Was it going to run? It had been plucking apples, she noticed. One lay on the ground where it had fallen, still with the imprint of the beast's sharp teeth.

She stepped forward quietly. One harsh move and the beast would vanish. What sort of creature was it? She'd never seen its like before. A strange beast. An almost frightening beast. But there was something about it that called her to it. As though they belonged together, as though once they'd been a partnership, or would be friends ...

Another step. The beast looked wary, but it held its ground. A brave beast, she thought exultantly. A good creature for a friend.

Another step. Another. Now the beast stepped forward, too, the long hair down its neck shaking a little as it trembled. But it still came on ...

She could smell the beast now, a strange smell, deep and warmly musky.

One more step. Slowly ... very slowly ... she reached towards the creature.

The beast flinched, then smiled. She knew it was a smile. Who would have thought a beast like that would smile, too? The smile looked different, that funny mouth, those crazy teeth. But still she knew it was a smile.

Slowly ... very slowly ... the beast reached towards her, too.

Its skin was warm, and smoother than she'd thought. What now? What now?

Suddenly it was simple. As though not only were they meant to be together but she knew how ... and the creature knew it, too.

The beast laughed and she laughed too, and though their laughter was different each understood.

Then she was galloping, galloping through the shadows of the leaves, with the beast clinging to her back, its two long legs on either side, its face bent low so the long hair on its head tangled her mane and fluttered up towards her horn.

The wind tore away their laughter and mingled it and sent it flying through the trees.

The Lady of the Unicorn

The hill was steep, the grass a strange unearthly green. The unicorn picked his way uncertainly among the bones and rubble. His hooves looked very white among the green. His flanks were wet with sweat when Ethel patted them.The hill stank too, thought Ethel, as she clung to the unicorn's mane. This wasn't the Hall's familiar smell of chamber pots and dogs and winter sweat. This was a sharper smell, of bones withering in sunlight, of hot rock and decomposing flesh ... and something else ...

The unicorn dodged around a chunk of rubble, worn smooth by rain and wind till it almost looked natural, higher than Ethel's head even when she was riding. At least the piles of rubble shielded her from sight if anyone looked down.

But of course no one was looking down. No one lived on the hill. The giant on the hill was just a tale of Ma'm Margot's to frighten children if they yelled too loudly in the Hall. It was just a trick of Uncle Maddox's in the days when he could tell her what to do. Don't go to the forest, you'll be eaten by a dragon, don't climb the wild hills or a lion will tear off both your arms.

Don't climb up the hill or the giant will suck your bones ...

Giants were olden day myths, Ethel thought, like werewolves and koalas and dragons. No one she knew had ever really seen a werewolf or even a giant, though Ma'm Dorothy the Baker had seen a lion when she was young.

But lions were real. The old books agreed that lions were real, just like sheep and goats had once been real before they interbred as geep. There'd been lion parks in the old days, then in the wild days the lions had escaped. But werewolves and giants and dragons and monsters were all imaginary. The old books said they were.

The unicorn stumbled, then righted himself. Ethel glanced down at a large bone, a thigh bone from a cow maybe or from a horse. Who would eat a horse? A giant maybe or a ...

There were no such things as giants.

The bone was splintered at one end, as though it had been crunched in giant jaws. A few bits of meat clung to the other end. Raw meat, rancid and festering in the sun. A fly buzzed, slow and sleepy, then settled back onto the meat.

Ethel hesitated. Many things might carry away a bone ... foxes, eagles ... Just because there was a bone didn't mean there was a giant.

Would a fox or an eagle splinter a bone like that?

The bone had been baking at least two days. Whatever had crunched it was probably long gone. Ethel patted the unicorn again to tell him to keep climbing. The unicorn stumbled again. Ethel dismounted and began to lead him.

Round a hunk of concrete, crowned with twisted steel, then round another. A snake slithered slowly into a crevice, its belly red against the sandy stone. The grass was soft and still, and that strange and brilliant green. Maybe grass just grew well between the rocks. Maybe the giant cast a spell ...

There was no such thing as spells either, Ethel told herself firmly.

The stench grew stronger instead of weaker. High above a pair of crows yelled into silence.

Surely she must be nearly at the top. But the piles of rubble stood too high, with chunks of concrete, fat as Ned the Barrel Maker. It was impossible to see above them to see how far she had to climb.

The unicorn whinnied softly, distressed by the stench. Ethel shivered. What if the giant heard it — though of course there was no giant. But there was no need to take the unicorn further either. She'd be faster, quieter on foot.

Ethel assessed the rubble quickly. Surely there must be a place to tie the reins. There were no trees, no bushes, the steel was all too rusty, it would never hold ... But there must be something ...

Finally she chose a cow's skull, wedged firmly between great hunks of stone. She slipped the reins around the horns, then patted the unicorn, murmuring to him in the no-words language that they shared. The unicorn butted her shoulder with his warm white nose. The whites of his eyes were showing around the clear soft blue of the iris. His ears were narrow and pointed. They twitched towards the top of the hill as though listening to sounds that Ethel couldn't hear.

'I won't be long,' whispered Ethel, hoping that the unicorn understood the tone if not the words. 'You'll be safe here.'

She hoped that she was right.

Up the hill, twisting between the rubble, through the too-green grass. Suddenly the rubble cleared. The top of the hill opened in front of her.

Ethel gasped; she closed her mouth, afraid that she'd been heard.

Once the top of the hill must have been bare as Uncle Maddox's head, a grassy clearing grazed perhaps by nimble geep. Now it was divided neatly into gardens, each edged by jagged rocks, as though the chunks of rubble from below had been split and shattered. Fruit trees clustered against sun-warm walls. A mound of even larger chunks of rubble clustered in the centre of the clearing. Ethel blinked and saw it was a hut.

A strange hut, a massive hut, more like a cave than any hut should be, but built by human hands none the less. Tree trunks poked out above thick walls, roofed with long thin slabs, like shingles that someone had turned to stone. The hut would just look like a pile of rubble from a distance, thought Ethel. You'd never know a hut was here from below.

Now she was closer she could see smoke as well. It came from the far side of the hut — clear, hot smoke from long-dry wood, so the air merely shimmered instead of clouded grey.

The stench was even worse.

She should run. She had to run. She had to get her feet to work. Ma'm Margot was right. Even Uncle had been right.

She had to run ...

Suddenly her feet began to move. Down between the rubble, to the right and to the right again, never mind the easiest way now, just the quickest to get down, to get away, down to her unicorn and home.

'Aaaaah!' Ethel bit the sound back. Something gripped her foot. A snare of plaited leather grew tighter as she pulled.

Ethel froze. She mustn't make a noise. She mustn't panic. She wasn't a wallaby or wild geep to be caught blindly with a bit of leather. She only had to stop and wriggle her foot free ... but even as she thought it she realised that it made no difference what noise she made. A bell was ringing high up on the hill.

The snare must have set off an alarm.

It was a dull bell, not like the sharp tuneful bells at home, more like a clapper against a ring of steel than a proper bell cast in a forge, all its proportions right to sing its note. But this wasn't a singing bell, or a bell to call you in from the fields. This was a hunter's bell, a command to come and fetch your prey.

Ethel tore urgently at her foot. A wild dog might bite through the snare. Her teeth weren't as sharp as a wild dog's teeth, but maybe she could manage it — but not in time, not in time. Maybe if she pointed her toes downward her foot would be narrower and might slip out. Yes, that was it. She took her slipper off. But the snare stuck around her heel and held it firm.

A noise came from above. Like a crow learning to sing, thought Ethel with half her mind. She struggled frantically, but knew it was too late.

Footsteps. Heavy footsteps. A chunk of rubble rolled as something large brushed against it — *ca-thunk, ca-thunk, ca-thunk* down the hill, till it crashed against another and was still.

The booming sound came closer.

'And he sang as he stuffed that jumbuck in his tucker bag ...'

Ethel froze. It was a song from the olden days. She'd read it in a book in the Hall. One of her greatest joys at the Hall was the big room full of books. There'd been music written for this song too, but no one at the Hall could play it ...

The giant stepped around the boulder.

It was small for a giant, was her first thought. She'd always thought that giants would be much bigger. Though this was big enough.

The giant was no taller than two men, though its

arms and legs were slightly longer in proportion, so the hands hung down below the knees.

It was cleaner than Ethel had expected too, the long hair plaited neatly and wound about its head. Its head was bare. Ethel had thought only the T'manians had bare heads. Perhaps neither they nor giants ever got the sun sickness. It wore a shapeless tunic, like faded dark green curtains, belted roughly several times with a leather thong below its breasts and sewn roughly at the shoulders and down part of the side so that its lower legs gleamed long and bare and hairy.

The giant was definitely a woman.

The giant stopped singing. She blinked at Ethel. Her eyes were just a little larger than they should be too. And then she grinned.

'A mouse,' she boomed. 'A little mousie! How are we meant to dine upon a mousie then? There's not much meat upon a mousie.' Her teeth were whiter than any Ethel had ever seen, and longer than they should be. It looked like she still had all of them, though she must be Ma'm Margot's age or more.

The giant lifted her great hands, wide as pitchforks, brown as any field hand's, though the nails were clean. 'Maybe I'll have the little mousie stewed, or fried. It be most tender boiled inside my pot ...'

The giant cackled. It bent down and snapped the thongs that bound her ankle. The giant stood back. 'I will cook the little mousie and suck her bones. I will hang her like a wombat in my larder till she be soft.

She'll be a delicate little morsel for such as me.' The giant blinked and folded her arms. 'For mercy's sake, why aren't you running girl?' the giant said in a normal voice.

'I don't know,' said Ethel truthfully.

'Look child, if a giant catches you in her snare and talks about turning your bones into soup, it's prudent to run, run as fast as you can, then tell everyone about your narrow escape. You understand me?'

'Yes,' said Ethel.

'Well, go on then. Scamper.'

Ethel shook her head.

'Stubborn,' grinned the giant, showing her too-white, too-long teeth. 'Stubborn as ... well, I know of only one thing as stubborn and that's me, so I suppose I shouldn't complain. What am I to do with you if you don't run?'

'Turn me into soup?' offered Ethel.

'Don't joke about it child, it's no joking matter. I only have two options up on my hill. I can hurt people or I can scare them, and big as I am, I couldn't defend this place myself if a whole mob came at me. So I'm left with scaring people. Sensible people, who allow themselves to be scared.'

'I was scared,' objected Ethel.

'But you still didn't run. Why didn't you run?' inquired the giant, as though she really wanted to know. 'Maybe I can improve my performance next time.'

'Because I was more interested than scared,' decided Ethel.

The giant leant against a chunk of weathered concrete, her wide hands almost dropping against the ground. Her fingers were broader at the tips than below, like fattish spoons, thought Ethel.

'So,' remarked the giant. 'Scared but not running. Curious. Lonely perhaps? So lonely you would dare even a giant?'

'I'm not lonely,' objected Ethel. 'I'm the Lady of the Unicorn.' She waited for the giant's face to change. The giant looked unimpressed.

'Don't you know who the Lady of the Unicorn is?' demanded Ethel.

'More or less,' said the giant. 'I've never been much interested in who is what in the villages down below my hill. How did you become the Lady? Was there a competition?'

Ethel shook her head. 'When the old Lady died, they sent out searchers to find a new unicorn because hers wouldn't go to anyone else, of course. And when they found one they took it to the Hall, and sent it out to find an owner.'

'And it found you?'

Ethel nodded. 'I was up a tree picking apples. The unicorn stopped under my branch. I threw him an apple. He looked hungry ... and sort of lonely. I didn't know they were choosing a new Lady. I just thought — I don't know what I thought. And so I slid down the tree and the unicorn butted my arms for more apples, so I fed him more, even though Uncle Maddox would be angry.

And then, and then ... I sort of slid onto his back. I don't know why I did that either. And suddenly these six old men and women were racing up to us and they bowed and called me "my Lady" and they've called me "my Lady" ever since.'

'What about your parents?'

Ethel shrugged. 'I don't remember them. The T'manians killed them down south in a raid when I was small. I moved up here with Uncle Maddox and my cousins; but there were a lot of cousins and I was just a nuisance. They made a great fuss of me of course when I became the Lady — I think they thought I'd have them at the Hall. Or give them presents. But why should I? They didn't want me when I was just Ethel. Why should I want them when I became the Lady?'

'No reason that I can think of,' said the giant matter-of-factly. 'So now you have a great Hall and people to do whatever you want ... and yet you still come looking for a giant.'

'Yes,' said Ethel slowly. 'But I'm not lonely. I can't be lonely. I've got Ma'm Margot — she's sort of the steward, in charge of everything at the Hall. And the Grand Marshal, he's building walls to keep out the T'manians if they ever decide to come up north again, and all the servants — everything I do has to be what the Lady does,' she went on in a rush. 'I wanted to do something for myself.'

'So you came giant hunting,' said the giant.

'I suppose,' said Ethel.

The giant looked at her consideringly. 'As it happens,' she said, 'I'm lonely too. Come on then. What's your name?'

'Ethel.'

'Come then, Ethel. Let's see how you like a giant's company for a change.'

Her ankle hurt now the thong had been removed, but not enough to slow her down. Ethel followed the giant through the piles of rubble. The crows had vanished now, as though they recognised who had the rights to the dead animals on the hill.

'Are you ... are you really a giant?' Ethel asked.

The giant turned and grinned her toothy grin. 'What kind of a question is that?' she demanded. 'Look at me! What do you see? Am I a giant or not? Or maybe you think I'm an elf in disguise, just pretending to be big.'

'Well, of course you're big,' said Ethel. 'I just thought giants would be different.'

'Giants are giants,' said the giant. 'We're big, that's all. If you're big you're a giant.'

'Oh,' said Ethel. 'You mean there are more of you? More giants? But I thought giants didn't exist. The old books say giants don't exist.'

'Maybe they didn't then,' said the giant. 'I bet those olden days writers said unicorns didn't exist either. And geep. But they do now.'

'Why?' asked Ethel.

The giant shrugged. 'All I know is that once there were many horses and now there are hardly any horses and every so often one is born as a unicorn. And once there were many people but now there are fewer, and every so often one is born who becomes a giant … or something else.'

'Weren't you always a giant?'

The giant shook her head above the heaps of rubble. 'Once I was a baby just as you were a baby. I was a child just like you are a child. But I grew. I kept on growing. I grew till my father could no longer pretend I might change back to true proportions. I became a giant.'

The giant trudged between the final circle of rubble, out into the clearing. 'Come,' she said. 'The door is on the other side.'

Ethel gazed around. The world below was flat, and marked like a game of noughts and crosses. There was the village, with its paddocks of corn and pumpkins and seedy wattles and potatoes. There was a square that must be the Hall, a smudge that was the coast, a green haze that was the forest, a sweep of blue that was the sea and a wider arch that was the sky. She hadn't noticed how high the giant's hill was before. 'You can see everything from here!' she breathed.

The giant smiled a little sadly. 'See everything and be part of nothing,' she answered. 'I can see the boats on the sea and the travellers on the road and the children playing hay fights after harvest.'

'How come you didn't see me coming then?' asked Ethel.

'Because I was inside,' said the giant simply. 'Most days I'm outdoors in the garden. Nothing much escapes me then. Though I don't know whether it makes you more or less lonely to watch others. But if the T'manians ever come to this part of the world I'll be the first to see them; and if a battle's fought I'll watch it too; and weddings and processions and funerals and harvests ...' The giant's voice trailed away.

'You said ...' began Ethel hesitantly. 'You said there were more giants. Why don't you live with them?'

'And make a land of giants?' The giant laughed a little shrilly. 'There aren't enough of us for that, child. If we were together where folk could see us they'd be scared, and scared people do all sorts of things they wouldn't otherwise. No, we're safest by ourselves, most of the time at any rate; monsters that people can forget, unless they want a reason to be scared. This way, child. This way.'

Ethel followed the giant through the garden. It was very like the enclosed garden at the Hall, she thought, sheltered from frost and harsh salt winds, though the Hall's garden was surrounded by a neat stone wall and this wall was ... she grinned to herself. She had been going to say like a giant had just dropped great chunks of rubble round the edges, which was probably exactly what had happened.

But these gardens flourished, even more than the Hall's. There were beds of white flowered beans, tall as her knees, and beds of parsley, kumera, medi-grass, thyme and sage, and rows of purple cabbages, and green ones, fat as Sam the Miller's belly, and a high stone bed with tomatoes, red and yellow and green striped, trailing over its edges, and tall plants with slightly furry leaves that looked like weeds to Ethel but were too carefully placed to be weeds. Perhaps the giant liked to eat weeds, she thought; or maybe the plants were just hardier up here on the hill than many of those that grew at Uncle's or the Hall.

'You were lucky,' said the giant conversationally. 'Usually anything that comes this way is caught in my traps long before they reach as high as you did. Maybe I need to set more snares.'

'Do you catch a lot of people?' asked Ethel, skirting a bed of strawberries, fruit dark red against the darker leaves.

'For mercy's sake, no,' said the giant. 'It's been … how long has it been? Three years at least since I last caught a person, and that was just a geepherder who had wandered up this way. I caught his geep too, but that I kept. Fear is the best barrier, better than any moat or wall. The snares are mostly to catch animals, wallabies and rabbits and geep, and sometimes even a cow … ah yes, I do like the taste of cow. Meat to eat and meat to keep on a cow, if it's not too old and bony.'

'I saw cow bones,' offered Ethel.

The giant nodded. 'I throw the big ones down,' she said. 'They smell a bit, but they help keep people off.

There's nothing as frightening as a good sun-bleached skull. Speaking of smells ...'

They rounded the corner of the hut. The giant nodded towards a barrel. 'I'm sorry about the stench. I keep my pottings and the leavings of the animals and soak them well, then pour them down the hill. It makes the grass grow green, and green grass lures the animals. More than I need mostly. Are you hungry?'

Ethel nodded.

'It won't be what you're used to at the Hall,' the giant warned.

'I don't mind. Um ... excuse me please for asking ...'

'Yes? What is it child?'

'What's your name?' asked Ethel.

The giant paused. 'Do you know how long it is since I had a name?' she asked. 'I'm the giant on the hill ...' She looked down at the world below for a moment, then back at Ethel. 'My name is Alice,' she said finally. 'Alice of ... Alice of the Hill.'

'Thank you, Ma'm Alice,' said Ethel. She hesitated. 'My name is Ethel.'

The giant blinked at the word 'Ma'm'. And then she smiled.

The interior of the hut was larger than Ethel had thought it would be from the outside. Ma'm Alice must have had some skill in piling chunks of rubble together, she thought. The walls sloped gradually up to the tree trunk ceiling, the crevices packed with mud and hay to stop the draughts. A blackened smoke hole at one end covered a broad flat hearth, with a spit for roasting meat and a thick pot of precious iron swung on a hob.

A line of smoked meat hung from the tree trunk beam above the fireplace: legs of geep and wallaby, shoulder of cow, even whole rabbits with their paws hanging down like they were preparing to dive into the fire, all greyed and hard-fleshed from long smoking, and glistening slightly from old fat. The hut smelt of old fires and charred bone and bunches of bay leaves, mint bush, tea tree and lavender — not an unpleasant smell, thought Ethel.

The floor was dirt, but so hard-trodden it seemed like stone. A broom of tea tree branches leant against the wall.

There was little furniture in the room — a flat-topped chunk of debris that served as a table, a pile of untrimmed furs that must be Ma'm Alice's bed; a wooden chest, once finely carved but now charred at one edge, to keep cloth from the damp and moths perhaps, if indeed Ma'm Alice had any clothes other than what she wore. Another flat-topped rock that must be her scriptorium, with leather flask for ink and magpie feather pen and a large flat book still open.

A book … Ethel stared in the dim light. How would a giant have a book?

Ma'm Alice followed her gaze. 'Haven't you ever seen a book before?' she asked gently.

'Yes ... of course ... there's a whole room of old books at the Hall. Wonderful books. I bought a new book for the Hall just last month, too. I have the money now to buy books.' She approached the book slowly.

'Can you read?' asked Ma'm Alice suddenly.

'Yes,' said Ethel, her eyes still on the book.

'How did you learn?'

Ethel looked up guiltily, till she remembered that there was no reason to feel guilty now. She was the Lady of the Unicorn. She could do anything she wanted, even read.

'A storyteller came to Uncle's village. He had three books — not genuine old ones, but rewritten with pen and ink, not magic-print from olden days. And he had another book too, one that he'd written himself, stories that were all his own.'

'And he taught you to read?'

Ethel shook her head. 'He taught Katerina the Pig Keeper's daughter. They were wealthy from the pigs and could afford to keep the storyteller for a half year. Katerina taught me. She was a good friend, the only person who ever liked me when I was just Ethel.'

'Where is she now?' asked Ma'm Alice gently, as though she guessed.

'She died of the flushed cough the winter before the unicorn chose me. She would still be my friend now that I'm the Lady, if she'd lived. But it was her who taught me to read.' Ethel looked up a little shyly. 'You're the first person I've met since I became Lady who likes me

287

just because I'm me. You have nothing to gain from my being the Lady.'

'But you must have other friends now?' asked Ma'm Alice.

Ethel shook her head. 'Someone who wants something from you can't be your friend,' she said.

'You may be right,' said Ma'm Alice. 'Friends give both ways. The Ma'm Margot that you spoke of ...'

Ethel shrugged. 'She likes the Lady, not me. If I wasn't the Lady she'd pay no attention to me. And she's always telling me what to do, what the last Lady did.'

'And you resent it?'

'I am the Lady!' cried Ethel. 'They are my lands, my Hall, my people. The unicorn chose *me* — but it's always Ma'm Margot who decides what I should do.'

'And you think a girl of your age should decide what to do?'

'Of course. I'm the Lady of the Unicorn.'

The giant shook her head and stepped carefully to the other end of the hut. Her head nearly touched the ceiling, Ethel realised. A room that was tall for her was cramped for a giant. The giant reached over to the hob.

'Listen to me, girl. Maybe the day will come when your people will follow you. Maybe it won't. But it will depend on you, not on whether a unicorn chose you or not.'

'I don't understand. How would you know about these things?'

'How would a giant on a hilltop know about people? I was a person too once.' The giant nodded towards the book. 'And I read. Books are the essence of people. I know more people on my hilltop than you do in your Hall.'

'Where ... where do you get the books?' asked Ethel tentatively.

'How do you think?' asked Ma'm Alice with a touch of aggression. 'I steal them. I sneak down from my hill at night, down to Halls and churches, and I rip the doors off their hinges and grab the books, the old-steel goblets, the precious plastic relics, the hangings from the walls ...'

'Don't be silly,' said Ethel.

Ma'm Alice grinned. 'As to that,' she said, 'I don't know where they come from.'

'You mean a dragon just drops them from the sky?' demanded Ethel scornfully.

'Some were always here. Some a friend brings. He knows I like books. He's better than I am at scavenging from farms and villages. I'm too big. No one could fail to notice me. But I don't know where the books come from.'

'Maybe he steals them,' Ethel pointed out. 'Why don't you ask him?'

The giant laughed. 'It would do no good. He does what he wants. Maybe one day you'll meet him. Then you'll understand.'

'I would be honoured to meet a friend of yours, Ma'm Alice,' said Ethel politely, though in truth she wasn't sure.

'Maybe. Maybe,' said Ma'm Alice. She pulled the pot from the hob, then two plates from beside the hearth. They were ordinary earthenware plates, roughly glazed, the sort you'd find in any cottage, thought Ethel, with high rimmed sides to stop the gravy spilling. Ma'm Alice poured a mess into both of them and handed one to Ethel.

'Thank you,' said Ethel.

'No spoons,' said Ma'm Alice. 'My friend hasn't brought me spoons, though he brought me a knife once. Maybe he doesn't know what spoons are for. I use a stick to stir my pots. It serves well enough.' She shrugged. 'If my fingers were nimbler I could carve a spoon. But my hands are better at tossing boulders than carving.'

Ethel scooped up a little of her stew in her fingers. The meat was unfamiliar and strongly flavoured. Wallaby perhaps, thought Ethel, certainly not cow or geep, flavoured with onions and some kind of herb, and thick with beans and wattleseed and carrots.

Ma'm Alice ate hungrily, the gravy dripping down her arm. She licked it clean, then saw Ethel watching. She shrugged. 'It's been a long time since I shared a meal with a person,' she apologised.

'What about your friend?'

'He's different,' said Ma'm Alice.

'You mean he's not a person?'

Ma'm Alice wiped her plate clean with her fingers, then hesitated. 'Am I a person?' she asked.

'Of course,' said Ethel.

'Even though I'm a giant?'

'Yes. You are a giant and a person.'

'Well,' said Ma'm Alice. 'My friend is a person and he is not a person too.'

'Tell me more!' insisted Ethel.

Ma'm Alice shook her head. 'You would have to meet him to understand,' she said.

'Then let me meet him!'

'You'd be scared.'

'I'm not scared of anything.'

'Not of the T'manians?'

Ethel thrust out her chin. 'Certainly not of the T'manians,' she declared. 'The first thing I did when I became Lady was to prepare the Hall in case of an invasion.'

'How did you do that?' inquired Ma'm Alice.

'I hired Grand Marshal Kevin and his guard. He's in charge of the new defences. A new wall and ... and ... all sorts of strategies. He's fought the T'manians many, many times. He told us so. He was even the Marsh King's Grand Marshal for a while.'

'What's he doing this far north then?' inquired Ma'm Alice. 'There's never been a T'manian invasion near here.'

'He said he needed a new challenge,' Ethel said vaguely. 'Like our Hall. Our Hall was never built to be defended.'

'There's never been anything to defend it against,' said Ma'm Alice.

Ethel shrugged. 'The City Lord was telling me last trading day that the T'manians are moving northwards, and that they no longer just raid and kill and leave. There are rumours that their islands are overcrowded, that they want new lands now, and slaves to work them. So they are sailing their boats to lands that aren't prepared for them, so they can take them for themselves. But if the T'manians come here we'll fight them, and we'll win.'

'Will you now?' said Ma'm Alice softly. She paused. 'Well, what of the night then? Are you afraid of the night? My friend only comes here in the night.'

'The night.' Ethel hesitated. Night was shadow time, whisper time ...' Why at night?'

'So no one sees him.'

'I'm not scared of the night either,' said Ethel firmly.

'Tonight then,' said the giant calmly. Too calmly, thought Ethel, suddenly aware she might have been manipulated. Had Ma'm Alice planned for her to meet this friend all along? Would they ...

'Don't worry,' said Ma'm Alice. She grinned again, showing her too long teeth, a piece of meat caught between them. 'He won't hurt you, I give you my word. He'll be glad I have another friend. Perhaps you will be his friend, too.'

Ethel nodded.

The Hall smelt staler than usual, even though the windows were wide open, and the shutters, too, and there was fresh-smelling mint bush in the holders along the walls. Ma'm Margot looked after the Hall well, thought Ethel.

It was an old Hall, almost as old as the olden days, built like most Halls of the rubble from an olden days building, so it resisted all weathers, not slowly crumbling like the mud and wattle cottages. The walls were thick and the top windows even still had glass — not olden days glass, it was true, but the thick bluish glass from the next-to-olden days, when such crafts as glassmaking were still practised.

The main room was the Hall, from which the building took its name, a long room that took almost two minutes to walk, it was so long. According to legend it had been the trading Hall, the meeting Hall in the next-to-olden days, and the other rooms had grown around it to accommodate the Lady.

Behind the Hall itself were the storerooms, full of tallies from farm and village. No cottage stores were as secure from rats or weather as the Hall's. Produce was stored at the Hall and strictly tallied, so each knew what they had brought and could take back again. And by tradition the Lady and her household took what they needed.

The Hall looked after the granary as well, the mill where oats and wattleseed and bunya nuts were dried into flours. According to tradition the Lady controlled all that she could see but, by tradition too, she did very little ruling. She was here to make decisions if decisions were needed — but they rarely were.

Ethel looked out over the courtyard, at the rust-coloured chickens clucking through the unicorn droppings, at the sparrows eyeing them thoughtfully from the eaves, as though they would like to join in but didn't dare, at the unicorn itself, only his nose visible through his stable, and the flash of his silver horn.

'My Lady.'

Ethel turned. It was Ma'm Margot.

Ma'm Margot was no taller than Ethel and not much wider. Her hair was hidden under a shallow headdress in plain colours, blue sometimes or red. She wore the traditional narrow skirts of the Hall, unlike the wide dress of the cottager who needed to be able to move freely round their fields or gather oranges perhaps in the generous fabric of their skirts. Ethel was thankful that as the Lady her skirts were wide as well — the Lady's skirts had to be wide or else she wouldn't have been able to ride the unicorn.

'The pumpkin harvest tallies are ready for you to inspect, my Lady,' said Ma'm Margot, her face expressionless as always below her headdress. She coughed gently. 'They were ready this morning, but you weren't to be found.'

'No,' said Ethel. 'I was out.'

'So it would appear,' said Ma'm Margot, her voice as blank as her face. 'Of course the Lady of the Unicorn may come and go as she pleases.' She paused slightly for emphasis. 'But the farmers always bring their pumpkin harvest tallies to the Lady on this day. They expected to see you.'

'Well, I didn't know,' said Ethel impatiently. 'No one told me I was expected to be here today.'

'No one expected you to leave the Hall without announcing it, my Lady,' said Ma'm Margot, fitting her fingers together calmly. They were wide, practical fingers, calloused slightly, but without the ingrained dirt and scars of outdoor workers.

Ethel shrugged. 'I'll count the tallies now,' she said. 'I'm sure they're correct anyway.'

'As you will, my Lady,' said Ma'm Margot. 'Then tonight there'll be the formal acceptance of the pumpkins. The farmers will arrive at dusk and then you'll ...'

'Yes, yes,' said Ethel. 'Whatever you like. No,' she said suddenly. 'I can't tonight.'

'You can't, my Lady?'

'I ... I have to go out.'

'But ... Ma'm Margot closed her lips. It is not my business to question the Lady, her face seemed to say. Even if the Lady is unreasonable.

'Look,' sighed Ethel. 'I'm sorry. I mean it. If I'd known today was special ... Can the farmers come tomorrow night? The pumpkins will still be all right tomorrow. I'll be here then, I promise.'

'There's no reason why they can't come tomorrow,' admitted Ma'm Margot finally. 'It isn't how it was done before. But I can send a message to them all.'

'Thank you,' said Ethel.

'As my Lady pleases,' said Ma'm Margot.

Dinner was formal. Dinner was always formal, thought Ethel from her position at the head table in the Hall, Ma'm Margot on one side and Grand Marshal Kevin on the other.

There was always a cloth on the head table and flowers, a fancy of Ma'm Margot's, even though you couldn't eat them. The chairs were always in the same positions, everyone sat in the same places and the meal never started until the Lady took her first mouthful. Ethel had never dared be late in case everyone else went hungry.

The fire licked and puffed and snickered behind the main table, filling the Hall with extra heat, even though it was already hot with the warmth of so many bodies.

Of course it made sense to have a formal meal with so many to be fed. It just looked so ... so complicated, thought Ethel wearily. The guards, the millers, the tanner, the chookman, the servants down the far end of the Hall, the platters in place along the tables, roast geep and mounds of small white geep cheese wrapped in herbs, yesterday's leftovers turned into pies, dishes of potatoes, their skins just lifting, spread with butter and still steaming, pumpkins baked whole and filled with long-cooked wattleseed and fruit, apple fritters that would be cold before anyone got to eat them, lillypillies baked in honey and bunya bread and wilted turnip tops with bacon and ...

Meal times had seemed so luxurious to the village girl, used to the grudging soup at Uncle Maddox's. But to the Lady of the Unicorn it was yet another day's chore to get through, a time when she must be public and watched by all.

'A fine meal,' said Grand Marshal Kevin, his face as smooth as an egg and slightly greasy round the chin. 'But then every meal is fine in your Hall, my Lady. The hospitality of your Hall compares even to the great Halls and I've seen many of them in my day. Why, I remember when I was Grand Marshal to the Marsh King, his Hall once served ...'

'Excuse me,' said Ma'm Margot. 'My Lady, will you have some cheese?'

'Thank you,' said Ethel. 'What were you saying Grand Marshal?'

Grand Marshal Kevin was tall, though not quite as tall as all heroes ought to be, and dark haired. His hands were smooth as his sword, a genuine olden days one he claimed, though Ma'm Margot sniffed when he was out of hearing and muttered that there were precious few references to swords in any of the olden books.

'I was speaking of the Marsh King,' continued the Grand Marshal affably. 'It was the victory feast after we'd routed the T'manians that third time. Three hundred of them attacked that time ...'

'Are you sure, Grand Marshal?' asked Ma'm Margot politely. 'You would need many boats to carry three hundred. Of course I've never seen a T'manian boat, but I have heard they only carry a crew of ten or even less. Now that would mean that to carry three hundred there would have to be ...'

Ma'm Margot didn't like Grand Marshal Kevin. Ma'm Margot didn't like anyone new, thought Ethel resentfully. Including her.

'What do the T'manian boats look like, Grand Marshal?' put in Ethel hurriedly, though in fact she was glad she'd been too young to remember anything about the T'manian attack that had killed her parents. 'Are they really made of metal? Surely they'd sink?'

For once the Grand Marshal looked serious. 'Yes, my Lady. They're made of metal. Some people believe that the T'manians have great stores of metal, olden days cities perhaps that weren't covered by the floods. But I don't believe that is the case. Metal is the first thing they steal on their raids; metal and slaves and just enough food to see them home to their islands.

'But this is a poor subject for a lady's table, my Lady! And there's no need for you to worry about the T'manians now. Not when you'll soon have fine walls ...'

'When will the walls be started?' put in Ma'm Margot.

'Soon, soon,' said the Grand Marshal good-temperedly. You can't hurry these things. As soon as we have the stone ...'

Ethel swallowed another mouthful of cheese. What was Ma'm Alice eating, she wondered, high up on her hill? Perhaps she should bring her some chicken tonight. Did Ma'm Alice ever catch chicken in her traps? The roast at the end of the high table was still untouched. Suddenly she realised the Grand Marshal was still speaking. 'I'm sorry Grand Marshal Kevin,' she said. 'What was that again?'

'I was saying, my Lady,' said the Grand Marshal jovially, 'that when I was in the service of Lord Jason ...'

'I thought you were in the service of the King,' said Ma'm Margot.

'I served the Lord Jason before I was in the service of the King.' Grand Marshal Kevin was unfazed. 'Lord Jason was Overlord of the estuary up beyond the great salt marshes. But as I was saying ...'

What would it be like to live by yourself like Ma'm Alice? wondered Ethel. To snare your own food and grow your own crops, to watch the sunset spread across the world all by yourself. Lonely, perhaps; but you could be lonely in a crowded Hall as well ...

'My Lady? My Lady?'

Ethel blinked, brought back abruptly to the present. 'I'm sorry?' she asked. 'I didn't catch what you said.'

'It doesn't matter, my Lady,' said Ma'm Margot.

Ethel glanced at the water clock in the courtyard. You could just see its steady drip, drip, drip through the open doors. 'Grand Marshal Kevin, Ma'm Margot, if you will excuse me. I have an appointment.'

'An appointment?' Grand Marshal Kevin raised his eyebrows. 'Ah, a young man. What other appointment could a lady as beautiful as yourself ...'

'The Lady is too young for young men,' said Ma'm Margot shortly.

'When a lady is as charming as our Lady,' began Grand Marshal Kevin. He took another mouthful of stuffed tomato. 'I remember when ...'

Ethel slipped from the table.

The unicorn sniffed his way between the rubble, his hooves sounding hollow on the soft grass. He seemed to see better in the darkness than a horse would, thought Ethel. Which was strange, as you'd think that a creature so bright and white would only love the day.

The moon sailed like a cheese rind above the hill, thickening the shadows between the rocks. The smell wasn't as bad as it had been during the day, Ethel decided.

She shuddered as the unicorn stepped over a giant skull, milk white in the moonlight, then sat herself firmly upright. It was just a bullock's skull. She ate beef on festival days. Why should she be scared of its skull? Why should darkness make everything so strange?

How could anyone live mostly in darkness, like Ma'm Alice's friend? she wondered. How would it change you to know only shadows and never the clear light of day?

The rubble grew thicker. Ethel dismounted and led the unicorn up the final path. She halted at the edge of the clearing and looked for a stout beam or post to tie him to. Yes, there was a bean pole. She looped the reins over the top and knotted them firmly.

Suddenly the unicorn reared, his pale hooves flashing in the night. The bean pole cracked, torn from the garden, and swung in a wild arc against his back.

'What's wrong?' cried Ethel.

The unicorn reared again, snorting his fright.

'What is it? Quiet boy ... quiet ...'

'You'd better take him down the hill again.' It was Ma'm Alice's voice. Ethel turned. The giant seemed even taller in the moonlight, her bulk blocking out a good portion of the stars.

'But what's wrong with him?'

'He smells someone strange,' said Ma'm Alice. 'It upsets him. You'd better tether him further down. There's a post over that way. There's a snare on it, but it's not set. You'll see it in a minute.'

'But ...' Ethel had been going to say that Ma'm Alice was strange and the unicorn hadn't been afraid of her. But she didn't. She patted the unicorn's neck instead to soothe him and led him across the hill and down.

The unicorn was breathing heavily but not from exertion. His sides were sweaty.

'I should rub you down,' said Ethel. 'But there's no breeze here. You won't get chilled will you?'

The unicorn snorted, but not as loudly this time. His eyes flashed white, and then he sighed and bent down to the grass and began to eat.

Ethel turned up towards the clearing again.

Ma'm Alice was waiting for her. 'Scared?' she asked abruptly.

Ethel shook her head.

'Maybe you should be,' suggested Ma'm Alice. 'Your horse is scared.'

'He's a unicorn,' stated Ethel.

'Ah yes, of course he is, how could I have missed it?' said Ma'm Alice.

'He really is,' said Ethel. 'It's not just the horn. If you put him with other horses they attack him. They know he's different.'

Ma'm Alice nodded again, her face serious now. 'They always attack what's different,' she said. 'Humans or horses ...' She paused in front of the door. 'Child,' she said hesitantly.

'I'm not a child,' said Ethel. 'I'm the Lady of the Unicorn. Whatever is in there won't hurt me.'

'Won't hurt you perhaps,' said Ma'm Alice softly. 'But you might hurt him.'

'Me? How?'

'By showing revulsion. By turning away.' Ma'm Alice hesitated again. 'Perhaps I shouldn't have asked you here tonight,' she said. 'I don't know why I did — loneliness perhaps. He's a good friend, the one who's here tonight, but not someone to talk to as you talked to me.'

'I won't hurt him,' said Ethel softly. 'I promise Ma'm Alice.'

Ma'm Alice looked at her closely. 'I believe you,' she said finally. 'Very well, child. Come in.'

The inside of the hut was dim, lit by a single taper on the table. The fire licked red tongues up the rough chimney, the stones behind it black. Ma'm Alice took the taper and lit a slush lamp and then another. The room flickered in the growing light.

Ethel looked round. 'But where ...' she began. And then she stopped.

A creature sat by the hearth, its back to the flames. It was small, which was why she hadn't seen it at first. It had four legs, furry legs like a dog, or cat perhaps, thought Ethel. Its face was furry too, and its ears and snout were long and covered in hair as well. Its teeth were very white and protruded a little at the edges of its mouth, like a wolf. But this was human.

How she knew she couldn't tell. It was like no human she had ever seen. But somehow Ethel knew that despite the fur and teeth and hairy ears, this was no animal.

The creature saw her. It started in sudden alarm, as though its sight and hearing were too poor to have seen or heard her when she first came in. He backed away towards the fire. The heat stopped him. He crouched trembling in the firelight.

'Sit down,' said Ma'm Alice to Ethel gently. 'Try not to startle him.'

Ethel sat. The weathered concrete chair was too tall for her to reach comfortably, but she clambered up anyway and sat on its edge, her legs dangling and her back very straight.

'Tell him I won't hurt him,' she said softly.

'Tell him yourself,' said Ma'm Alice. 'He doesn't understand words. Just voices and how you say things. Say you're his friend and he might understand.'

Like the unicorn, thought Ethel. 'Hello,' said Ethel tentatively. The creature looked up at her with large brown eyes. 'My name's Ethel,' she added softly. 'What's yours?'

'I call him Hingram,' said Ma'm Alice. 'It's not his name, of course. I had a brother once ...' She shook her head. 'Hingram, this is a friend,' she said quietly. 'Would you like another friend?'

Hingram blinked at her inquiringly, then looked back at Ethel.

'Try feeding him something,' suggested Ma'm Alice. She walked over to the store cupboard by the door and pulled out a shank of geep, greasy with cold fat. 'Try this.'

Ethel wriggled off the chair and took the meat. She crossed the room warily and held it out towards the boy. 'Here,' she said slowly. 'Are you hungry?'

Suddenly the boy snatched the meat. He held it close to his chest and warily retreated again. He sniffed it, and then began to gnaw.

Ethel went back to her seat and clambered up. 'How can he be a friend? You can't talk to him, or ...'

'Friends help each other,' said Ma'm Alice. 'That's how we met. I'd been trapping down below and Hingram, well I reckon he came after the scent of meat. He can't catch much for himself so he scavenges.'

'You mean ... stuff that's already dead?' Ethel suppressed a shudder.

Ma'm Alice shrugged. 'He forages what he can. I had known someone was around. I'd seen him out of the corner of my eye. Never fully, you understand, Hingram was too wary for that. So I left bits of meat out for him, and vegetables too, though he never ate those, and sometimes fruit. He liked fruit, too ...'

'But that day something else came after the scent of meat. A lion. I should have seen it coming, but lions are the colour of the rocks. I've never seen a lion around here before or since, though I've seen prides in the distance, way off on the plains beyond the forest. They hunt in packs, you know. Maybe this one had been cast out of its pack. Animals can do strange things when they're cast out.'

Ethel shook her head. 'I've never seen one.'

'Let's hope you don't,' said Ma'm Alice. Her thick fingers brushed a strand of hair from her face. 'It must have been hungry because it leapt on me, big as I am.

. And big as I am it had me down and I was fighting it off my throat. I still have the scars.' She held up one broad arm.

'And then it dropped away, right off me. It just lay there ...'

'Dead?' asked Ethel.

'Not dead. Stunned. It lay there for a while then blinked and slunk away and it's never come back either. Frighten something enough and it doesn't return.

'But it was Hingram who had saved me. He'd grabbed a rock and leapt up onto the boulder — that big one straight out there — and threw it down onto the beast's head.

'He didn't have to save me. He could have let the lion take me, then taken my hut for his own, and scavenged from my traps and had all the meat he wanted ...

'But he was my friend. And he's been my friend ever since.'

The fire crackled and flared. Hingram started back and then relaxed. He sucked at the marrow from the shank, then threw the bone into the fire. The scent of charred bone filled the hut. He looked around hungrily.

'May I give him some more?' asked Ethel.

Ma'm Alice nodded.

'Oh,' said Ethel. 'I just remembered. I brought you some chicken. From the kitchens at the Hall. It's in the saddlebag on the unicorn.'

Ma'm Alice smiled. 'That was kind of you,' she said. 'It'll be good to taste something I haven't caught myself and cooked myself. And chicken ... well, I don't get chicken in my traps. But ...' She stopped as Hingram scurried across the floor.

He walked on four legs, not two, thought Ethel. She froze as Hingram stopped by her chair. He raised his head and quickly licked her leg, then backed away, as though he was ready for a blow. Another pause and he was gone, a shadow through the door.

'I thought he would leave soon,' said Ma'm Alice. 'He never stays long.'

'Who is he?' asked Ethel. 'Where does he come from?'

Ma'm Alice shook her head. 'I don't know,' she answered. 'He can't speak ... I don't think he hears well enough to learn to speak, and his eyesight is none too good as well. But his sense of smell seems to make up for it.

'No, I don't know where he came from. If he had parents who cast him out, or who died and left him alone. If he was born like that or just grew ... differently. I don't know.' She crossed over to the fire and threw more wood on — a giant root, a tree root perhaps, thought Ethel. Only someone as big as Ma'm Alice could have managed it.

'Why did you want me to meet him?' she asked finally.

Ma'm Alice sat heavily on the other slab chair. 'I don't know,' she said quietly. 'Perhaps ... perhaps I thought that the Lady of the Unicorn should know someone different, to learn a little understanding perhaps. Or maybe I just wanted one friend to meet another.'

An owl boomed outside. 'Am I your friend?' asked Ethel finally. 'I would like to have a friend.'

'Doesn't the Lady of the Unicorn have friends?' asked Ma'm Alice.

'No,' said Ethel. 'Loyal subjects. But I left my friends behind when I became the Lady. When I was ... different.'

'Friends then,' said Ma'm Alice. She licked her wide dark lips. 'Now, where is that chicken you said that you brought?'

The moon was low on the horizon, as though someone swung it from a string high up in the night sky. Ethel untethered her unicorn. He whinnied at her softly and pressed his nose against her, as though checking that she smelt the same despite the unfamiliar scents that clung to her.

Ethel glanced down the hill. She could just see the Hall from here, a dim light in the dark. 'It's later than I thought,' she said. 'Ma'm Margot will be worried.'

'Won't she be asleep?' asked Ma'm Alice. The roast chicken looked tiny in her hand, like a roast sparrow, not a hen, thought Ethel.

'No. She never sleeps before I do, I think.'

'A loyal woman,' said Ma'm Alice.

Ethel sighed. 'Loyal to the Lady,' she said. 'To the idea of the Lady. Not to me. I don't think she even likes me. She loved the last Lady very much.' She gathered the unicorn's tether in her hand. 'I'll mount when we get down the hill,' she said. 'It will be lighter there, away from the rubble. Thank you for your hospitality, Ma'm Alice. And for introducing me to your friend.'

'It's good to have friends,' said Ma'm Alice vaguely. She met Ethel's eyes for a moment. 'I do have other friends,' she said slowly. 'Not ones I see often, but friends none the less. Maybe one day you would like to meet them too?'

'Friends like Hingram?'

'No. Not like Hingram. There's no one else like Hingram. But not like the people of the village or the farms or the Hall either. These are forest people.'

'I didn't know there were forest people,' said Ethel. 'Grand Marshal Kevin says there are dragons in the forest.'

'No dragons,' said Ma'm Alice. 'A few kangaroos. Possums. A colony of bats. And people. Different people.'

'People like you?'

'Some like me. A bit. Some different in other ways.'

'I would like to meet them,' said Ethel slowly.

'Are you sure?'

'Yes,' said Ethel.

Ma'm Alice nodded. 'Next full moon then. That's when we meet — at the full moon.'

For a moment Ethel hesitated. Witches met at full moon, and werewolves bared their teeth ... it didn't take much of a leap of imagination to see Hingram as a werewolf.

Then she shook herself. She was being silly. Hingram was no werewolf. He was a boy, a different boy. And it made sense for the outcasts of the forest to meet at full moon when there was more light to see by.

'Will I meet you here?' she asked.

Ma'm Alice nodded. 'At dusk,' she said. 'When everyone is indoors. There's just time for me to walk to the forest and meet my friends then come back here before the world is awake and people see me.' She grinned in the darkness. 'I travel fast,' she said. 'I have long legs. But perhaps your unicorn can keep up with me.'

'Of course he can,' declared Ethel proudly.

'We'll see,' said Ma'm Alice.

'I hate darning,' said Ethel.

'But it must be done, my Lady,' said Ma'm Margot.

'Not by me,' said Ethel.

'But the Lady always mends the tapestries, my Lady.'

'I am the Lady,' said Ethel. 'And this Lady doesn't darn. Anyway, I'd make a mess of it.' She glanced out the window. The sky arched like a blue glazed bowl held upside down, the breeze smelt of forest and far hills. She wanted to be outside, not stifling by the fire. 'I'm going to inspect the defence wall,' she said. 'Grand Marshal

Kevin said they would start to dig the foundations today.'

Ma'm Margot looked back down at her darning. 'I believe he has had to postpone it again, my Lady,' she said. 'He said something about needing more materials. He has gone to Far-marsh Castle with his men.'

'But he'd just got back from getting new materials,' said Ethel. 'He said he needed to arrange a supply of dressed stone.'

'And now perhaps he needs stonemasons, my Lady,' said Ma'm Margot.

'But ...' Ethel hesitated. Ma'm Margot was antagonistic enough about the Marshal. There was no point making it worse. And after all, there was no real hurry for the walls.

'He knows what he's doing,' Ethel said finally. 'After all, he was the King's defender. He's built defence walls all along the coast. He told me about the walls he built at the salt marshes just last night.'

'Yes, my Lady,' said Ma'm Margot, attending once more to her darning.

Ethel wondered if she'd even listened.

The moon rose fat and yellow, like it was a duckling stuffed full of grass ready to make its first swim across the sky. Ethel ignored the stares of the Hall workers as she crossed the hard-packed rubble courtyard. The unicorn lifted his head as she approached, his mouth full of thistle from the crevices between the stones, his coat gleaming white against the mud and rubble walls.

Ethel rode slowly between the gates then turned the unicorn point forward to the hill. Let them stare, she thought. She was the Lady. No one had any right to question where she went, or why.

Especially not Ma'm Margot.

A child waved to her as she rose between the cottages, then giggled as she waved back. A girl gathering washing from the line gazed at her, curious, the men and women with their hoes nodded respectfully.

I am the Lady, thought Ethel.

The dusk settled as she approached the hill, pink clouds shading into grey. Ma'm Alice waited among the boulders, her head with its thick ring of plaits towering above them. 'I saw you set out,' she explained.

'You see everything,' said Ethel.

Ma'm Alice laughed, a booming sound that sent the unicorn skittering. 'Not quite,' she said. 'Not what goes on behind the windows or in the sheds. But I see enough. Come,' she said. 'We have to hurry.'

It was strange travelling through the night, thought Ethel, watching the trees' thin fingers brush against the moon and send the shadows dancing across the road, glancing unseen into the dim interiors of cottages, watching people sitting by the fire or carving, mending or knitting by the light of a single slush lamp on the table.

It was even stranger to be with Ma'm Alice. What did Ma'm Alice think when she looked through cottage windows, watching the peaceful everyday life indoors? As far off to her as if she'd been — the Lady of the Unicorn, thought Ethel.

Not that she wanted to live in one of those houses again, mend sheets by the light of a spluttering lamp — Ma'm Margot came briefly into her mind. Was she still mending by the light of the Hall candles, waiting for her Lady to return?

Ma'm Alice turned, a solid lump against the night. 'Not too fast for you am I?' she asked softly.

'No,' said Ethel. The unicorn wasn't even straining. A unicorn is hardier than a horse, thought Ethel proudly — stockier and more enduring, even if it didn't have a horse's speed.

'Not far now,' said Ma'm Alice.

Ethel nodded. Somehow Ma'm Alice seemed even odder away from her hill, as though up there her size seemed normal against the massive boulders. Even her walk seemed different — not a normal walk like other people's, but a sort of lunging hunch. Perhaps, thought Ethel suddenly, there were other things different about Ma'm Alice apart from her size.

'Tired?' asked Ma'm Alice.

'No,' said Ethel. 'I slept this afternoon.'

Ma'm Alice's grin was white in the moonlight. 'What did your people think of that?'

'It's none of their business what I do. I'm their Lady.'

The grin grew wider. It was a big grin even in the enormous face, a little bigger than a normal grin might be. 'I should think that made what you do even more their business,' said Ma'm Alice.

'But ...' Ethel stopped. She had been going to say the people didn't own her. But maybe they did in a way. '*My Lady*,' said Ma'm Margot.

She didn't want to be theirs. She wanted ... What did she want?

'Nearly there,' said Ma'm Alice.

The forest was a dark mass against the stars, almost purple after the pale gold of the plain. Only the odd branch broke the smooth dark line, dancing firelit against the moon. It was strange to think the forest had been there even in the olden days, too marshy for the olden-dayers to bother with clearing.

The forest would be full of shadows, thought Ethel.

'Ma'm Alice?'

'Yes?' The giant grinned again. 'It still seems strange to hear you call me by that name.'

'Do you want me to stop?'

'No,' said Ma'm Alice. 'What were you wanting to ask?'

'Will Hingram be there?'

'Maybe,' said Ma'm Alice. 'He often is. You can never tell though.'

'Will he mind my being there? Will he remember me? Does he realise I'm the one he met at your place?'

'Oh, he realises that well enough. I think he's intelligent, for all he can't hear much or speak or see. More intelligent than you or me perhaps. How would we survive if we couldn't see or hear, if we had to scurry on all fours from babyhood like Hingram?'

'I don't know,' said Ethel.

Ma'm Alice shrugged. 'Every time I don't see him for a few days I worry. Maybe he's been caught in a trap, or someone has set the dogs on him.'

'But, but they wouldn't!' cried Ethel.

'Of course they would,' said Ma'm Alice. 'Think back to your farm life girl. What would your aunt have done if she saw a thing like Hingram out the window one dark night?'

'She'd have …' Ethel didn't finish. 'But she'd have been wrong!' she said finally.

'There are lots of wrongs in this world,' said Ma'm Alice softly.

Of course, Ma'm Alice would know, thought Ethel, and was silent.

She could smell the forest before they reached it. Why had she never noticed the forest's smell before? Was it stronger at night? Or did the colours of the day just blind you to the scents of night? A damp smell, a soil smell, a rotting smell — but not like garbage rotted. A scent of a thousand years of leaves soaking into swamp. A mosquito buzzed against her arm. She swatted it absent-mindedly.

'We leave the track here,' said Ma'm Alice. 'You'd better dismount and lead him now. The branches can be low.'

'But how do we find the way?'

Ma'm Alice chuckled. It was a louder sound now that she no longer had to fear people hearing her. As though she could be more herself in the forest, thought Ethel. 'I know the way,' she said. 'Thirty, no almost forty years I've come this way. You walk behind me, and keep the unicorn behind you too, or you'll find yourself knee-deep in mud.'

'How did you find the way the first time?'

'I was led here,' said Ma'm Alice, stumping through the trees. Her head was taller than the lowest branches, so she had to duck or hold them back. 'Just as I'm leading you now.'

'By whom?'

'A friend.'

'Who was the friend?' persisted Ethel.

Ma'm Alice stopped. 'You really want to know?'

'Yes,' said Ethel.

'His name was Justin. He was a leper.'

A leper. For a moment Ethel started back. Perhaps Ma'm Alice was infected too. But her skin had seemed clear. Surely if she had been infected it would have shown in forty years.

'No, I'm not a leper,' said Ma'm Alice, as though she'd read her mind. 'Leprosy isn't particularly infectious. In fact for all I know Justin didn't have leprosy at all. But his skin was different, marked and mottled, and these days that makes you a leper. You can read all about leprosy and skin diseases in the old books, though no one bothers. They had cures even for leprosy in the old days.

'Justin found me after I'd been cast out, after I'd begun to grow and kept on growing, so that they could no longer pretend that I was normal. I had no idea how to survive in those days. I went from village to village, hoping someone would take me in ...'

There was no self pity in Ma'm Alice's voice, thought Ethel wonderingly. Her voice was matter-of-fact.

'But of course they didn't. It was at the last village I tried. A woman gave me scraps and told me to go ... but that little kindness made me hope for more. I sat on her doorstep, hoping she'd smile at me again, but she screamed at me instead and the children began to throw stones.

'And then Justin came. In his leper's cloak, with his leper's bell, just as in the old days. The children ran away. I nearly ran as well. But he spoke to me kindly and I realised I wanted kindness more than I feared leprosy. In those days of course I couldn't read. I didn't know how little I had to fear.

'Justin lived on my hill. It was his hill then. They called it Leper's Hill then, just as it's the Giant's Hill now. He took me home. He had a shack — just bits of wood propped over the boulders to make a roof. He didn't have my strength,' said Ma'm Alice, still matter-of-factly. 'He was too weak to hunt, and the lack of food made him weaker still. But he did have books. He'd been a Manor Lord before the disease struck.'

'A Manor Lord wouldn't have been cast out if he had leprosy!' protested Ethel. 'They'd have kept him isolated, but his people would have looked after him.'

'They did — till the T'manians came. The T'manians burnt his Hall, they — slaved his people — but not Justin. No one wants a leper as a slave. In those days the T'manians plundered, then they left. They didn't try to keep the land as they do now. So when they'd gone Justin foraged in the ruins of his Hall and took his books high up on the hill, where he could see if T'manians came again. But they didn't. He saw me instead, and weak as he was he came to rescue me.'

'Did you live with him?' asked Ethel.

Ma'm Alice nodded, the movement almost hidden by the night. 'Justin had read about traps in his books, though he didn't have the strength to make them. I did. First of all I dug pit traps; just big pits covered with thin bits of wood and with straw on top, so anything that walks on top falls through. But that way injured the animals ... it's a cruel way to kill them, and sometimes there were more than we needed, with broken legs perhaps so we couldn't let them go. So I made snares instead.

'I built the hut too, with Justin reading from his books and telling me to put this here, or that bit there, to fetch a tree trunk to brace the doorframe or how to tan skins to make more snares. Gradually I learnt to read as well. I don't know what I would have done up on my hill without my books. Books don't care what you look like. Books speak to anyone who knows their words.

'When he was stronger from good feeding, Justin led me here, into the forest. He hadn't been for years. He'd been too weak to walk this far. But the people were still here. Not the same people — even every month they differ. Some come every month, some live too far away to come too often; some come once and never come again, so you wonder if something has happened to them. Or if being with others who were different made them too aware that they were different too. Come, we must hurry now.'

'But what happened to Justin?' demanded Ethel.

'He died,' said Ma'm Alice abruptly.

'Of the leprosy?'

'Of old age. He was very old when he found me. But he taught me many things,' said Ma'm Alice. 'He taught me that by ourselves neither might have survived. But the two of us did very well. And that's why the people of the forest meet.'

'I don't understand,' said Ethel softly.

'You will,' said Ma'm Alice. 'Friends help each other,' she added softly.

The moon was above the trees now, its beams piercing between the branches, reflecting from the distant pools, the shadows sharp and flickering on the forest floor.

Something shrilled above them, then was silent. A possum, Ethel realised, annoyed with the intruders in its world.

'How far now?' inquired Ethel.

Ma'm Alice pointed to a slight rise in front of them. 'Just through here,' she said.

Ethel squinted through thicker trees, their branches low to the ground, not high and silver trunked like the swamp gums. Fig trees maybe, or pittosporums. Ma'm Alice parted the branches and crouched low.

Ethel followed her, leading the unicorn behind her.

It was damp and sour smelling under the trees, with ankle deep water. Maidenhair ferns tickled her ankles. The unicorn snorted, or perhaps it was a sneeze. Ma'm Alice looked even larger, bent double as she squeezed under the trees.

'Up this way,' she instructed, and parted the branches again.

Light poured through. Moonlight, starlight, and firelight as well, red among the gold. Ethel held the branch up to let the unicorn through, then looked around.

They were on a rise above the swamp, fringed with dark trees all around. No one would see the firelight from here Ethel realised, though it was a small fire, the coals glowing red and smokeless; a pile of dry branches set to one side, and a large pot beside it, steaming in the firelight.

Ethel stared at the fire. It was safe to stare at the fire. It meant she didn't have to look at the faces all around.

Slowly she lifted her eyes, and then she stared.

A face looked at her. But it wasn't a face. It was half a face. The rest was ... was what? Burnt away by flame, eaten away by illness, savaged by an animal. All that was left was bone and scar and a gaping hole where once there'd been a mouth. And the mouth was smiling. Or trying to smile. She could see a tongue, some teeth ...

This wasn't like Ma'm Alice. This wasn't like Hingram, so small and so defenceless. This was a ... monster, monster, monster shrieked Ethel's mind. But it can't be a monster, whispered another part of her. This is Ma'm Alice's friend ...

Her gaze shifted slowly from the ruined face and dropped with relief onto the person beside them. This was an old woman. Her back was bent in a sharp curve, so her face nearly touched her knees, then bent out again as though someone had tried to pull it straight. She was smiling, a strangely sweet smile though her face was lined with pain. That sweet smile gave Ethel the courage to look further.

A man, another giant, but not like Ma'm Alice. Where Ma'm Alice was tall and broad this man was simply tall, like he'd softened in the sun and been stretched like sticky toffee. His head was almost hairless, his lips were thick and his nose and chin were much too long. He blinked as though confused by the newcomers.

A boy sat beside him, an ordinary boy, till you saw his face was marked by circles, like raised pimples on his skin. And then a girl with sad brown eyes, and hair —

thick hair across her face and even down her neck, her hands and feet were hairy. And another giant and another, even larger than Ma'm Alice, her face blank as the moon, until she smiled, the wide unthinking smile of a tiny child ...

Ethel was going to be sick. She was going to run. As soon as her legs would move she'd run. She'd dive under the branches and mount the unicorn and she'd be gone ...

Why was she here? She was the Lady of the Unicorn. She had no place with people such as these. Ugly people, people who had no home, monsters ...

Suddenly her mind halted. They'd call Ma'm Alice a monster. But she wasn't. You might even think she was ugly, till you knew her. The first time she'd seen her she'd been the giant; the second time Ma'm Alice who was big; and now she was Ma'm Alice and you hardly noticed her size.

And what would happen if she ran? No one would stop her, not even Ma'm Alice. But she would have lost a friend.

Slowly she raised her head again. The old woman with the hump still smiled at her. Her voice was soft but harsh, a worn out voice. 'Welcome child.'

And suddenly it didn't seem so strange, it didn't seem so horrible. As though words had made a magic to make it all all right.

'Hello,' said Ethel softly.

'So, you can speak,' said the old woman. 'And you

look like anyone might look. Why have you brought her here, Alice? Why, if she's not one of us?'

Ma'm Alice crossed to the fire and held out her hands as though to warm them, although the night was hardly cool. 'She needs friends,' she said slowly. 'So I brought her to meet mine.'

'To laugh at us?' The harsh voice was firm. 'To run away in horror? Look at her. She's still in shock.'

'But she hasn't run,' said Ma'm Alice. 'Come closer Ethel. Bring the unicorn.'

Obediently Ethel pulled at the reins. The unicorn moved closer to the firelight.

'Ah,' said the old woman. 'I begin to see. You're the new Lady of the Unicorn. Welcome, my Lady.' The tone was only slightly ironic.

'Welcome, my Lady,' a voice echoed. It was the male giant. But the voice was empty, as though there was no meaning in his words.

'That's Philip,' said the old woman. 'He grew too much and his brains went as he grew. For some reason Ma'm Alice kept her brains. She's the only one of the big 'uns who has. She uses them too. So girl, you are the Lady of the Unicorn?'

'Yes,' said Ethel, her voice steadier now.

'Do you know who we are?' asked the woman.

Ethel nodded. 'You're the people of the forest.'

'Yes. We're the people no one wants. We're the people who have to hide away because we're different.'

'I know,' said Ethel.

323

The old woman nodded. 'Good, good,' she said. 'You did well to bring her, Alice. You did very well indeed.'

Ethel froze at the tone of her voice. 'What do you mean?' she demanded.

'Why, nothing. Nothing,' said the woman. 'Just that I'm glad that you are here.'

'What do you want of me?' asked Ethel quietly. 'You do want something, don't you? I've learnt how people look at me when they hope that I can give them something.'

The old woman shrugged. The movement looked grotesque in the flickering light, her narrow shoulders protruding far beyond her head. 'Hasn't Alice told you why we come here?'

'No,' said Ethel.

'We come to do what we can for each other,' said the old woman. 'Some,' she gestured with an elbow toward the male giant, 'just bring food, a couple of dead roos perhaps, enough food for some of us for days or weeks if we look after it. We look after those who have been hurt and don't have the wits to tend themselves. Some of us exchange news. But all of us bring what we can.'

'Ma'm Alice didn't bring anything,' said Ethel slowly.

'She brought you,' the old woman's laugh sounded like bits of rusted metal scraping down a pot. 'You're the Lady. You're the best that anyone has brought.'

Ethel turned to Ma'm Alice. 'Is that true? That you brought me here to be of use to your friends?'

Ma'm Alice hesitated. 'In a way,' she said.

Ethel clenched her fists. All at once she was angry, angrier than she had ever been in her life.

'What do you intend to do with me? Ransom me? Make Ma'm Margot deliver bags of corn or iron pots to the forest? Then you'll deliver me to her?'

'No,' said Ma'm Alice. Her face was expressionless. 'That wasn't what I intended. But yes, I brought you here so you might help.'

Ethel shuddered. Desolation swept across her sharp and swift. 'That's the only reason you said you were friends with me wasn't it? Because I'm the Lady! Because I might help you! Help your friends!'

'No,' said Ma'm Alice gently, but Ethel spoke over her.

'I thought you were different! I thought you really liked me! But you're just like everyone else! You just want my help!'

'Would it be so very bad to help us?' said the old woman sharply. 'Friends help each other.'

'I'm not your friend!' cried Ethel. You want to use me — not be my friend!' Her voice broke off. *Acceptance*, said the old woman's eyes, the scarred half face, the pock-marked boy. *Can you give us acceptance?*

'I'll do what I can! I don't know how I can help but I can try. If you send me a list of what you need ...' choked Ethel. Then she was running, running, under the branches out into the forest.

Dimly she heard the unicorn canter behind her. Someone must have sent him after her, lifted the branches for him. The old woman or Ma'm Alice ...

The unicorn nudged her back. Ethel clasped him for a moment, her face against his neck, the old woman's words thudding in her ears. Friends, friends, friends — friends help each other.

'What if I need help?' cried Ethel to the dark branches. 'Then who will help me?' The unicorn turned curiously at the sound of her voice, his ears laid back in alarm. Ethel shook her head. She didn't need help. The Lady of the Unicorn never needed help. She had everything she needed.

Except friends.

Ethel mounted the unicorn. He lifted his head, as though to sniff the path, then picked his way delicately through the swamp, back into the cleared lands and the Hall.

'And twelve pots of macadamia oil,' said Ethel. She gazed around the storeroom, its thick walls roughly plastered with thick clay to keep it cool, the packed rubble floor, packed smooth with mud and straw, the dim light from door and taper. 'Haven't we done enough yet?'

'There are still three more storerooms to be counted, my Lady,' said Ma'm Margot calmly. 'The Lady always takes stock of the storerooms once a year, to see what needs to be used before the new tallies. It's tradition.'

Ethel sighed, a deep breath filled with the scents of withered apples and sprouted onions, heavy fruit cakes to store the eggs and fruit and nuts, jars of honey crystallised around the edges. Tradition. Just as the Lady always had to eat at the top table with everyone around, instead of eating as she read in the book room, thought Ethel dismally; just as the Lady had to learn the old tongue in case she met another Lady (who would probably rather talk in everyday speech too) or the Lord of Coasttown, instead of exploring the hills and forest on her unicorn ...

What would Ma'm Margot do, Ethel wondered, if she just flung down the tally book and ran across the room, out the courtyard and rode away, up to the ...

Up where? she thought bitterly. To Ma'm Alice? But Ma'm Alice was just like everyone else. If Ma'm Alice had met her before the unicorn, she'd have ignored her too. Ma'm Alice only wanted help for her friends — her real friends.

For a moment she remembered Ma'm Alice's face in the firelight that night. The too-wide eyes dark, her mouth a straight line. She looked almost as if someone had struck her and she refused to show the pain.

But why should Ma'm Alice be hurt? The Lady of the Unicorn would help, if she could, when she could ...

A flicker of guilt washed over her. She dismissed it firmly. No, she'd done nothing yet for the people of the forest. She'd asked them to send her a list of what they needed. What else could she do? She didn't even know where they lived — the other side of the forest from the Hall, maybe. Except for Ma'm Alice and Hingram.

Hingram! He hadn't been at the moonlit meeting. What had Ma'm Alice said? *Every time he doesn't appear, I worry that someone has hurt him. Or maybe not a person, an animal perhaps — a lion ...*

Hingram couldn't write a list of what he needed. Hingram couldn't even talk.

'Ma'm Margot?'

'Yes, my Lady.'

'Is it possible to send a message to all the villages and farms?'

Ma'm Margot looked surprised. 'Of course, my Lady. The last Lady did it all the time.'

'Then I want it done now.'

'Of course, my Lady,' said Ma'm Margot cautiously. 'What about?'

'I want it to say ...' Ethel tried to think. 'If anyone sees a ... a strange boy, with fur down his back and long teeth and ...'

'A monster, my Lady!'

'He's not a monster!' said Ethel fiercely. 'Anyway, if anyone sees someone like that ...'

'They're to capture it, my Lady?'

'He's not an it. He's a boy. A different boy. They're to ... oh, I don't know — to send a message here, at once. To leave out food so he'll come back again — yes, that's it! They're to leave out food. And not to frighten him in any way.'

Ma'm Margot looked at her curiously. 'And then what, my Lady?'

'Then I will act as I see fit,' stated Ethel. She didn't have to explain to Ma'm Margot. She didn't have to explain to anyone!

'Yes, my Lady,' said Ma'm Margot. 'I'll attend to it directly. Is it my Lady's pleasure to keep on with the tally now?'

Ethel sighed. No, it wasn't her pleasure. It was her duty.

One of the Grand Marshal's guards entered the storeroom. What was his name again? thought Ethel. Tor, that was it. He coughed tentatively to attract her attention. 'My Lady?'

Ethel blinked. 'Yes? What is it?'

'It's a letter, my Lady.' Tor offered it carefully. Letters were rare.

'From whom?'

'I don't know, my Lady. A messenger handed it in at the gates.'

'What did they look like?' demanded Ethel.

'I didn't see them, my Lady. Neither did the gate keeper. He just looked round for a moment ... only just a moment ... and when he looked back someone had stuck it by the door.'

'Open it, my Lady,' suggested Ma'm Margot. 'Then you'll know. You may go, Tor.'

'Yes, Ma'm Margot,' said Tor regretfully, obviously hoping to hear the letter read. He shut the door behind him.

Ethel broke the seal and unfolded the letter. The paper was good quality parchment but yellowed at the edges, as though it had been stored for a long time before it had been used. Ma'm Margot looked carefully down at the store list, as though to indicate if Ethel wished it to be private she would not inquire.

The letter was brief.

My dear Ethel,

There is smoke in the Coasttown and ships on the sea. The T'manians have come. I will help if I can.

Alice.

Ethel sat without moving. It couldn't be true. It couldn't. The world couldn't shatter as fast as this.

T'manians ...

'Bad news?' asked Ma'm Margot gently beside her.

'The T'manians,' said Ethel stupidly. 'The T'manians are coming.'

'But ... but how do you know?'

'The letter ...' Ethel halted. How could she explain Ma'm Alice to Ma'm Margot? 'It's from a friend,' she went on quickly. 'From a lookout high on the hills. The T'manians are at the Coasttown.'

'Are you sure? Is this friend trustworthy?'

'Yes,' said Ethel quietly.

Ma'm Margot calculated quickly. 'It takes four hours to walk here from Coasttown. Or even less ...'

'Maybe they won't come here ...' said Ethel hopefully. 'Maybe they'll stay at Coasttown or travel another road ...'

'They'll loot Coasttown and send their loot to the ships,' said Ma'm Margot calmly. 'Then they'll take the main road inland. And that leads to here. The T'manians want land. They want farms. They won't stay in Coasttown.'

'But ... ' Ethel faltered. There was no way around it. The T'manians would be here ...

'You are sure about this friend of yours?' insisted Ma'm Margot.

'Yes,' said Ethel, for suddenly she was.

'Then we have to hurry,' said Ma'm Margot.

'Yes.' Suddenly reality hit like a fist in the face. 'Grand Marshal Kevin,' she said. 'We have to tell him! He'll know what to do, how we can defend ourselves! Thank goodness we have Grand Marshal Kevin! We must call the villagers in from the farms! They must bring everything they need to the safety of the Hall ...' She hurried from the room, Ma'm Margot behind her.

'T'manians!' Grand Marshal Kevin's bright round face seemed to shrink, like an apple that had been stored too long. 'Coming here? No, girl ... I mean, my Lady. You must be mistaken. The T'manians would never come to a place like this, not after all these years, so far up the coast ...'

'I'm not wrong!' cried Ethel. She waved the letter. 'I arranged a lookout.'

'You arranged a lookout? Without consulting me! That was wrong, very wrong, my Lady.' Grand Marshal

Kevin was indignant. 'I'm in charge of the defences here. Lookouts are to be arranged then I should do the arranging. When I was in the service of King Dennis no one ever thought of ...'

'Surely that's of no matter now,' said Ma'm Margot quietly.

'Yes!' cried Ethel. 'The T'manians will be here! We've got four hours to get ready! To defend ourselves!'

'Four hours!' stammered Grand Marshal Kevin. 'But ... but the walls aren't finished.'

'I don't think they'll wait for us to finish the walls,' said Ma'm Margot dryly.

Ethel stared at her. Ma'm Margot had changed. No, she hadn't changed, that was the strange thing. Just when you'd have expected her to be different, she was just the same as she had always been, organised and matter-of-fact. But this wasn't a tally of the storerooms now. This was war!

'No. No — of course not,' Grand Marshal Kevin said. He seemed to take hold of himself. 'You are right ... of course you are right. We must act at once!'

Ethel let out her breath in relief. Of course Grand Marshal Kevin knew what to do.

'Stevens, call the guard!' announced Grand Marshal Kevin. 'We must go at once!'

'Go? Go where?' cried Ethel.

'To the Far Mountain Stronghold of course. To ask for assistance. More troops, more guards, more swords and shields!'

'But it will take you a day's ride to get to Far Mountain! Maybe more. The T'manians will be here by then!'

'Lady, be sensible!' said Grand Marshal Kevin. 'We can't hold off an attack ourselves! We don't have the means! Even the walls aren't finished.'

'But you said ...'

'Well, never mind that now,' said Grand Marshal Kevin hurriedly. 'The sooner I set off, the sooner we'll be back — with reinforcements! You can be sure that we'll bring reinforcements — Stevens, there you are! Call the guard together. We must leave at once!'

'But you can't take the guard!' cried Ethel.

'Of course I must, Lady! There are T'manians about! I must get through to Far Mountain safely if I'm to bring help to you. In two days I promise — three at most, or four ...'

'No.'

Grand Marshal Kevin hesitated at the sound of Ethel's voice. 'My Lady?'

'No, you will not take the guard. We need the guard here. They are the only ones who have ever fought the T'manians.'

Grand Marshal Kevin's face stilled. 'They are my guard, my Lady,' he said quietly. 'Not yours.'

'They stay,' said Ethel.

Grand Marshal Kevin smiled. Ethel had never seen Grand Marshal Kevin smile like that before. 'Call the guard then, my Lady. Let's see if they will stay with you, or come with me.'

Ethel glanced at Ma'm Margot. Ma'm Margot nodded, and slipped out the door. A moment later she reappeared, with the noise of many feet behind her.

Ethel gazed at the line of guards. There were five of them, tall men like the Grand Marshal, and the herald and standard bearer too. They wore swords, and tunics, and their hands were calloused in different ways from a farmer's hands, or a tanner's.

'Will you explain or will I?' she asked Grand Marshal Kevin.

'You explain. You are the Lady,' said Grand Marshal Kevin. His voice was polite.

Ethel watched the faces of the men. Why did it seem so normal for Ma'm Alice to look down on her, while these men made her feel so small?

There was no time to waste feeling insignificant, she told herself. She held her chin high. 'The T'manians are invading Coasttown,' she announced, as calmly as she could. 'The Grand Marshal believes that the best tactics are to get reinforcements from Far Mountain. He would like you to go with him,' she lifted her chin a fraction higher, 'to hold his hand perhaps when it gets dark. But I'm ordering you to stay here, instead, to help with the defences here, though the Grand Marshal,' she shot him a scornful look, 'may go if he likes. Do you understand me?'

No one answered. The men glanced at the Grand Marshal.

The Grand Marshal smiled his strange new smile again. 'I think you will find that my men follow where

I lead,' he answered softly. 'I'm the Grand Marshal, my dear.' He paused, the smile deepening. 'I mean, my Lady.'

Ethel glanced round at the guard. None met her eyes.

'But you gave me your word!' cried Ethel. 'You've lived here all these months, eaten our food!'

'For which we thank you, my Lady,' said the Grand Marshal. 'But now it's time to go.'

'Did you ever intend to fight if the invaders came?' asked Ethel quietly.

One of the men grinned. The Grand Marshal shook his head. 'Why would T'manians come here, so far up the coast? They had small enough pickings last time. No metal — who wants to haul pumpkins to the coast? Although it seems now they have come. No girl. I've done enough fighting not to want more. Oh, I'd have built your walls for you, given enough time. But only a fool fights when they don't have to.' He hesitated for a moment. 'Look girl. I won't stay for you. But I will give you advice. Good advice. I may not have done all I said I did back in your Hall, but I have fought the T'manians before.'

We don't want your advice! screamed Ethel's mind. But her voice was silent.

'My best advice — though you probably won't take it — is for you to tell your people to take what they can, and escape now. Otherwise they'll be killed, or kept or sold as slaves.'

'But where should we run to!' cried Ethel.

The Grand Marshal shrugged. 'But if you do decide to fight,' he continued, 'keep your people fighting. If they start to run they're lost. Armies need leaders. If one person runs everyone will run. But if one person leads, then ... maybe ... your people will, too.'

'Anything else?' asked Ethel quietly.

The Grand Marshal shook his head. 'You have no weapons,' he said. 'No one with any experience. As I said, my best advice, my dear, is to go now, taking what you can. I'm sure Far Mountain will shelter you and Ma'm Margot, even if it doesn't have room for the villagers.'

For the first time Grand Marshal Kevin met her eyes.

'I'm not a villain, Lady. I'm just a man who has seen too much fighting, just as my men have.'

'Then why didn't you turn farmer? Tanner? Builder?' cried Ethel.

'Us? Farmers!' The Grand Marshal laughed. He was still laughing as they left the room.

Ethel watched him go.

'Just like that,' she whispered. 'As soon as there's danger he's gone ... What do we do now?'

'We make do with what we've got,' said Ma'm Margot.

It was almost as though they were back at the stocktaking — four barrels of salt fish, eighteen smoked legs of geep ...

'Sound the bells,' said Ethel quietly. 'Call in the villagers. Call everyone together in the forecourt. You're right. We must make do with what we've got.'

The forecourt was full — men in shepherd's aprons jostled with men in tanning leathers; women in farmer's skirts next to cooks and silversmiths. Ethel watched them helplessly. She had never felt younger, never felt more alone. What was the use of being able to ride a unicorn now? Did it make her a better leader? Did it tell her how to harness villagers into a fighting force to repel the T'manians?

Ethel felt the unicorn's damp nose against her arm. It gave her confidence. She was the Lady of the Unicorn. She must know what to do! She vaulted quietly onto his back. At least up here she could see and be seen.

'Villagers, farmers, people of the Hall ...' Her voice shook. To her surprise the courtyard was suddenly silent, the faces, round as plates along the sideboard, looking up at her.

'The T'manians are coming!' Fool, she told herself — they know that, that's why they're here. 'We have two choices. We can fight, or we can run.

'If we run, we leave everything — our harvest, our land, our homes. And even then the T'manians may catch up with us and make us slaves, or worse.'

'There's nothing worse,' said a voice.

'Oh yes, there is,' said someone else.

Ethel ignored them. Somehow now she had started to speak it was easy to keep on, as though she was no longer Ethel, as though for the first time she *was* the

Lady of the Unicorn. She could feel the power seep into her — the power of their expectations, the power of their love. Even if it was for the Lady and not for her, it was still there.

'This is OUR land!' For the first time her voice rang clear. 'Let anyone who wants to leave, leave it now! Now! While there's still time — perhaps — to run!'

Ethel looked slowly around.

No one moved.

'Then we will fight!' she said.

'But ... but how ... ' the voice was bewildered, not antagonistic. Somehow it broke the tension. Ethel grinned.

'With our hoes and rakes and kitchen knives — with everything we have!'

'But they have spears and shields.' Again the voice was only questioning, as though of course the Lady would know the answer.

And somehow the answer came. From books? From stories that she'd heard? Or because she was the Lady. The unicorn shuffled slightly. Ethel held him still. 'They have their spears,' said Ethel. 'But we have something else. We love this land. We have to fight for it. They don't.

'And we have something else. We know our own villages. We know every track and tree. And that's what we'll use to defeat the T'manians!'

'What about Grand Marshal Kevin?' came another voice from the back of the crowd. 'Where is he? Where are the guards?'

Ethel gritted her teeth. 'The Grand Marshal has ...' she stopped. She couldn't say that the Grand Marshal had fled, announcing the case was hopeless. But she had to say something. They were waiting ...

'The Grand Marshal has gone to get reinforcements,' came a voice behind her. 'He'll be back when he can.' Ethel stared. It was the youngest of the Grand Marshal guard's, the one who had brought the message from Ma'm Alice, Tor Underhill. 'Till he returns,' he turned to Ethel. 'I'll help the Lady organise our defences here.'

Tears stung Ethel's eyes. We have three hours to get ready,' she said instead. 'Maybe four.'

The crowd was quiet as she spoke.

The water clock dripped slowly in the courtyard. A cart creaked in through the gateway and then another, piled high with blankets, pumpkins, beds, sacks of seed and sheaves of hay — everything that could be gathered in was piled around the courtyard, with Ma'm Margot still with her tally book, accounting for it all.

'Weapons,' demanded Ethel.

Tor Underhill nodded. 'I'll see to it, my Lady. It's best that everyone uses the ones they know. A soldier can use a sword because he's been trained to them for years. But a farmer knows the balance of her hoe or rake. And the blacksmith knows the feel of hammers ...'

'Tor?'

'Yes, my Lady?'

'Why didn't you leave with the others?'

Tor shrugged. 'I had to choose,' he said. 'Either be loyal to you, or to the Grand Marshal. I met the Grand Marshal only six months before we came here, my Lady. I had no reason to be loyal to him.'

'And you had to me?'

Tor nodded. 'I was brought up around here, my Lady. My family has always followed the Lady of the Unicorn.'

'Oh,' said Ethel. 'Have you ever fought the T'manians, Tor?'

'No, my Lady. But I've listened to the other guards' stories. And the Grand Marshal taught me sword craft. I can drill troops, my Lady.'

Ethel gazed out at the crowded courtyard again. 'If only there was some other way to defend ourselves.'

'If this was a castle,' said Tor slowly, 'we could pour boiling oil down on the invaders. Or rocks ...'

'But this land is flat.' Ethel shook her head. 'If only there was some way to trap them before they got to the Hall, some way to ...' Suddenly she stopped. 'Tor!'

'Yes, my Lady.'

'I've had an idea. Maybe it's a silly idea.'

'No idea is silly now, my Lady,' said Tor seriously.

'Maybe ...' said Ethel slowly. 'Just maybe ... it will work ...'

The clock in the courtyard dripped down onto the rocks. The moisture seeped into the crevices, feeding the watercress and swamp dock that grew below the clock.

Two hours. Three hours. Four.

'Any sign?' demanded Ethel.

'No, my Lady,' said Ma'm Margot calmly.

'The lookouts?'

'In place up on the roof, my Lady.'

'The hay?'

'Pul the Shepherd says it's scattered, my Lady.'

'The barricades?'

Ma'm Margot nodded. 'Everything we could lay our hands on, my Lady. It's all piled up before the Hall. Tor is drilling.' She gave a slight smile. 'Drilling the troops out front.'

The Lady's troops, thought Ethel. Farmers and bakers and geepherds, with hoes and rakes and sticks ...

The barricades would keep no one out — only the Grand Marshal's walls might have done that. But they would at least provide shelter against the spears till the T'manians drew close.

Suddenly Ethel's mind was blank. There had to be more that they could do. But she couldn't think. She had to think, thought Ethel desperately. She had to make decisions for her people.

'Then get everyone together,' said Ethel's voice, the Lady's voice. 'In lines behind the barricade.'

They waited outside the Hall behind the piled up firewood and furniture and carts. The sun beat down, shadowless.

'Send the children in for water,' ordered Ethel. 'Tell them to bring buckets and cups so everyone can drink. Bring water for the unicorn too.' The unicorn snorted beside her. The activity had upset him. He tossed his head restlessly. His tail flicked, though the day was still too cool for flies.

Four hours, Ma'm Margot had said. It took a man four hours to walk from Coasttown to the Hall. But these men would be moving swiftly, hoping to arrive before the alarm went out, before fleeing Coasttowners brought their message to the Hall.

'Five hours,' muttered Ethel. 'It's been five hours since we had word.'

'Then they'll be here soon,' said Ma'm Margot calmly beside her.

'Ma'm Margot ...'whispered Ethel.

'Yes?' answered Ma'm Margot.

'Nothing. It's just ... it's just I wish the Grand Marshal were here ... Or not the Grand Marshal — someone who really knew how to lead ...'

'You're managing, pet,' said Ma'm Margot. 'I mean, my Lady.'

'That's the first time you've called me "my Lady" since the message came,' said Ethel irrelevantly.

Ma'm Margot grinned. A lock of hair had slipped from her headdress, rusty against her indoors face.

'Maybe I had to keep reminding myself that you really were the Lady before. But you're the Lady now well enough. You're doing fine, pet. You're doing fine.'

Suddenly down the road a dark grey plume of smoke twisted towards the sky. A farm roof set on fire, thought Ethel. The T'manians were nearly at the village.

Someone muttered fearfully behind her. The whispers rose and fell along the lines — 'They're here, they're here, they're here ...'

'They're here, my Lady,' said Tor unnecessarily.

'Send the children into the Hall,' ordered Ethel. 'Joel Blacksmith, tell them to fetch the oil.'

'Yes, my Lady,' said Joel Blacksmith.

Then she saw them.

They were far away still, just past the hills between the Hall and the coast. Like earwigs thought Ethel, not like people yet at all. The sun glinted on their spears, the metal garlands round their necks and arms. It was like something in a book, thought Ethel. It was all just the same as everyone described, except here it was real.

It didn't feel real. It felt as though you could turn the page and it would all be over. If only she could just turn the page and skip this bit. Or put the book away and say, 'I don't want to read this anymore.'

But this was real.

Could she hear them? Surely not at this distance — and yet she could. The muffled thump of many feet, the jangle of armour. But no voices. That was the most ominous aspect. The silence. There was too much silence. As though the birds too knew there would be a battle, as though even the animals had retreated.

A muffled creak passed behind her. Ethel didn't turn. That would be the oil pots being dragged down to the village where the straw was laid. She could smell them, hot in the cool air.

Closer, closer, closer — the T'manians moved together, like a tortoise or a snake, thought Ethel, but you could see that they were men now, although they were still too distant to see their faces. No, thought Ethel suddenly. They weren't men. You couldn't hurt someone if you thought of them as men. They were just the enemy.

'They're nearly at the village, my Lady,' someone whispered, as though the T'manians might hear if they spoke any louder.

'Not yet,' said Ethel. She stared at the T'manians till her eyes began to blur. They were short — even from here she could see that — their shoulders broad and their heads entirely hairless. Ethel wondered if their women were hairless, too. Their skins gleamed slightly silver, an oil perhaps, to protect their skin from the sea glare.

Ethel could hear her pulse ringing in her head. When should I give the order? she thought desperately. What if I get it wrong? When? When? When? In fifty breaths' time maybe — she listened to her breathing, began to count.

One, two, three ...

You could see the spears now, high above their heads, like saplings that had lost their leaves. Metal spears, and spears of fire-hardened wood, almost as lethal.

Twenty, twenty-one ...

The first T'manians disappeared hidden between the cottages.

Thirty-two, thirty-three ...

Now, thought Ethel, now ... any longer and they may separate, pillage the cottages before descending on the Hall.

'Now!' she yelled.

Immediately a pigeon shot into the air; and then another and another.

Ethel stared down at the village.

Nothing happened.

What was wrong? Was the oil too cool to light? Was the straw too damp to fire? Surely there must be smoke soon. Surely ...

Then someone screamed.

It was a long scream, on and on and on. Another came and then another — the village was full of screams.

Someone ran along the road, writhing and turning, their hair on fire. Others boiled out into the fields, throwing themselves onto the cool damp earth, rolling, rolling, rolling ...

'It was a good plan,' said Ma'm Margot quietly. 'Filling the streets with straw then pouring hot oil down and firing it. We should stop a lot of them that way.'

'It was Tor's idea,' said Ethel. 'He said they pour oil down from the castle walls onto the invaders. I wasn't sure if it would really work. I thought there would be smoke.'

'Not from burning oil and straw,' said Ma'm Margot. 'Not from this distance. It just looks like a heat haze in the air. Ah, there's smoke now — one of the cottages must have caught. Now they'll be running towards the pits.'

Like Ma'm Alice's pits, thought Ethel, only covered with wet straw, so they looked just like the road, but wouldn't burn. She wondered suddenly if Ma'm Alice was watching the battle from her hilltop. Could she see her on her unicorn? But surely it was too far away for that.

Suddenly the screaming changed.

'Your plan worked, pet,' approved Ma'm Margot.

'But how many have been caught?' whispered Ethel. 'How many are still left?'

'We'll know soon enough,' said Ma'm Margot.

Someone gave a sob of fear in the line behind. The sound stopped abruptly as though they were ashamed.

How long could it take for the surviving T'manians to leave the village? wondered Ethel. Maybe, maybe there were no survivors. Maybe they'd all been trapped or burnt. She turned to Ma'm Margot, then stopped.

The first of the T'manians appeared between the cottages, and then another ... and another. They were close enough to see their round chins now, the smudges on the arms and legs, their armlets and their shields.

So many, thought Ethel desperately. There were still so many. The unicorn stamped beside her, alarmed by the screams. She patted him till he was still.

'We must have got half of them,' said Tor beside her.

Ethel nodded. Even half were so many. They looked determined, undeterred, as though they met burning oil and pit traps every month.

Of course, realised Ethel, those were the tools of war. You survived them or you didn't. And you grew used to them. You couldn't scare the T'manians with oil or traps.

The T'manians drew together — like a beetle, thought Ethel, a beetle with many legs and antennae waving at the sky. Someone gave a signal at the front.

The beetle began to march again.

A villager muttered in the lines behind. The muttering spread like melted butter down a hearth cake.

Ethel gripped her spear. It felt strange in her hand. It had hung in the Hall above the hearth. She wondered who had used it before. How long ago? Another Lady of the Unicorn perhaps? Then it should know her hand. But it felt strange.

'Listen!' she cried. The words were lost in the muttering behind. 'Listen!' she cried again, and now someone took up the cry — 'Listen to the Lady! Listen!'

Ethel tried to keep her voice steady. 'The time is nearly here! Remember! If one of us runs the rest may run but if we run we will be killed. If we stand we may be killed. But at least if we stand together we have a chance.'

The muttering stopped. 'If we die the enemy gets our land. But if we win ...' Tears filled Ethel's eyes suddenly. Who would give *her* courage? Who was there for her to lean on?

'Advance when I give the order!' cried Ethel. She mounted the unicorn. His coat was warm against her legs. She gripped the reins.

The enemy advanced, still beetle-like, steady and determined. Then suddenly the leader signalled again. The clump spread out to become a line, three deep perhaps, or four, curving slightly at the edges. They intended to surround the Hall, Ethel realised. Kill or be captured ...

The line advanced. The unicorn snorted and twisted his head.

So many ... so many ... so many ...

When would it start? Would they charge? Or just keep walking steadily, strike them steadily, kill them steadily ...

No, she decided. The leader would give a signal and they'd run, their spears held low, their sword arms raised. And those behind her might run too. For who could stand when armed T'manians poured towards them?

They had to advance instead! It would give her people confidence if they were the attackers instead of waiting for the spears! She glanced at the people behind her — Tor with his sword, waiting for the Lady's order, Ma'm Margot with a kitchen knife, Gary Tanner with his sharp, steel scraper, the farmers with their hoes and potato forks ...

Would it really make any difference in the end?

The unicorn stood steady beneath her, his breath soft and even. At least he wasn't afraid.

Ethel opened her mouth to call the charge.

Someone screamed. It was a different scream from the one before. This was a scream of terror.

Ethel turned.

It was, what was her name? One of the women from the dairy. She pointed at the T'manians — no, not at the T'manians. She pointed up beyond them to the hill behind.

Something was coming from behind the hill. People, many people. Were they people? Ethel squinted into the sun. The shapes were wrong for people. Too tall, too small, the wrong colours — no one was as tall as that, except Ma'm Alice, and ...

A cloud shifted across the sun and Ma'm Alice lumbered into view.

She wasn't alone. The others were all with her — all the people from the clearing that moonlit night and more besides, as though they'd spread the word through all the forest and the hills and plains. There was the white-faced giant, taller than Ma'm Alice; the old woman carried on his back; and other giants, thin lips in long-chinned faces, and a dragon creature. Was there really a dragon in the forest ... or was it human, too? And others, so many others, the hidden people facing daylight for their friend.

Was she their friend? Not yet, thought Ethel. But Ma'm Alice was their friend. They'd come for her.

Slowly they came forward, steadily across the plain, Ma'm Alice in the lead. Something scurried at her side. Hingram, Ethel realised. She could see him clearly now. He stopped, and as though he sensed her too, he lifted up his head and howled.

Caroooooooooooooo!

The sound filled the hollow air. Another person screamed and pointed. One of the T'manians turned around, and stared ...

'Attack!' shouted Ethel.

No one moved.

'Attack!' she yelled again

'But ... but, my Lady — the monsters!' The voice was low. An enemy they could face. But not the monsters.

'They'll fight for us! Don't you understand? They are our friends!'

There was no way to convince them. Or only one way ... *Armies need leaders.*

Ethel dug her heels into the side of the unicorn. He reared, almost toppling her. He yelled in challenge to the horses facing them.

It was the first time she had ever heard him make a sound.

And then he charged.

She could hear his hooves against the dust-brown grass. She could hear his breath panting in her ears. There was no other sound.

And then the cries began behind her — a battlecry from Tor and Ma'm Margot's warlike scream (who would have thought that Ma'm Margot could scream like that?). Fifty cries, a hundred, and the sound of running feet.

Ethel faced the enemy.

But the enemy had turned. They paid no attention to the villagers with their rakes and knives. They stared at the monsters coming from behind.

Their line broke without a sound. They ran, but not like an army ran. They ran towards the villagers, their spears cast down in their terror to be away.

The monsters shambled behind them.

Ethel pulled frantically at the unicorn's reins. He halted, shying to one side. Someone ran in front of her — Gary Tanner, his rake raised high, striking at the fleeing men. Others came after him, their weapons raised. There was a new scent in the air, of blood and steel and hatred.

'Stop them!' Ethel turned. 'There's no need to fight now! The T'manians just want to escape! Stop!' she cried, but her voice was lost in the yells and screams. 'Stop!'

A man lunged against the unicorn, sending him skittering to one side. For a moment Ethel thought he was attacking her, then she realised he was unconscious, blood seeping from his skull.

'Stop it!' she shrieked, and this time the unicorn rose with her cry, his hooves flying towards the sky. But still the fight went on.

'She said, stop it!' The voice boomed across the battlefield. Ethel glanced around.

It was Ma'm Alice. She loomed above the fighters, twice as high as the tallest of them, her hands wider than two men's heads, her voice louder than the cries of pain. Why did she look so much larger here, thought Ethel wildly, than on her hilltop? Because here you saw her surrounded by the world of ordinary sizes and proportions ...

Ma'm Alice reached down. She grasped Gary Tanner in one giant hand and held him high; the other reached for a smooth headed T'manian. His metal necklace swung against his chest as she shook him like a rat.

'Lay down your arms,' boomed Ma'm Alice. 'Every one of you! I mean *now*!'

There was silence. A rake clinked, a knife thudded on the grass. Then suddenly all over the battlefield men and women were laying down their hoes, their plough blades, Solvig Sweeper's broom. Someone groaned, and then was still.

Ma'm Alice lowered the men to the ground. Gary Tanner blinked, his legs buckling as he collapsed onto the grass. His face was green.

The bearded invader recovered faster. He glanced once at Gary Tanner, once at Ma'm Alice looming above them, then he was running, running, running swerving through the silent crowd.

'Catch him!' someone yelled.

'No!' cried Ethel. 'Let him go! Let them all go!'

And suddenly the field was full of running T'manians, their weapons left behind them, their feet thudding on the flattened grass, back to the road and to the sea.

'We should go after them,' someone called.

'No!' said Ethel again. 'Let them run! Let them tell everyone what happens to T'manians here!'

'The monsters get them,' someone muttered, looking uneasily across to the hill.

'The monsters,' whispered another and the whisper spread. 'The monsters, the monsters, the monsters ...'

Ethel followed their gaze.

The people of the forest had stopped advancing. Like Ma'm Alice they looked even more different out here on the plain, their strangeness accentuated by the ordinariness around them. Were screams and battles normal? Maybe it was the gentle peace of the forest people that was strange, and not their faces ...

'Ma'm Alice?' said Ethel unsteadily.

Ma'm Alice strode towards her. 'Are you all right, child?' she asked, her voice low.

Ethel nodded. There seemed no words to say. 'Thank you,' she said finally. 'I ... I'm sorry for what I said ...'

Ma'm Alice smiled, her eyes intent on Ethel's. As though she didn't dare look to either side, thought Ethel, and see the revulsion on other people's faces.

'We told you in the forest,' said Ma'm Alice gently. 'We help our friends.'

'Thank you,' said Ethel again. For some reason the world seemed strangely clear, the sounds retreating to a distant buzzing in her ears.

'Catch her,' said a voice — Ma'm Margot's, but very far away ...

The bookroom was quiet when she opened her eyes. The books piled on their shelves, just as they should be, with the bags of mint bush and garlic to keep away the silverfish, the high wooden ceiling free of cobwebs — Ma'm Margot would never allow a cobweb.

'Here,' said Ma'm Margot. Something warm touched Ethel's lips. She sipped.

'Ma'm Alice?'

'I'm here,' said a voice.

'She carried you in,' said Ma'm Margot.

'My unicorn?'

'He's in the courtyard munching thistles,' said Ma'm Margot. 'He's safe. Everyone's safe. I've had the wounded carried in. They're in the Hall.'

'The wounded?' Ethel tried to sit up. Ma'm Margot pushed a pillow behind her.

'Don't you worry now, pet,' she said. 'I mean, my Lady. There are none that won't heal with a little nursing.'

'How many are there?'

Ma'm Margot counted on her fingers. 'George the Weaver, he took a nasty blow on the head, and Eric the

Binder, Gary Tanner fetched him a blow accidentally with his rake. He's got a cut right down his arm but it will heal, it will heal, and Tor took a blow as well. Little Agnes from the farm by the creek, she's hurt the worst — the T'manians got her before they reached the field, the child must have been hiding. A few others, nothing to what might have been, thanks to Ma'm Alice and her friends.'

Ma'm Alice said nothing.

Ethel sipped the drink again. It was bitter and hot, one of Ma'm Margot's 'good for you' teas, but she felt stronger with every sip.

'There's one who would speak to you, when you're feeling better,' said Ma'm Margot slowly. She met Ethel's eyes. Her look was strange.

'One of the wounded?' asked Ethel.

Ma'm Margot nodded. 'Do you feel strong enough?' she asked.

Ethel struggled to her feet. She felt silly to be so weak now. 'Of course.' She looked over at Ma'm Alice.

'Off you go,' said Ma'm Alice. 'I'll be all right here.'

The Hall stank of blood and fear. Ma'm Margot had been busy, ordering hay beds for the wounded, salves and bandages to tend the wounds, and boiled strips of old petticoat that had been left to dry in the sun and rolled with lavender flowers to keep them pure, pots of powdered basil and calendula and comfrey root, all the silly things that Ma'm Margot had collected and that didn't seem so silly now.

'Over here,' instructed Ma'm Margot.

Ethel trod between the pallets. Old Bertram, his eyes shut with the pain, his arm and one side bandaged. Little Agnes from the farm by the creek.

Why had the T'manians bothered with a tiny child?

Ethel wondered whether to smile, to reassure or comfort. But the wounded were buried in their world of pain.

Ma'm Margot stopped. Ethel looked down.

A man lay on the pallet before her. His skin was smudged with silver, whatever lotion he'd been wearing partially cleaned away. His face must have been bloody, for long gashes ran down his cheek as though they had been cut with a rake perhaps, rather than a sword. Now it was clean and the gashes covered with a layer of salve, like sliced strawberries set in jelly, thought Ethel, her stomach lurching suddenly. His side was bandaged too. His face paled as he tried to sit, then fell back among the straw.

Ethel stared at his blue, clear eyes, the round, bare skull, the iron around his neck, the silver skin.

This was the enemy.

For a moment Ma'm Margot met her eyes. Ma'm Margot, who had always been so loyal to her and to her people. Ma'm Margot had brought a T'manian inside the Hall.

The man gasped, as if he tried to speak. Slowly Ethel nodded. Ma'm Margot smiled an almost smile.

'I'll leave you with him,' she said. 'He wishes to speak to you alone.'

Ethel knelt by the man's side. 'Speak,' she said.

The man frowned, as though it hurt to concentrate through his pain. 'I beg a favour,' he gasped. His accent was strange but intelligible. 'Oh gracious Lady ...'

'Don't waste your strength,' said Ethel. 'If you have something to ask of me, just ask.'

'I would like to stay,' said the man simply.

Ethel stared. 'You mean stay here?'

The man nodded.

'But ... but you're our enemy. You can't stay here. We must send you to Coasttown. They have a prison there. You can be ransomed. Don't worry. We don't keep prisoners slaves.'

'I wish to stay here,' said the man. His voice was even weaker.

'But why?' cried Ethel. 'This isn't your home. We're not your people!'

'I have no home,' said the man. 'The water covered all my island. I came here hoping for a home. No one will ransom me. I was loyal to my leader. I didn't run with the others. I stayed till I was struck down. Now I would be loyal to you.'

'But ...'

'I would be loyal,' promised the man. His eyes closed, bruised smudges in his too-white face. His breathing deepened.

Ethel stood and walked back through the Hall. Who are friends and who are enemies? she thought. How can you ever know?

A hand clutched her skirt and she looked down. It was Tor Underhill. His skull and thigh were bandaged.

'Tor! What happened! How badly are you hurt?'

Tor shook his head, as though his wounds were irrelevant. 'The monsters ...' he said urgently. 'Lady, have the monsters gone?'

'What monsters?' asked Ethel, though she knew.

'We were just about to fight ... then the monsters came ... and we attacked ... and something struck me ... there were monsters all along the hill ...'

'Don't worry,' said Ethel gently. 'They fought for us.'

'For us, my Lady?' The pain-thickened voice sounded confused. 'Then we've won.'

'We won,' said Ethel. 'We're safe. Go to sleep, Tor. We're all safe.'

Ma'm Margot met her in the courtyard. 'Will you let the T'manian stay?' she asked.

Ethel nodded. 'We've land to spare, if that's what he wants. Do you think I'm right?' she asked.

'I think so,' said Ma'm Margot.

'I'd better go,' said Ethel. 'Ma'm Alice will wonder where I am.'

Ma'm Margot shook her head. 'She's gone,' she said.

'Gone? But she can't have gone! I haven't thanked her properly! We have to bring her back! She must stay here!'

'Let her go, pet,' said Ma'm Margot softly. 'Help tend the wounded now. You can see her later.'

'But she saved us ...'

'And now she wants to go. She can't stay here.'

'But ...' Ethel stopped. 'Have the monsters gone?' Tor Underhill had asked.

Ma'm Alice would always be a monster here.

Suddenly the unicorn snickered from his shelter in the corner of the yard. His horn glinted in the dusty orange light. His blue eyes, blue as eyes of the man who had once been an enemy, met hers across the cobbles.

Ethel looked at the unicorn who was her friend. If you put a unicorn with horses they'd stamp it to death. She was the girl who rode the unicorn. She was different, though her difference made her the Lady, not an outcast. The unicorn was different. And her other friends. Are only those who are different at ease with others who are different? she wondered. Maybe when you were born different you had to become wise.

And Ma'm Margot? Ethel smiled. Maybe some people just learn how to be wise. Or perhaps their differences didn't show ...

'Take me with you when you visit her again,' said Ma'm Margot softly. 'I would like to meet Ma'm Alice properly next time.'

Ethel nodded.

The world had seemed so simple when enemies were simply enemies, and giants sucked their victims' bones.

The world was more confusing now. But for the first time she knew what it might mean to be the Lady.

The unicorn whinnied again. Ethel gazed up at the hill. There was Ma'm Alice trudging up the slope. Something dark scurried at her heels. Hingram, come to meet his friend away from the stares of other people.

Her friends. The monsters who were generous, the enemy who would now be loyal, the old woman who was strong.

Ethel looked back at Ma'm Margot. She was smiling, the smile of an old friend for a young one. 'Let's go in,' said Ethel. 'There's a lot to do.'

Things had changed in the past. Maybe tolerance could come once more. Somehow it no longer seemed so impossible that she, the Lady of the Unicorn, might lead her people once again.

They walked back into the Hall together.

Titles by Jackie French

Australian Historical

Somewhere Around the Corner • Dancing with Ben Hall
Daughter of the Regiment • Soldier on the Hill
Tom Appleby, Convict Boy • A Rose for the Anzac Boys
The Night They Stormed Eureka • Nanberry: Black Brother White
Pennies for Hitler

General Historical

Hitler's Daughter • Lady Dance • How the Finnegans Saved the Ship
The White Ship • Valley of Gold • They Came on Viking Ships
Macbeth and Son • Pharaoh • Oracle
I am Juliet • Ophelia: Queen of Denmark

Fiction

Rain Stones • Walking the Boundaries • The Secret Beach
Summerland • A Wombat Named Bosco • Beyond the Boundaries
The Warrior: The Story of a Wombat
The Book of Unicorns • Tajore Arkle
Missing You, Love Sara • Dark Wind Blowing
Ride the Wild Wind: The Golden Pony and Other Stories
Refuge • The Book of Horses and Unicorns

Non-Fiction

Seasons of Content • How the Aliens from Alpha Centauri
Invaded My Maths Class and Turned Me into a Writer
How to Guzzle Your Garden • The Book of Challenges
Stamp, Stomp, Whomp • The Fascinating History of Your Lunch
Big Burps, Bare Bums and Other Bad-Mannered Blunders
To the Moon and Back • Rocket Your Child into Reading
The Secret World of Wombats
How High Can a Kangaroo Hop? • A Year in the Valley
Let the Land Speak: How the Land Created Our Nation
I Spy a Great Reader

The Animal Stars Series

The Goat Who Sailed the World • The Dog Who Loved a Queen
The Camel Who Crossed Australia
The Donkey Who Carried the Wounded
The Horse Who Bit a Bushranger
Dingo: The Dog Who Conquered a Continent

The Matilda Saga

1. A Waltz for Matilda • 2. The Girl from Snowy River
3. The Road to Gundagai • 4. To Love a Sunburnt Country
5. The Ghost by the Billabong

Jackie French AM is an award-winning writer, wombat negotiator, the Australian Children's Laureate for 2014–2015 and the 2015 Senior Australian of the Year. She is regarded as one of Australia's most popular children's authors and writes across all genres — from picture books, history, fantasy, ecology and sci-fi to her much loved historical fiction. 'Share a Story' is the primary philosophy behind Jackie's two-year term as Laureate.

jackiefrench.com.au
facebook.com/authorjackiefrench